REVISITING EMPTY HOUSES

REVISITING EMPTY HOUSES

Una Flett

CANONGATE

First published in 1988
by Canongate Publishing Limited,
17 Jeffrey Street, Edinburgh

The publisher acknowledges subsidy of
the Scottish Arts Council towards the
publication of this volume.

British Library Cataloguing in Publication Data
Flett, Una
Revisiting empty houses
I. Title
823′.914[F]

ISBN 0-86241-158-0

Typeset by Hewer Text Composition Services, Edinburgh
Printed and bound in Great Britain by
Billing & Sons Limited, Worcester

1

I dreamed about Alma Crescent last night, Marius, a tribute from my fantasy to the shock of seeing you after all this time. You walked into the gallery smiling quietly, as if this were some little joke, and I looked up from my desk and hid the stunned gape of disbelief behind a smile of what I hope was dignified welcome.

Hullo, you said, I thought I'd just look in. Well what a lovely surprise, I said. And so we continued for an unmomentous half hour, smiling quietly and guardedly at each other and being polite with almost mandarin courtesy, asking after each others' sons and very cautiously about each others' lives. And then we said good-bye with an old friend's kiss on the cheek, and unmomentously you disappeared again to catch the train back to Edinburgh, as if dropping in once every six years was something quite unremarkable.

My dream-life, which is prolific and easily troubled, should have produced one of its nostalgia-special B features, all about being re-united and mysteriously losing you, or finding you've turned into somebody else. I've had these in bouts over the years. For you are part of my repertoire of recurring people, coming up for review every so often when an enigmatic hint is provided.

But last night the hint got indirect treatment. I was simply back there, alone, in Alma Crescent, a lovely empty dream in which nothing had changed. How could it? I had never left, this was the beauty of it. And yet, to add further joy as only dreams can do, there was also this sense of return. At last, at last, I felt. I've come back.

The dream took me down so deep that when I woke up I felt totally disbelieving. Do you understand, Marius? Do you know about the curiously unconvincing feeling the present can take on? You cannot argue against the physical facts. I live here, and I do this, and I have this sort of face in the mirror. But deep in your bones you know that it's all a conspiracy, an illusion. Your spiritual centre is still quietly living out its time in those one or two places and times when harmonious coincidence took over and the result was a sort of jet of happiness, bursting up, apparently inexaustible.

You mustn't think, because I reflect in this way, that I'm not happy now. I am. That is to say, I tick along very well. I enjoy running the gallery, even with its rather hair-line financial balance. I enjoy spotting new talent. I enjoy travelling. I even get along with people well enough for someone of my curious striped temperament. Oh yes, I enjoy life, though that is not quite the same thing as finding it has magic.

The dream reminded me of that.

Externally there was very little about Alma Crescent to suggest magic. It was, as you may remember, merely a funny wedge-shaped slice of a house set in a Victorian crescent. From the outside it looked small and narrow, but inside the rooms turned out to be quite large although they were all oddly shaped, because number six was at a point where the crescent curved over-abruptly and the builder had had to make some rather curious adjustments to negotiate the bend.

I always think of a builder, not an architect, whoever it was that put up that row of houses. He had so obviously set out to imitate the stiff propriety of Victorian houses in more fashionable parts of Edinburgh, and failed utterly. All the familiar features were there – the ornate rose medallions in the middle of ceilings, the moulded cornices, the high rooms, but everything had either slipped or slurred a little. The rooms were high but not square. The rose medallions were lumpy and had more than a hint of cabbage. The mouldings had none of the frightful precision of the real thing, but ambled along in low relief and indeterminate outline. There were real marble mantelpieces in the public rooms but they were not centred, and the shape of the hall was the despair of tile-fitters. But the staircase was elegant, indeed it was, with a suggestion of pre-Victorian grace, winding its way in a serpentine twist to the upper floor with a charming patterning of wrought-iron bannister rails.

Something about this confusion of good lines and bad calculation appealed to me at once. I felt an affinity towards the unknown man who had failed to produce the genteel primness of his intention but ended up with something much kinder, sloppier, human, fallible. It seemed to say that there are some things even Victorian high-mindedness could not crush. And perhaps I felt that, in consequence, it would be a tolerant house, that would allow me in my turn mistakes and miscalculations, even forgive me for past ones – though that, I realised, was asking a lot.

We chose it, Nick and Louis and myself, one autumn afternoon when father had kicked up a worse than usual row over the damage the boys were doing to his garden. Compared to the broken greenhouse windows and the trampled plants for which they had been scolded first by him and then by me without much effect, the sin of scuffing through piles of swept-up autumn leaves seemed so trivial that I suddenly rebelled and thought 'To hell with it!'. And I went there and then to the daily paper, looked at the property columns and ink-marked two or three. Then I collected up the boys, muddy as they were, and we drove over to Alma Crescent.

It belonged to a nice, elderly couple who were about to retire to the country, and I don't suppose they had any idea why I was trembling when I said, yes, we were interested and I would get my lawyer to contact theirs. They couldn't know that my lawyer was also my father, and that I had yet to persuade him that I wanted to sell my mother's jewellery, held in safe-keeping all these years, so that I could buy a house of my own. For father's attitude to me and the boys was split between a sense of civilised grievance at the disruption to his life and an equal sense of his own indispensability in keeping *our* lives on the rails.

I fell for the house at once, but the real deciding factor was the boys' reaction, Nick, then an outsize nine-year-old, dark as his absent father, and Louis, four years younger, small for his age and golden-haired. So far that gold hair had not improved the quality of his life. Set against the adoration of elderly ladies, and indeed most women of any age, was the fact that his smallness and fairness and pretty, elfin features acted on Nick's precocious machismo like a raging irritant. Nick bullied him, appallingly and uncontrollably. My father was horror-struck but refused to 'become involved'. He would be gruff from the head of the dining-table about the ravages to his garden, but he would not take on Nick over thumb-twisting, bruising and terrorising his younger brother. Mary, my stepmother, tried to make it up to Louis with cuddles and sweets, which only made matters worse. It was left to me, feeling sick, murderous and despairing by turns, to do what I could. This was not much for I was further hampered by the fact that if I got angry with Nick, I was in danger of crossing the borderline into frenzy. Nick was one of the many ways of being haunted by Robert whom he so uncannily resembled – his father, not dead, merely on the other side of the world in Australia. Just the same he haunted me, asleep and awake.

To my unbelieving joy, the house at Alma Crescent was instantly taken over by the boys.

'Come on! Let's explore – ' Nick even grabbed his younger brother's hand before galloping out into the back garden leaving me to apologise to the owners.

'Oh, let them be,' said the old man comfortably. Shortly after I heard them partitioning out the rooms, Nick saying, 'I'll have the big room at the back so I can set out my railway and you can have the little room *and* the cupboard under the stairs for all you puppets and wood and stuff. That's fair, isn't it?'

To hear Nick bothering about fairness was miracle enough. To hear them sounding like other people's boys, having fun together instead of the usual savage mayhem, made up my mind on the spot.

For the first time in years I smelt hope – the possibility of stepping clean out of the mucked-up past and the monotonous stalemate of our existence as my father's lodgers, ruled by his habits and his time. I had visions of the children playing happily in a house where no piece of furniture would matter, where the walls would be painted so brightly that untidiness and confusion would be drowned out in the general carnival of colour. It would be a house for children, including myself. I would have the big front room as a bedsit studio, where I too would play to my heart's content. There would be no carpet to ruin with my paints, and I would turn the record-player up fortissimo.

Of you, Marius, there was not the faintest forewarning, nor of any of the riches you would bring. My sights were set on a humbler kind of happiness, simply that my poor embattled children might draw a few unscolded breaths and with luck leave each other in peace.

2

After we got home that afternoon, the boys still talking as if we already owned the place, I went straight to my father while my courage was high and said I wanted to sell my share of my mother's jewellery and buy myself a house. Meanwhile, could he advance me a loan so that I could put in a bid?

Although he demurred about the price – 'too high for that area' – I think it was probably more a lawyer's reflex action than anything else, for with surprisingly little argument he agreed to lend me the money.

'But don't sell the jewellery, Carla. It's family stuff.'

'What good is it sitting in a safe-deposit?'

He shook his head. 'I'd just hate to think of it being sold, that's all. I can spare the money for the house.'

'But I don't want to be –'

'Beholden to me any longer?' Father sounded weary and flat, most unlike himself.

I didn't say anything.

'Well, you won't be. I'll make it an advance on your share of my estate.' He paused. 'It's time you led your own life, I can see that.'

The fact is, there was rather more behind my impulse to go and view Alma Crescent than an unpleasantness over scuffed leaves. That was only the tail-end of a stormy week, starting the previous Sunday with a monumental row between my sister and myself, a real shouting-match such as had probably never happened – ever – in our family. Stella had been married for years and had her own faultlessly appointed house, but the old family home – I hadn't fully realised it until we had this awful row – was in her eyes a sort of shrine to childhood, and nothing must ever be changed, neither the arrangement of objects nor the kind of behaviour which took place within it. My boys she regarded as demons of destructiveness. I did my best to keep them within the limits of our basement rooms, but since we all ate together, they erupted periodically into the hush and neatness of the upper house with great strain to all nerves concerned, particularly Stella's if she happened to be visiting.

Stella and I, of course, grew up in the middle of hush and neatness and good manners, but time had moved on and so had circumstance. Ever since the boys and I had been given shelter – and she, like everyone else, never argued for a moment against this rescue – she had been keeping an eye on the wear and tear to the house, an even more watchful eye than father. Nick being stronger-willed than any of us, there wasn't much she could do about him. So inevitably I came in for a certain amount of deflected anger. The causes were usually quite astonishingly trivial – for example, the fact that I'd moved a blue-and-white Chinese vase from one side of the sitting-room to the other.

'You've moved that vase!' Stella sounded as vexed as though I'd grubbed up a tree. Another time it was a pretty little Turkish rug which I had placed in a better light.

'What's that doing there?' she asked, agitated. 'It's always been under the sideboard.'

'I wanted to be able to see it without going down on my hands and knees.'

'It'll fade there. You should be more careful. I thought you were supposed to appreciate these things, being arty.'

'Exactly, that's why I want to *see* it.'

Stupid bickering, breaking out because there were tensions no one was prepared to admit. And then Stella made two dreadful discoveries in quick succession. She discovered that I had entertained a lover (well, actually, a man I'd met at a party, both men and parties being rare events in my life) *under our father's roof*. She discovered this thanks to our neighbour, Mrs. Mackie, who must have been up very bright and early that

Sunday morning, and who reported to Stella that she had seen a *man*, a strange man, coming out of the basement door, and was it all right? She was worried in case – And then, as luck would have it, the very same day poor Stella discovered, years and years after it had happened that I had 'pillaged' the closet where our mother's clothes and other things were stored.

At that she blew. She called me a 'wrecker and a whore' and a lot of other things as well. And I called her a 'prosy married virgin' with a rampaging obsessional neurosis. The resulting bad feeling was more than anyone could deal with. At Sunday lunch Stella broke down and wept, and we all ate through it with our heads down, even the boys subdued or at least silent with curiosity, and only father tried to act normally by asking 'Could you pass the horseradish, Carla?' But my nerve eventually gave way, and I got up and left the room, not to weep, but to sit quietly in my basement room and ponder over the fatal way I seemed to create disturbance and upset – to people I loved very much at heart. And I imagine everyone's thoughts were heading towards the conclusion that it was probably time I went.

That is how I explain father's extraordinary acquiescence in buying Alma Crescent. He didn't even ask to see over it and I didn't suggest it. I wanted to be living there and safely settled in before letting him over the doorstep. I was extremely bad at keeping masterful men at bay, and I winced at the thought of father's appraising eye being cast over my strange lop-sided dwelling and hearing him decree what improvements should be made. Of course he insisted on a survey, which was favourable as to structure and the state of the roof although pointing out that kitchen and bathroom were badly in need of modernisation, but otherwise he showed no curiosity. Poor father, I think he'd had enough, more than enough.

'Well,' he said on my last night under his roof after nearly five years of uneasy co-existence, five years in which I'd been neither flesh, fowl nor good herring, that is to say, a separated woman, finally a divorced woman, a dependant with dependants, 'I wish you luck, my dear.'

'Thanks, father.'

14

'I realise you want to strike out on your own. It's only natural.'

'Mm.'

'Just the same, I would counsel you not to do anything rash. Don't throw up your job with the firm or anything like that.'

Was he clairvoyant, or had he had a snoop round my correspondence? There lay the application form for a grant, and there also lay the precious letter asking me to attend an interview on the strength of the portfolio of work I'd presented. I wanted to go to art college, backed by the lecturer who took the life class I'd been attending twice a week evenings for the past year. 'You have a very sure line, unusual for a beginner' he'd said, and asked me to bring anything else I'd done. I went along with a collection of sketches of the boys which I'd done more to pass the time than anything else, and he thought they would probably get me in if I wanted to study full-time. So at the same time that Alma Crescent became mine, early in the new year, it seemed as if the gods, rather belatedly, were at least considering whether to chuck in a few more bits of good fortune.

'I shall certainly think very carefully before making any changes.'

That was the best route I could pick between agreeing and disagreeing with father. No point in chafing the raw state of relations further. It was important for both of us that this second departure from under the family roof should take place in civilised fashion. In my family, behaving in a civilised fashion was a test of maturity. I had failed it too often not to want at least to exit gracefully. Whatever I did next could be done at a distance; my resignation as secretary to one of his partners from the safe and comparatively distant roof of Alma Crescent might well be viewed as 'Carla's folly', but it would not be direct insulting disobedience.

My first exit was, of course, the start of the whole story which I so decidedly did not want you to know, Marius, not so much through a conscious policy of concealment but because I really believed that at last it was over – that you loving me the way you did had painted it out. Besides, I was already a new woman leading a new life by the time we met. If

I was a little 'mature' to be wearing quite such brief minis and quite such crazy boots, never mind. I swung with the rest in the mindless sixties, determined to banish the spectre of middle-aged frumpery that had crept up on me as I lived (like some travesty of a Victorian unmarried daughter) under the shadow of my fretful, masterful little father who had so loyally, bless him, stood by me in my time of need and got such little thanks.

It was past, it was all past. Life was hectic, it moved. It was full of hard work and excitement and then quite suddenly it was also full of love – love in the form of a mild-mannered, hesitant psychologist called Marius Gardiner, with a smile to charm flowers out of concrete, let alone a 'mature' art student already high on rediscovered freedom, catching up for life's lost time.

Life's lost time? Time never gets lost. It only gets stored away in vaults or cells, dripping away quietly like poisonous honey. Nothing gets lost down there, in the regions where things get turned into dreams, and *they* were never taken in by all that liberated fun. They simply waited and stalked me patiently through the years until the cracks appeared again –

So, let me go back to the beginning, to the time of my first exit in 1953, when I was nineteen and left home to get married.

3

Though he would have spat at the comparison, my father did share one important characteristic with the man I was to marry. They both exuded a kind of dominating energy, an assumption of mastery that was almost impossible to argue against. There the resemblance ended. Father was austere, correct, painstaking – lawyer's qualities, and certainly none of Robert's. But when it came to the crunch he was loyal in a way that was neither austere nor correct but truly passionate.

The crunch, of course, was brought about by me. I can't think that Stella gave him much cause to lose sleep, except for a few hectic months when it looked as though she were getting 'entangled' (father's word) with a Greek doctor from Alexandria. However, the Greek's mother came over to visit her son after which the liaison seemed to lose some of its attraction and Stella became subdued and undecided. Then the Greek returned to his home city and the affair tailed away leaving her ready to respond to the more conventional Edinburgh charms of Henry Johnson, a plump chartered accountant with tory instincts and commercial ambition. And he wooed and won my sister and father could relax.

I don't know what word he used to describe my involvement with Robert. Perhaps the whole thing was too awful to be summarised in a word, or indeed any number of words. Before our marriage there had been, as far as I remember, only one encounter between them and they had sat and bristled and rattled their quills at each other, and after that I was careful not to bring Robert to the house again. The next time I had occasion to mention him to father it was to tell him I was expecting his baby.

'Oh, my God!'

Father put his large head between his small hands. He was sitting at his desk in his study and had his reading glasses on. These he now took off and set carefully on the desk in front of him. His hand was quivering. He looked at me beseechingly, begging for this monstrous fact to be hustled away out of sight.

I would have given anything – anything to be able to oblige.

'I – I'm sorry, father. I didn't know it was so – easy to conceive.'

He stared even harder at that.

'There is one and only one sure way of conceiving,' he said, slowly and drily. 'Surely your step-mother told you – all the things you should know?'

She hadn't, she had merely said when I had my first period, 'Now your body is ready to have a baby' which to a girl of thirteen is not of enormous interest. And Stella had been evasive, rather more so after her marriage than before. But still I couldn't plead total ignorance. I had not been to school for nothing. Latin last period on Thursdays was the traditional time for discussing the facts of life. Those of us who thought ourselves emancipated, or wanted to be, sat in the back row and whispered and passed little notes to each other. Unfortunately a few ingenious fantasies got passed along with the factual stuff, most of which was not really very helpful. By this means I learned the meaning of the word 'dildo', but also believed that if you drank half a cup of unsweetened lemon juice within two hours of 'doing it' with a man, the sperm would curdle and you would not get pregnant. It was Patty Sparks who had provided this piece of information, and Patty wore black lace panties under her school uniform and generally let it be understood that they had been seen by more appreciative eyes than ours.

When I started sleeping with Robert my knowledge of contraception was still at this rudimentary, or rather, mythical level. I spent a lot on lemons and eventually developed stomach cramps but not the kind that would have been good news. When I told Robert he went pale and said, 'I thought you knew what you were doing. I thought you must be using something.'

Father had also gone pale. He picked up little objects on his desk and put them down again carefully. His hands were always well manicured, part of the dapper sensitive side of him that combined so peculiarly with the small-city man of business. He was rock-solid, but still there was this dash of stylish, almost stagy vitality, a quiver of temperament and sharpness at the edges, a touch of the dandy – I once caught him painting out the grey in his thin black moustache. I would have adored him openly if he'd let me but he kept both of us at bay with a kind of exasperated common-sense. If our mother had lived, perhaps he would not have been so scared of actually showing tenderness. As it was, father, small and neat with his gnomish large head and clipped moustache, simply stood centre-stage and directed operations.

'Well, this is a precious mess,' he said, sounding petulant as well as despairing.

'Yes, I know. Can I sit down?'

'Yes, yes, of course.'

'I'm sorry,' I said, starting to feel tears rising. 'I'm dreadfully sorry. About the disgrace.'

But it was worse than that, it was menace. The solid order of things was falling apart. The lamp-light, the flicker of flames, the book-cases with their fat, still volumes – all these were part of the snug inner lining of father's orderly, rational, hard-working, unquestioning life, that life which I simply gripped like an amulet knowing myself secure because he was there. And now, with my grotesque revelation in the air, the enchanted safety was vanishing, vanishing while I watched. My father, my rock, was drawing deep quavery breaths and his hands were shaking.

There was a long frightened pause. Finally father looked up from the silver paper-knife he kept turning and clutching.

'You have two choices, my dear.' For all the fright his voice still carried authority. 'You can have the baby quietly somewhere away from here and have it adopted – or marry its father. An illegitimate grandchild under my feet I will not

19

have.' He paused, as though he wasn't sure that was what he had meant to say. 'But I have to admit it's the man as much as the child that distresses me.'

With great difficulty we looked at each other. In father's face was a terrible scared distaste as he tried to cope with the insult of my sexual choice. In my own, I imagine there was shame and distress, also a bit of defiance, but above all, swamping all, utter confusion.

'Do you – love him?'

What was I to say? Either answer was to be dreaded. If I said 'no', then there between us floated the image of a sexual woman, the dreaded bogey of respectable folk – loose, lewd and anarchic. It was an image which terrified me as well as him. Where would I end up? Already I was not nice, not nice at all.

If I said 'yes' – oh, how could I know? Was fascination love? Was obsession love? Both of these I felt for Robert. He had seduced my imagination far more thoroughly than my body. He filled my mind the way a mountain blots out the sky. He was adventure, he was the unknown. He was the 'Older Man' – twenty-nine to my nineteen – beside whom the mannerly boys of my own background seemed like inspid children. He was wild, bitter, heretical, outrageously funny. He saw all life in terms of a dirty fight against the gods and the upper classes. I was going to change all that, make him see that life could be joyous and light-hearted. I wanted to rescue him from his black despairs. A serious mistake, for Robert, I later discovered, had taken out a monopoly in random, undeserved pain. Nothing made him madder than a positive approach to life.

Most fatally of all, I had fallen for the seduction of my own power to charm sweet words from him. 'You're my flower' he used to murmur after we'd made love. It was the only part I really enjoyed, being called his flower and his hand stroking me after the action was over. But it was all by candlelight, mark you, candles in wine bottles and candles in saucers, and our clothes lay in a tumbled heap on the floor, so it was fulfilling in the theatrical sense.

Meanwhile, my father's question.

'Do you love him?'

'Yes' I said suddenly.

I wanted to try out the sound, see if it rang true. It certainly rang out clear and defiant.

Father's face folded down into a small creased version of itself. I was suddenly appalled at having beaten him, scored a victory I didn't know I wanted. I saw him forlorn and tremulous and I couldn't bear it. 'Oh father,' I wanted to say, 'It'll be all right. You will feel safe again.' But I should have been more concerned about myself. Father's kingdom, thirty years in the making, might have to repair its defences a little. It was I who would live in the wasteland.

He said resignedly, 'D'you think he'll agree to marry you? And if he does, what has the fellow to offer you in the way of security? He's some kind of temporary lecturer at the University, isn't he?'

'Well, he's almost certain to be given a permanent appointment, I think.' My mind was wandering, trying to gauge Robert's reactions if he could overhear this conversation. 'Then there's his poetry. His last collection of poems is selling quite well – '

Father made a face.

'You can forget about that. I don't know much about literary publishing, but there isn't a poet on record, as far as I know, who's ever done anything except drag his family into drudgery–'

'There was Wordsworth – ' I put in, and immediately remembered Robert quietly removing the hide of a young student from England who had complained at the scanty treatment given to the philosopher of Windermere in our introductory course. Mention Wordsworth to Robert and you released a withering discourse on the folly of attempting to be metaphysical with a poetic technique 'about as subtle as a clog-dance.'

Father wasn't listening.

'Would you have anywhere to live?'

'He's got a flat.'

I thought of that third floor den. Love by candlelight. But a wife and baby? In there? Mentally I shook my head, and then remembered the wife and baby would be me.

'He may decide to have nothing to do with me.'

21

'Then he'll have something to do with *me* which may not be to his advantage' said father viciously. However horror-struck at the idea of Robert as his son-in-law, since I had given him the cue by admitting love, he was going to pursue the cause of my honour with determination.

My mind switched away again. One fact stuck out above all others. I say 'fact' but I mean nightmare, a distillation of pure panic. I, as I knew myself, had disappeared. I had existed the day before, the week before, even when the dreadful visit to the family doctor had confirmed all my fears. Now I did not. The girl who rushed from lectures to fencing-matches, who went to dances and parties and worried about nothing except handing in the next essay and spinning out her generous dress allowance – that creature was wiped out. Whether I married Robert (always assuming he agreed), or disappeared for several months to let this shocking fact in my womb turn into a human child, life as I had known it was over. In a man's experience, I can only think of going to war as an event similarly terrifying and inescapable. Don't get me wrong, Marius, I feel the enormity of making such a comparison, but there it is. I know nothing of the joys of happy pregnancy.

In father's study there was a moment of meekness when I wanted to say to someone or something, 'I never realised how easy it was to smash up your chances.' Then numbness settled in, the kind of numbness which leads to brilliant acting.

'I'm not going to say anything about this to your step-mother until the situation is a little clearer.' Father put on his reading glasses again, signalling that our talk was concluded. 'And I'd rather you didn't either.'

For a moment I thought he was going to add 'This is a family matter'. It would not have been so very out of keeping with their relationship which outwardly had not changed much since the days when Mary was our housekeeper and nanny. Although they had been married for years, their manner (at least in front of anyone else) was almost as formal as it had ever been and even embarrassingly suggested that Mary, despite plump gold wedding ring and solitaire diamond still 'knew her place'.

Stella had been furious when they married, unreasonably

22

and cruelly furious. Of course it was much worse for her. She remembered our mother, whereas I did not since I was only three when she died. Stella was nine. She was sixteen when father re-married – beneath him, she said, and then went into a cold rage which lasted for weeks during which family meals became unbearable. Stella said such appalling things to Mary, about her figure, her background, her 'scheming' and plenty more, that I do not know how Mary put up with it. In point of fact, she was a placid, pleasant-looking woman who had been an infant teacher before coming to run our household and look after us children. Perhaps she was not in the same league as our mother whose chilly handsome features stared out of a large portrait in the sitting-room. And perhaps father was quite content to have it so. Nevertheless, even masterful men have their Achilles' heel, and he rather cravenly left poor Mary to face his elder daughter's abuse alone, making for the safe retreat of his study as soon as he could decently bolt from the table.

Just as I was going out of that same study he looked up at me over the half-moons of his glasses.

'One thing I absolutely will not have and that is a backstreet abortion. So if that was anywhere in your mind, you can rule it out. I'm not paying to have some butcher perform an illegal operation on you. There's too much risk - of every kind.'

4

It was almost the first thing Robert suggested when we met the next afternoon at Meldrum's cafe, our usual trysting place. We hadn't seen each other for several days.

'Is it definite?'

I nodded. Robert breathed out noisily, like a scared horse. He looked terrible, hollow and stricken. How much that was to do with the threat of a scandal and losing his job I don't know, but I suspect quite a lot. Universities then were small uncrowded places, well supervised and surveyed by their authority figures. Lecturers were not supposed to seduce students, certainly not get them pregnant. There would be questions asked and steps taken if he did not do the right thing by me.

A waitress came over fussing kindly, making sure we had everything we wanted, for we were great favourites in the tea-shop. All the world loves a lover, especially elderly waitresses with tired misshapen feet and motherly express-ions. We had been petted and spoiled through all the weeks and months of our courtship, with extra butter slipped onto the dish and the toast rack re-filled without asking, and even occasionally a wrapped chocolate biscuit slid onto our plates that didn't figure on the bill. It was their way of taking part in the pastime of love. In return, Robert flirted with them gallantly.

'Right then, Mary,' he would say to the stout manageress, armour-plated in her beaded black suit. 'When are we going to the dancing? How about Saturday night?'

She laughed every time.

'Yer aff yer heid. Ma feet'll be up in front of the fire and the old man snoozing behind his paper. That's ma Saturday night!'

'Well, shame on you. That's for old women.'

'And wha' d'ye think I am?'

'You? Just a lassie. Still in yer prime!'

More laughter – 'Wait till I tell the old man! He'll die laughing. Look, there's a nice table for you over by the window. I'll get Kathleen to clear it.'

She gave me a big smile. It was blessings all round – the daytime, innocuous face of our affair, shaped more by my school-girlish habits than Robert's. I knew nothing then about all the time spent in pubs, those rank and revolting male drinking-dens which have all but disappeared now, their place taken by plush and pink-lit lounges and shop-girls quaffing vodka-and-orange in the lunch-hour.

The day we decided to marry, if you can call it that, everything was the same, a table of school-girls (from my old school), student couples holding hands, elderly women nodding their tea-cosy hats and discussing sickness and death. Our favourite waitress came over with a fresh pot of tea which was slipped onto the table with a wink meaning it wouldn't appear on the bill. We both smiled our thanks with an effort.

Robert was a large restless man. That afternoon he sat quite still with that whitish look on his face showing up the rather bad shave he'd given himself.

'I suppose I kept hoping for miracles,' he said at last, low-voiced.

'Miracles?'

'Yes, that you might miscarry, that it was all a false alarm – anything. Can't you – '

'What?'

'Try to get rid of it?'

'I don't know how. And I'm not going to try. I'm terrified of being messed up. And besides, father has said absolutely not.'

My eyes started filling, and this was no act. My body had already become strange enough with swollen aching breasts

25

and attacks of nausea which made me panic. I'd never been ill in my life, apart from mild bouts of measles and chickenpox.

'No, all right – ' he took my hand with one of his funny impulses of tenderness, gestures that escaped unawares and left him stranded. His grasp slackened but I held on. 'I shouldn't have said that. I'm sorry. But it is – ' he closed his eyes – 'pretty disastrous. And you're so bloody young.'

Perhaps at this point things were a little easier for me. I had had a day or two to get used to the queer fact that things go on, much the same, even when the will to live has gone. I don't mean that I wanted to take my life – no, it was simply that I had gone numb and passive in the face of this blundering set of forces which had so much more power over events than any conscious ideas of mine. And vanished along with my old self was any notion that I could either defy or control, which, considering that 'wilful' and 'arrogant' were teachers' favourite epithets during my teens, seemed strange. It's also true that life had been remarkably easy. I was pretty and popular and unreflectingly pleased with myself, a bubble that can easily be pricked. But then, what about the sharp tricky fighter who had so recently earned her position in the fencing-club's first championship team? Perhaps that is the clue. I liked to know what I was fighting against, the size and strength of the adversary. It was beyond me to know how to fight something as shapeless and shadowy as the traitor in my gender.

'You won't finish your degree now' said Robert, after a long silence.

'No. But it's not important.'

'Well it should be,' he said sharply. 'Oh I know *you've* never taken your work seriously, but I have. Don't you realise? You're one of the very few since I got this farcical job who actually shows some signs of a capacity to think. You even have some original ideas, but do you care?'

'Don't tell me' I said, rallying with a pinch of sarcasm 'that your main worry is ruining a promising career?'

'No, it's not my main worry. But I have thought about it. Which is more than you seem to have done.'

'I don't think that's very surprising. I'm only in second year.

26

I thought there would be plenty of time. No one takes work seriously until – well, junior honours year anyway. And for you, I've worked very hard. You know that.'

'Yes.' Robert chuckled. 'One of the penalties of going out with your tutor. By the way, I've got your last essay somewhere to give back to you – '

We stared at each other. That other penalty loomed large. I shook my head.

'I don't want it.'

And for the first time since it had happened, learning that I was pregnant, I had a most terrible wrenching sense of loss. It was all past, all over, the silly dizzy time of nothing mattering. And looking ahead, that world that my friends would walk into when they graduated, looking for work and challenge and adventure, that too I glimpsed, sparkling with promise, before it was whisked away for ever.

Over the thick china cups and the metal teapot with the handle too hot to hold I cried into my hands. I cried with incomprehension. I cried at being sent into distant exile, here, without moving a foot from my accustomed places. I cried at the sight of Robert's face, stunned as though hit by a hammer. I cried at being turned into the instrument that could deal such a blow.

'Don't cry, Carla.' Robert quite gently tried to take my hands from my face. 'For God's sake, don't cry, not in front of all these folk. Mary'll be over to ask what's wrong. I can't stand it. I'll try and make you happy, I promise I will. I'm not much good at it, but I'll try. Now *please* – '

'Do you still love me?'

'Yes, yes – ' he broke off and swung round to stare hastily at the window as if gauging the jump to the ground. I knew his desperation was the only honest response. But I was pregnant and I had my role to play.

He ran his hands through his hair, and I saw my romantic lover come to life again – dark, shaggy, intense. Then he took hold of my wrists and gripped them tightly.

'We'll marry,' he said. 'We have to, don't we?' I nodded. 'Only for God's sake, no family celebrations.'

5

That is how I remember that afternoon. It is still so vivid that it takes me a few hours to shake off the sinking sense of panic and foreboding and emerge thankfully into the present, made safe and sane by problems which only require competence and drive to solve.

But as I've been telling it to you, Marius, I realise that I'm still not at all clear whether I believe my 'story' is the outcome of a personal engagement with fate, Robert and I in some sense destined to tangle with each other, or whether my unknown self, a creature hidden from its own eyes by a kind of purdah veil of niceness, would have broken out and made obsessively for some other source of sexual trouble.

Then again it occurs to me how much that very thing that upset me so much, the vanishing world of potential, was an illusion, a dream of freedom for us women. My contemporaries probably did no better in terms of actual *freedom*. They probably made better terms for themselves, went for a better class of submission to the inevitable, but inevitable it was and we didn't even know we thought that. At least I didn't.

And yet, if I had not married Robert I would almost certainly have married someone else, two, three, perhaps four years later, in the 'natural course of events'. It might have been more comfortable, more pleasant, but I do believe that there would have come eventually the same sense of devastating mystery – 'I was – and then I vanished'. For kinder and saner men than Robert have reduced their women to existential crumbs, simply because they feed without thinking on that rich apologetic uncertainty, that nourishing pap for male energy, which society has so dogmatically built into the definition of 'being a woman'. Even you, my gentle Marius, had the unmistakeable signs of knowing how to tap it. For you I became, at least in private, passive and wanting only to give and give . . . and felt wondrously fulfilled for a time.

'No celebrations' Robert had pleaded. But of course there was a celebration, of sorts. Father, with a kind of icy bravado, booked a table at a restaurant where he was known and respected. Whether he wanted the moral support of the restaurateur who would have walked through fire for him ever since he had won a case of threatened eviction, I don't know. Possibly he felt it was best to exhibit his undesirable son-in-law and get it over, though on the occasion of his wedding Robert's performance was not outrageous. He left that to his best man, the appalling life and soul of the party, his party, his private drunken buffoon's party happening in the context of our wedding.

He was called Eddie and he had stuffed himself into a snuff-coloured suit which had been pressed but not cleaned for the occasion. 'Gotta keep out the cold' he said cheerfully, producing a hipflask from a distant pocket and taking a swig. We were by this time gathered in the waitingroom of the registrar's office. It was November and the office was panelled in wood and reeked of official death, or more correctly, demise. It was, as Eddie had noticed, cold.

'C'mon, pal – ' Eddie offered his flask to Robert, but he shook his head morosely. Bravely, in the silence of total disapproval, he raised it to his lips and then, even more bravely, made a half-hearted gesture towards my father, who gave him a stare of such frightful hostility that my guess is the flask de-materialised then and there.

'Just get yourself together and find the bloody ring,' Robert whispered through his teeth. He had come alone and unsupported to his wedding, apart from this dubious ally. He was wearing a grey suit, cleaner than Eddie's, but like his a bit on the tight side. I had the feeling it was borrowed.

As for myself, my outfit was the most amazing anticipation

of the drab mouldiness of hustle-through weddings. I toned in
almost to disappearing point with the decor of the office,
having bought myself an extraordinary garment, a wool suit
in a small pernickety check of brown, cream and olive green. It
was an outfit intended for a woman of forty, someone
moreover who has shunned colour with the shudder of sin
avoided, and it forcefully symbolised a vanishing (or a
banishing) because my normal taste ran to the brightest of
bright. I adored colour, fed off it, and although I blamed God
for the shape of my nose and my large feet I never once
quibbled over the fact that I was dark as a gypsy, for it meant
that I could dress up in all sorts of flamboyant craziness.
Privately – and perhaps not so privately – I hugged myself that
I was not like Stella who had small neat features and the kind of
midway colouring that feels safest in pastels. I identified with
Carmen Miranda, she with Anna Neagle.

Yet here was I, in my middle-aged outfit, sallow with
anti-nausea drugs and pregnancy sickness, and here was she,
fresh and pretty as a posy of flowers standing beside her
plump and cologne-clean husband. And this was my wedding
day.

'Please come in.'

The registrar had appeared. Yet another ill-fitting suit, only
this time slack and creased. He ushered us into a side room
where there was a deal table with two Woolworth's glass vases
and a few chrysanthemums in each.

'Who is the best man?'

The registrar scanned the men present in turn and saw no
likely candidate.

'Go on,' Robert nudged Eddie. 'It's you.'

Eddie stepped forward, looking suddenly stricken with
stage-fright. The registrar looked at him wearily.

'Are you also going to act as witness?'

'Oh aye,' said Eddie uneasily.

'And the second witness?'

He turned to the rest of us, again looking like a casting
director faced with a bum lot presenting for audition.

Mary indicated that she was second witness. Anyone would
have done, but in a way it seemed quite appropriate that she,

rather than either of my genuine relatives, had been given this small part.

The ceremony was very short. Robert and I didn't look at each other. Eddie mercifully did not drop the ring. Father said his lines as if he were giving evidence at a particularly unsavoury trial. And when it was over there was a very definite sense of relief. Father even shook hands with Robert. Stella came forward and gave me a hug. Mary, my step-mother, said what nobody else tried to say, 'I hope you'll be very happy, my dear'. She also gave Robert a hug, and he accepted it. Stella said coldly to him, 'Congratulations' and did not offer her hand.

In the Powder Room at Luigi's I plastered some pan-cake over my peculiar olive-green complexion. Stella patted her posy-fresh cheeks and pulled a curl or two into place. She saw, and I saw, not only the contrast in our complexions but the look of defeat that had settled unawares on my face some time during the past two weeks.

'Carla –' She turned me away from the mirror and put her arms round me. For a few seconds she was the sister of my childhood, the kind older sister who had mothered me not always patiently but with passionate responsibility and love – the kind of love that takes a hammering when men appear on the scene. It felt warm and comfortable with her arms round me. 'Are you all right, poppet?'

'Yes.' My voice was muffled by her shoulder. 'I'm all right.'

'Do you think you'll – I mean, will the meal be too much for you?'

'Oh no, I'm quite peckish for once.' I tried to sound bright and cheery. 'I'm dosed up to the eyeballs with Fergus's pills. They make me terribly sleepy, but I don't feel sick.'

I raised my head and we stared at each other.

'I'll help you when the baby comes,' Stella said abruptly. 'I promise. You mustn't think –' she broke off and looked away. 'After all, you are my sister.' She sounded as if she were arguing with someone, someone she was afraid would over-rule her. Perhaps it was a whole court full of people, nice people. She was, after all – we all were – first and foremost, social beings.

Stella had come once to Robert's flat at my request. He'd given me the keys and let us get on with our measuring for more adequate curtains and a rug or carpet for the bare boards in the bedroom. She was clearly dumbfounded.

'I thought you said he was a university lecturer,' she said at last.

'So he is. An assistant lecturer, anyway.'

'Well, this doesn't look like – I mean, *surely* he could afford some rugs or something? And some decent furniture? And why aren't there more books?'

'He keeps most of them in his room in the department. And assistant lecturers don't get much pay, you know.'

She stared round glumly. Clearly her heart was not in the business of helping me choose curtain material. In the end I went out and bought it myself, warm red wool with a faint stripe of darker red. That was before my colour sense packed up. I remember those curtains vividly. They created the one splash of brightness in that flat and they kept a thin thread of connectedness with a younger, more optimistic person from breaking altogether.

Our freshening up concluded, we went through to the restaurant. Luigi had put discreet floral decorations on our table without making it so festive as to attract attention. Perhaps he had consulted with father on this, but probably it was just another instance of his near-psychic tact.

I sat down beside Robert. He smiled at me faintly and we squeezed hands under the table. Wine was brought in decanters. Father proposed a toast, very simple . . .

'To Robert and Carla.'

There was a discreet murmuring like an 'Amen'.

'Robert and Carla! Robert and Carla!' brayed Eddie belatedly. 'Sounds like some posh double-act, doesn't it? Aristocrats of the High Trapeze . . . Tango-Time in Teneriffe. . .'

Everyone resolutely lifted their glasses to their lips and tried to ignore him.

'No?' Eddie clung with all the obstinacy of your truly great bore to his stillborn joke. 'But you can't waste it, man – it's made for a double-billing – ah!' He threatened to crack the chair by throwing himself suddenly backwards. 'That's it! Billing and cooing. . . .'

By this time we were all studiously engrossed in reading the menu, discreetly gold-bordered.

'Luigi does a beautiful *medaillons de veau*' said Stella, who was sitting on Robert's other side.

'Does he?'

For one awful moment I thought he was going to tell her about the phase of his childhood spent living near the abattoir and how the first poem he ever wrote was about watching calves being herded in for slaughter (the reason why the lesser celandine and other pretty snippets of nature figured so low in his estimation). But he didn't. He simply didn't say much at all.

The plates of hors d'oeuvres started to arrive. Stella's husband seemed to be transfixed by the way Robert was using his knife and fork, the knife held pencil-fashion, the fork gripped far down the handle. It was a clinical stare, coming through his gold-rimmed accountant's glasses, and it happened again when Robert picked up his glass and drank his claret, a good swig at a time, no lingering on the palate of a measured sip.

I wanted to shout 'How *dare* you stare at my man – my husband – as if he were some specimen of tribal life!' And yet I did wish that his table manners were not so conspicuous. I saw with most awful clarity, at my wedding, what I had never realised before, that I belonged to a caste and that I was about to become an outcast, if not an untouchable, with every caste feature and instinct still firmly in place.

'Carla tells me you're a poet.'

That was Stella, trying again.

'Well – I write poetry.'

Stella laughed a tinkly little laugh, not her everyday one.

'Isn't that the same thing?'

Robert turned towards her.

'No,' he said politely.

'No?' There was silence. 'Well, obviously I'm going to have to work that one out for myself. Would you like some more wine?'

'Yes, thanks.'

'Carla?'

33

'No thanks.'

It wasn't nausea this time, but a sense of the mild blasphemy we were committing by eating together with such little goodwill that was taking away my appetite for food and wine – that and the subdued agitation all round me. Father had safely flanked himself with Mary on one side and Henry on the other. But on the other side of Mary sat or rather, increasingly sprawled, Eddie, whom father was watching with bitter satisfaction.

'Why did you bring him?' I whispered to Robert. 'And who is he anyway?'

Robert stared at his best man with almost as much dislike as my father.

'A chap I met in a pub. He didn't seem too bad that night. I made a mistake, he's just a fat-arsed drunk.'

'Couldn't you have asked someone you knew? Your brother – why didn't you ask him?'

I knew Robert had a brother although I had never met him.

'Because – ' Robert looked round at my nearest and dearest and drew in his breath tight – 'he wouldn't have come. He's a militant red and you, my dear, are the class enemy. Nothing personal, of course.' He looked down at me and his expression changed. 'I shouldn't have said that. I'm sorry. Carla, stop staring like that. We're married now. We'll be good to each other. This is all – a load of crap. When it's out of the way it'll be just us, having a good time together.'

'D'you think we will have a good time together?'

'Well, we used to, didn't we?'

He smiled, one of his rare smiles. For a moment we caught the romantic bit again, the shaking and agitation before meetings, the tense hand-holding in the cinema, the clinging and kissing in the chilly shadows before hurling ourselves into bed and then – the event which was always puzzling and remote for me and exhaustingly violent for Robert. And after, I enjoyed after, soothing his damp body and stroking his hair and face and knowing I had given pleasure.

I smiled back at Robert, a shaky grin, lacking confidence.

It was at this point that Eddie swayed to his feet to give his imitation of a seal being trained to balance a ball on its nose, only he was using his wine glass. After the first breakage, which was almost instantaneous, father summoned Luigi and told him to get him out. It was done swiftly and with no protest, which surprised me. Perhaps it was part of Eddie's life to be flung out of places.

'I'm sorry,' said father grimly to Robert, 'but your friend was going too far.'

'I quite agree,' said Robert courteously, also grim. And that was the last we ever saw of Eddie, though you may see his double in the small hours of any Hogmanay party, a red and featureless blur of bonhommie which even committed revellers find curiously depressing.

I felt like telling on Robert, saying to my father, 'He wasn't a friend. He was someone Robert picked up in a pub. They probably made this whole wedding into an evening of dirty jokes.' Father would see how horribly I'd been hurt and insulted. He'd put everything into reverse – annul the ceremony, tell Robert to go to hell, take me back to the brown-and-russet warmth of his study, tell me for Heaven's sake to be more careful in the future. . . Then I remembered the baby growing inside me, the irreversible factor, the tunnel you walk into and have to keep walking down.

There was a sense of movement, the beginnings of a break-up. Stella had brought my coat from the Ladies. Apparently there was a taxi waiting to take us to the station.

'Bless you, my dear.'

Mary kissed me warmly and rather to my surprise kissed Robert as well. And he quite naturally gave her a return hug. She seemed the only person unaffected by the whole bizarre experience.

We went downstairs to the street where the taxi throbbed patiently. At the last minute, father drew me slightly aside, kissed me almost like a lover on the mouth, and then looked at me with the oddest expression. It was full of fatherly concern, yet at the same time he eyed me like a fellow-conspirator, as if between us we'd brought off a delicate secret operation. Then we kissed again more decorously, lips to cheek, and I made for the taxi.

Mary threw a handful of confetti after us. Some of it landed on my shoulders and fluttered to the taxi floor as Robert and I were borne off to the station, hands locked tight – in relief, in defiance, because of the taxi-driver – I don't know. And that was the end of my wedding.

Stella told me long after that she and Henry and father and Mary went back to our old home where father promptly shut himself up in his study and was found, when Mary went to tell him supper was ready, sitting at his desk with his head in his hands. She had difficulty persuading him to come and eat and he'd hardly spoken a word throughout the meal.

I've often dreamt my wedding over again. It's one of the cycle of dreams that comes round and round, or did, until very recently. Each time I wake up mystified. Why does it still go on? They are not good dreams, they signify troubled states. Even in the dream I'm sometimes mystified, asking myself why I am letting this all happen again? Why don't I protest? Sometimes the scene is very realistic, as it actually happened. Sometimes it gets mixed up with other scenes, like the awful parties Robert used to have at our flat, a kind of dingy bacchanalia.

Once I was dressed up as a proper bride in lacey white with a bouquet and Robert's shadowy presence was in some kind of dark correct outfit, and that caused me more agitation than any of the other versions. At first when I woke I simply thought 'How absurd! Am I really trying to "make it nice" after all this time?' And then I realised that once again, long-departed Robert was exercising his *droit du seigneur* over my unconscious. For that dream came shortly after an evening which we'd spent carefully, hesitantly exploring the question of marriage, you and I, both full of longing, but both wary of the transition from being lovers to being man and wife.

6

We spent our honeymoon at a west-coast seaside resort shut up for the winter except for one hotel keeping an eyelid propped up for passing trade. It was not actually such a bad choice. The weather was sharp and sunny and the light was amazing. The bare bones of the Victorian pavilion stood out sad but elegant at the end of the promenade like the fancy ribs of an old umbrella, while its saucer roof flaked and collapsed. Behind the town there were hills where we walked most days. Robert looked rugged and grand in that setting, and seemed to be aware of it for, perched on a rock and gazing out to sea, he would go off into soliloquies about himself.

'I'm really a very solitary kind of bloke,' he said. 'A loner – no, more than that.' He thought for a moment. 'I'd like the *whole world* to myself. I could use every bit of it, *be* every bit of it. It's a sort of mystical state, and I've tried to get it into words but it doesn't work, not yet, anyway. It's not in anything I've published. And in any case – '

He gazed out to sea again.

'What?'

'It doesn't last. I lose it. And then I go to the other extreme. I want to disappear. I don't want to be anybody, I just want to be a bundle of senses – no mind, above all no mind.' He looked at me sideways and looked away again. 'That's where the bevvy comes in, and the pub and all that.'

On our honeymoon we talked. He admitted he drank more than was good for him. I don't think he promised to mend his ways. I probably thought he meant that simply by making the admission. He made another admission.

'You know something? You're the first woman I've known who hasn't driven me crazy with boredom.'

'I don't believe you.'

'Well it's true.'

'What about the French girl who said you were like Guy de Maupassant?'

'Her?' he laughed. 'She was touched. Soft in the head. Must have been to say a thing like that.'

'But you said she had the most wonderful – um – breasts you'd ever – um – '

Robert chuckled and looked pleased.

'You're jealous. Well, you've no need to be.' He stroked my long hair. 'Her breasts were okay but you can't have a conversation with a pair of tits, can you? No, she was like all the rest, no spark. Whereas you – ' he grinned again. 'You've always got something to say. You're an arguer. Life and soul of the tutorial group. The rest of them – God I want to shake them sometimes, sitting there with their little buttoned-in faces, never saying a word. What gets into them, for God's sake?' He sighed. 'It's going to be pretty dull without you.'

We contemplated in silence the extraordinary fact that it was only a month ago that I'd stopped attending classes. Events had moved fast. I also contemplated his extraordinary remark.

'What do you mean, *without* me? I'll be with you all the time, at home.'

'Ah, but maybe that won't be quite the same thing, my dearest Carla.'

There was something unpleasant about the way he said 'my dearest Carla'. That kind of endearment wasn't Robert's style. He stuck to simple words like 'pet' and 'flower' on the rare occasions he felt the need to be tender. What he had just said sounded ironic, faintly insulting, a send-up of poshness, but I hadn't the courage to ask him what he meant. I was already losing those argumentative qualities he valued so much, in the tutorial group.

The next morning I woke up feeling disastrously queasy.

Even Fergus's pills had no effect, so instead of going into the hills we had to content ourselves with wandering along the empty seafront, I trying my best to convince myself that the queer salt smell off the beach was making me feel less squeamish and that the whipping wind was healthful and bracing. I held onto Robert's arm obstinately although he kept it tense against his side as if holding himself physically aloof. He hated any signs of illness or weakness. It seemed to bring out some kind of disgust in him. ('Fear' said a friend of mine years later, 'fear of his own childish vulnerable self.' People have a robust way of dismissing all domination as weakness turned upside down, yet it has always struck me that this 'weakness' has a most terrible staying power and a hideous amount of muscle, whether in the form of fascist dictators or bullying husbands.)

The manageress at the hotel, a gaunt spinster in appearance, but actually mother of four, had taken one look at me that morning and said kindly, 'Back to your bed, lass. You shoulda sent yer man down to tell me, and I'd a brought ye a cup of tea to yer room. It's all yer fit for, by the looks of things.' 'She's all right,' said Robert defiantly. 'Aren't you, Carla? The fresh air'll do you more good than lying in bed.'

I dithered uncertainly, longing for bed, unable to cope with the thought of Robert, caged, restless and angry. I had already suggested he should go into the hills alone but for one who wanted the whole world to himself he was curiously unattracted by the idea.

'Well, I'm going to have my breakfast,' he said abruptly, turning away. 'Make up your mind one way or the other.'

Breakfast with its attendant horror of frying bacon or kipper smells I could not face. The manageress put her arm round me.

'Come into my office and sit quiet for a bit. Maybe you could manage that cup o' tea? Sadie!' She called through to the waitress. 'Can you bring us a pot o' tea in the office?'

Her kindness threatened to demolish me. She almost had a flood of whimpering tears on her flat angora-covered chest. What saved her was not some last-ditch stoicism on my part, but the fact that she had reading glasses dangling from a fancy gilt chain that I would have had to bat out of the way.

She sat me down in an armchair. Sadie reappeared with a tray of tea and put it carefully on the desk.

'It'll be your first' said the manageress as she poured.

It was half question, half statement. I looked over at her. 'Yes.'

'First and worst.' She laughed. 'Don't worry. The next one'll be a treat, you mark my words.'

'There'll never be a second one if I have anything to do with it.'

The ferocity in my own voice shocked me. It shocked her too.

'Oh come away, you don't really mean that. It's just the way you're feeling. I'm telling you, it gets easier and easier. By the time I had ma third, Will – that's ma man – could run the house, do all the meals, get the others off to school. And by the time wee Angus came along, I just about handed him over to the family. Mind you, I'm lucky. Will's always been a helpful easy-going kind o' man. There aren't too many like him – '

She broke off and in the silence Robert's clearly unpromising characteristics as a family man passed before both our minds. I could picture him as he was at that moment, hunched massively over his plate of porridge or kippers, locked into that morose introspection I still fondly interpreted as the seedbed of his inspiration. One of the powerful charms of the days that turned out to be our courtship was my knack of teasing and coaxing him out of these black moods, to be rewarded finally with a look that suggested I had let light and hope into a gloomy prison. . . .

You may wonder, if this was the level of my private thoughts, how on earth Robert could possibly have spotted originality in my work? I don't know. Perhaps my mind was more inventive than my personal emotions, a condition of life, I think. I doubt whether writers or artists, however soaring their vision, ever move much beyond the simplicities of infatuation in their own lives.

But this business of gloomy heroes, it's not something to be dismissed with a light laugh. Women were (and still perhaps are) all too thoroughly convinced that manly strength implies the capacity to be cruel. For our generation, perhaps it was all the war-movies, the first heroes we encountered. After all, if that boyish, clean and upright guy couldn't contort his decent face into a mask of fury and gun them down he wasn't much use, was he? And then in civilian life, James Mason did his bit by whacking poor Anne Todd over the fingers with his walking stick and lo and behold, it's because he loves her, and worse still, she discovers she loves him!

We learned, by whatever means, that men were cruel to themselves, had to smother tenderness in case it 'unmanned' them. We were always hoping to release men from this exile from their softer selves, refusing obstinately to see what was staring us in the face. Men don't want to be released, in spite of occasional yearnings and murmurings that break through in the course of love. Exile is, on the whole, well-fed and reasonably paid and it earns respect – position and authority at one end of the social scale, the pride of the fist or the knife at the other.

Now the system shows signs of collapsing because the sexes have lost faith in each other. And women's bitterness, Marius, is not only on account of oppression but on account of *fraud*. Men never wanted us as companions. Men never wanted intimacy except in the manner of a locked room to which they kept the key. They have, by and large, not the slightest wish to emerge from the handsome armour of their 'public' selves – handsome, that is, when groomed and tended by a kind of emotional valet. Women supplied the human factor, vouched for men as well-rounded people. Why? Why can't men convince people without a supporting cast that they are warm, feeling, trustworthy? If that's what they want?

To be fair to Robert, that was not what he wanted. There was nothing he wanted less than all that. He was locked in all sorts of conflicts and tore poetry out of himself with more hatred than love, but he had never consciously tried to hand over this battle-ground to one particular woman. He treated his women as whores. Though I didn't realise it at the time, I was also treated, sexually, as a whore. What was different was the intrigue, for him, of discovering the 'boyish' side of a

41

woman, the fencer, both verbal and physical. If it had not been for the pregnancy, I expect we'd have carried on our hectic affair and it would eventually have burned itself out in terrible rows.

To get back to our honeymoon, breakfast had by this time come to an end. The only other resident, a travelling salesman, emerged first from the dining-room. Robert, still visibly in a bad mood, came over to the manageress's office where I had just been getting a pep-talk about sticking up for myself.

'If you need a day in your bed you take it, my dear. He'll not drop dead if he has to be left on his own for once.'

'Oh, I'll be all right' I muttered, getting to my feet and trying to look as if I were eager to be up and doing.

'Well, wrap up well.'

The manageress looked genuinely concerned.

We set off, I clinging out of necessity to Robert's stiff suspicious arm. We passed the Victorian sea-front villas with their pebbled pathways and frozen rose-bushes and faded green or pink front doors. They looked tatty and sad. There was no one about, except for one red-nosed woman polishing the front-door brasses in carpet-slippers and socks over lisle stockings, her breath coming out in clouds. She glanced at us, seemed to want to ignore us but at the last moment lost her courage and said grudgingly, 'It's a bitter day.'

We agreed and passed on.

'In summer,' said Robert, 'every one of these places has a "bed-and-breakfast" or a "guest-house" sign. I worked here one vacation.'

We took a flight of steps down to the beach.

'What did you do?'

'Taught kids how to swim.'

'In the sea?'

'No, there's an outdoor pool, or there used to be. Bloody cold it was.'

He hunched his shoulders and chuckled. I let go of his arm and started making my own way across the sand, stopping now and then to pick up a shell or a pebble, wondering if any were pretty enough to keep. I was starting to feel a little better.

In spite of the biting shore wind there was a cleanliness about the great open sky, the sea riffled into brisk waves, the stretch of pale sand empty except for our trails of footprints.

Then suddenly, among the rocks, I came across a sight of peculiar ghastliness, one of those revolting casualties of the deep, a dead and half-rotted cat tangled amongst some seaweed, with one eye still grotesquely intact in its empty skull and apparently glaring at me with a kind of crazy venom. I heaved, a spasm that felt as if my guts were being uprooted, and vomited not once but many times with a violence that shook me to rags. Gradually I recovered, got my breath back, blew my nose, wiped my eyes and mouth, and felt my pumping heart slacken off a bit. Robert had stopped some distance away and was waiting.

Slowly I went back to him. He eyed me uneasily.

'How long d'you suppose this is going to go on?' he asked.

'*I* don't know' I screamed suddenly. The sound was taken up by the gulls who had suddenly flown in from the sea and were wheeling above us. 'How am I supposed to know? I haven't had a baby before. And stop staring at me like that! I'm not a monster, I'm only a pregnant woman. And you haven't even the decency to – to put an arm round me, or anything. Oh I hate you, Robert Carmichael. Yes I do, you great muscle-bound hulk!'

I thought I had burst a blood vessel. My eyes seemed to be flooding with great whirling nebulae of red and spangled gold. Beside myself with anger and still blind, I set off across the sand, raging, raging with the injustice of it all.

Next thing I was walking briskly back along the promenade, powered by a resolution that must be acted on at once. It was perfectly clear. I could not go through with this. I should have agreed to go to a home for fallen girls of good family and quietly lived through my months of pregnancy. I could still do it. I would pack my case and leave. I would bribe a taxi to drive me all the way back to Edinburgh. And father? Oh I could fix him all right. If I had the courage to rage at Robert I could do anything.

Mrs. Crawford, the manageress, looked up in surprise from behind reception as I slammed into the hotel.

'Back already? I told you, you shouldna go out, though I must say you've got a sight more colour in your face – '

'Well, I'm not feeling too good just the same,' I muttered. 'I'm going upstairs for a while.'

'That's right. You have a lie-down.'

The glasses were on her nose, the fancy gold chain glinting and shifting as she moved her head. It struck me as odd to wear angora and fancy chains with an old tweed skirt, not to mention the brogued shoes and solid durable calves on which Mrs. Crawford's gaunt frame was firmly mounted.

However, I had more important things to think about. I unlocked our bedroom door and made straight for my suitcase, bearing my now out-of-date initials in gold. It was stowed away beside the flimsy wardrobe. In the distorting mirror set in its door I caught sight of my face, lop-sided, one eye lower than the other, but even in this palsied version, it was unquestionably an angry and determined face. I started pulling out my clothes, the awful checked wedding-suit, the spare skirts and one of my party outfits from student days. The metal hangers banged hollowly against the plywood and the wardrobe door kept creaking shut. I worked carelessly, recklessly, making things bang and creak for the hell of it. But through the racket came a still, small voice. Or rather, a polite knock on the door. Mrs. Crawford was outside in the corridor with a tray.

'I thought a drop o'soup would do you good.'

She stared in at the mess in the room, and was obviously puzzled. Nevertheless, she came in and put the tray down on one of the bedside tables. There was a clean white tray-cloth, a starched napkin in a tumbler, bread, a bowl of steaming broth, even a tiny spray of winter jasmine in a slender flower-holder.

'You shouldn't have bothered – '

My conscience smote me at the sight of all this care.

Mrs. Crawford sat down on the bed, her back to the tray as if to leave it out of the picture. She started all over again, quite differently.

'What's going on, lass?'

If I told her the truth I'd see no more of that concerned look.

44

She wouldn't call me 'lass'. She would stiffen and retreat. And yet – oh, I was too weak in every way to hold out.

'I'm running away,' I said.

'Running *away*?'

'Yes.'

'Whatever for?'

'Out there – ' I pointed vaguely towards the window, ' – I was sick. I was terribly sick, on the beach. He – he looked at me as if I had no business to exist, I was fouling his gaze. He said, "How long is this going to go on?" He didn't hold me or help me – why should I stay around to be treated so – so miserably? I'd rather have the baby on my own. Yes, I would. It'll be less lonely than having *him* around.'

My lips started trembling.

'How long have you been married?' Mrs. Crawford asked the question very quietly. It seemed insulting and pointless to tell lies.

'Five days.'

I waited for her to stiffen and retreat, fold her mouth down accusingly. But she did none of these things. She just looked rather sad, and sighed.

'It's certainly not the best way to start. But you can't run away from it now.'

'Why not?' I looked up from my packing.

'Because you have to act like a grown-up now. Because you're going to have a child. And children need fathers.'

'I wouldn't keep it. I'd have it adopted.'

'Even so, d'you suppose, after all that, you can go back to being a lassie like all the others?'

'No,' I said, my lips trembling again. 'I know that's all over. But anything would be better than facing that man again.'

'Is he that bad?'

'I don't *know*!' I said passionately. 'That's why I've got to get out. There's something wrong about being forced to live with a stranger. I know I've broken the rules, and I'm prepared to break some more. But none of that is as bad, as wicked, as two people tying up each other's lives in ignorance. And anyway, he's so strong, I don't stand a chance.' I sat back on my heels, overcome with the sense of Robert's awful

45

momentum. 'I've married a machine, a great machine that'll go tearing on down the track of my life, tearing it to pieces.' I got to my feet and picked up a pile of jerseys from an open drawer. 'I must get out. I *must* get out, before it's too late.'

'Leave that for a moment.'

Mrs. Crawford patted the bed beside her and obediently I came over and sat down. She put her arm firmly round my shoulders, a strange embrace for me. I was very moved. For the first time in my adult life I realised I didn't have a mother.

'You know, lass,' she said gently, 'you're not the only one who's felt like that about getting married. Most women'll tell you, when it's all safely passed, that the first six months were just awful, sheer bloody hell. I know it doesn't help if you've had to marry, like you and yer man, but maybe it's not as different as you think. We all marry strangers. We all marry in ignorance – and we learn to put up wi' it. It's the way o' things.' She paused. 'Sometimes you even find it's worked out pretty well.'

I felt the fire going out of me, and the first sinister intimation of acceptance – women's lot, women's destiny – creeping up. Also the bond of younger to older woman. I badly needed love, this kind of love, not the other kind. Mrs. Crawford had not drawn back in disapproval. Instead she was petting me, stroking my hair, soothing me like a child but exhorting me to be an adult. How could I run out in the face of all that? And some feeling that I was expected to be brave – for the sake of the baby, and herself, and all the other raisers of families who'd stifled the fires of rebellion and persuaded themselves it was a far, far better thing. . . .

Having watched me staring at the case without making a move for several minutes she spoke again.

'Come on, lass. Better get that stuff back in the cupboard and yourself into bed. I'll tell him when he comes in you're not well and need to be looked after. He'll be all right. They have a kind streak in them, most men, when it comes to the bit.'

Oh lord, the consoling folk-wisdom! Wrong nine times out of ten, but still passed along the line like a pebble with a faint flavour of sweetness which we suck to try and make saliva flow.

I was asleep when Robert came in. He woke me up gently. It was dark but still early, four o'clock in the afternoon.

'Mrs. Crawford says you're ill,' he said awkwardly.

'Where have you been?'

'Oh, wandering round the town. Thinking a bit.'

I wondered, very secretly, whether he'd had his own thoughts of running out. I put my hand out for his and he took it.

'Your colour's better.' He touched my face with his other hand. 'You're so pretty, Carla, I just hate it when you're ill and miserable. It seems all wrong. You should be sparkling and happy, the way you used to be. I feel like a murderer – '

We put our arms round each other, sharing our distress at having dragged each other into this – this what? I don't know. I don't know whether our distress, which was real enough, was at the level of monstrous insult at having such wretchedly unsuitable parts to play or something nearer and dearer to instinct, an animal dread of captivity, the desire for survival in freedom. Anyway for once we shared it. Robert felt warm and his bulk seemed reassuring, not menacing. If I could just lie back forever on pillows in a double-bed, perhaps everything would be all right. I'd wear frilly nighties and disarm Robert by looking pretty and helpless.

'Mrs. Crawford says I've got to look after you.' Robert lay back on the pillows, pulling me down with him. He tucked my head into his shoulder. 'She says I had no business to drag you out this morning. In fact, she gave me a real going over.'

We both laughed. To my dream of staying in bed forever I added in the figure of Mrs. Crawford, specs, angora jumper and long mild face, eternally presiding over us. If she were around, I thought, we'd manage.

'Anyway – ' Robert sat up abruptly. 'I did feel badly about what happened on the beach – long before Mrs. Crawford said a thing. I can prove it.'

He got off the bed and went over to the chair where he had flung his overcoat.

'It's all right – I believe you.' I had no idea what he was up to, only wanted the familiar squaring-up defiance to stay out of his voice a little longer.

'No, wait –' He pulled a little parcel out of his coat pocket and brought it over to me. 'A present.'

He plunked it in my hand and then sat down again. The mattress lurched under his weight. I stared at the little paper-covered cube. There was silence, except for Robert's breathing, always a little like escaping steam.

'Well, go on. Open it.'

I opened it. He'd brought me a ring, a very pretty ring. I looked at it nestling against its dark velvet bed, then tried it on the finger already wearing a plain gold wedding ring. It fitted, snugly, surely a good omen?

'Is it an engagement ring?'

We both found this mildly funny.

'If you like,' said Robert. 'I just happened to see it in one of the wee curio shops in the High Street, and it was open. I thought – I don't know, it seemed to be your kind of ring, and I wanted you to have it.'

I looked down at my hand, then held it away to try out the effect. It was an old Victorian ring, opals and pearls in a scrolled curling gold setting. I thought it was lovely. I was also wordless with surprise. There was something very tender about that little ring, and that Robert should have been moved to buy it for me seemed as if, even very briefly, he had acknowledged my world and me. He was not a great giver of gifts; he preferred to be reckless and generous with cash when he had it. To have paused and wondered and chosen, even then I realised it was a rare offering.

'D'you like it?'

'Yes, very very much.'

'That's good then.' He got up and went over to the window where the flash of an onshore lighthouse periodically came round to us. 'I don't suppose you want to get up for high tea, do you?'

'No, I'm afraid not.'

He nodded, Mrs. Crawford's voice, I suspected, still silently admonishing him.

'Well, I'd better get down. D'you want the curtains drawn?'

Much later I felt him carefully clambering into bed. I'd fallen asleep almost as soon as he left me, exhausted and for the time being at peace. As he snuggled up behind me I could feel his erection hard against my buttocks. 'Oh, please not to-night!' I prayed, and was heard, for although he held me close he never made a move to try and make love. And his abstinence expressed, in my eyes, far more 'love' than the act had ever done.

So now you know where it came from, Marius, that ring which I used to take off and put beside your watch and your wedding ring as we prepared ourselves to make love. There stood the wine glasses, half empty and usually forgotten, and the big goblet of water which we would share in the thirsty aftermath, and that little pile of objects which used to fascinate me so. They seemed to represent a ritual stripping, particularly the broad gold wedding ring which you still wore though Linda had been dead for two years and more. It was so much part of you and yet it was a reminder that you did not yet feel you belonged entirely to yourself. I don't know whether you used to take it off to make love to Linda, whether it was purely practical or out of a kind of delicacy.

As for my ring, don't ask me why the gift of a man I came to detest should mean so much to me. But it is a reminder, which I seem to need, that once, for a short time, he carried me in his imagination tenderly enough to want to buy me a pretty, feminine ornament. And it is really the only shred of evidence I have that he ever thought of me like that, once we were married.

7

Married! The word reeks of shock, disbelief, black farce, grim fact. I need hardly say that Mrs. Crawford's duties as mother and manageress kept her from taking up the role of fairy godmother I was so keen to offer her. We left as we arrived, on our own, her good wishes sounding in our ears, but nothing more. It was a pity. We needed help, we needed more. We needed a magic wand. Without that, or indeed any human agent much concerned with our wellbeing, we foundered and floundered, caught unprepared for the abrasive intimacy of conjugal life.

Let me attempt a sort of snapshot of myself in the months before Nick was born. I am down at heel, literally, wearing a jumper that needs a good wash, probably smelling a bit of sweat and cooking fat from all the fry-ups (Robert liked these, and besides I had never learnt to cook), my pregnant stomach stretching an unzipped skirt held up with tape and hanging squint. There are rings under my eyes. Being dark, they are a deep browny-purple. They appeared overnight about the fifth month and looked as if someone had taken crayon or paint and lined them in. Eager for some dramatic interest even of a morbid kind, I was convinced I had some rare illness. The doctor simply said it was probably one of the effects of the toxaemia of the early months. However, they stayed put for the next five or six years.

There is a phrase to sum up all that. It's called 'letting oneself go'. Yes, I let myself go all right. It is extraordinarily easy if you have never done anything more menial than wash out your own underwear, if your meals have always appeared regularly, if you've never had closer acquaintance with the problems of hot water than to draw off large tubfuls whenever the fancy took you. Without all this unconsidered support, I didn't even have to let myself go, I simply went.

You will perhaps see the origins of the disorder at Alma Crescent which was alternately a joke or a bone of contention between us. But I wouldn't want you to make the mistake of confusing this stale sloppy creature with the woman *you* knew, who went around with paint-stained jeans and a man's shirt hanging loose while she hammered and banged at her constructionist sculptures, designed her jewellery and sketched her sons. No, that was a very different Carla. Disorder there may have been, but it had a purpose. The one I described first, the pregnant one, was simply embarking on a long leave-taking from the shores of her childhood and there was not one single suggestion of anything out there, in the muddy ocean. It was as if flood waters had covered her world. All landmarks had gone in the obliterating scaring grimness of being hard up and pregnant.

I made so many alarming discoveries in the first months of marriage that I lost count. Most of them were to do with cash. I discovered that although Robert in our romantic days was a free spender, and still was in certain areas, over matters domestic he was as mean as sin – or as someone who has grown up in poverty. I don't suppose he was earning much, but whatever it was I was simply given a minute weekly sum for housekeeping and no discussion. His mother knew how to make such a sum last out and so should I.

But I had never managed anything more complex than a generous dress allowance from a lenient father who could be wheedled. Being poor takes a lot of ingenuity. I didn't know the first thing about housekeeping, on a large budget or a small. At the corner shop the carry-over of debt from one week to the next grew steadily larger.

If father hadn't agreed to continue my allowance for the first year, I don't know how we would have managed. It paid for the pram, the cot, the blankets, the baby clothes. Robert never asked any questions or offered to buy anything for the baby.

Apparently he'd done his bit by making an honest woman of me.

I had learnt a certain amount about Robert's order of priorities, and top of the list came his commitment to carrying on his life as little changed as possible from the days before he married. This meant that night after night the place filled up with men and beer bottles and the reek of fags and ash went everywhere and sometimes (quite often in fact) someone vomited carelessly in the tiny lavatory. I was there on sufferance, a bad-luck omen reluctantly taken aboard this shipful of drunken sailors. Usually I went to bed very early. I learnt to sleep through the noise.

Once Nicky arrived, and thank heavens he was not merely a boy, but almost a miniature of his rugged father, he occupied a place somewhere in Robert's life. Myself, no, not as far as I could see, except in bed. Occasionally we communed with some degree of harmony over our son – how clever he was, how advanced, how strong. But more often Robert was terrified I was going to bring him up soft. Long, long before we were at the stage of reading bedtime stories he had embargoed such elitist whimsies as the *Pooh* stories, Beatrix Potter and the *Little Grey Rabbit* books. I asked rather sarcastically if he intended reading him *The Communist Manifesto?*

There were altercations over Nick more related to the immediate context. Robert had this dreadful habit of waking the baby to take him through and show him off to his friends. Nick was still sleeping in our bedroom.

'Oh, don't pull him out of his cot now, he's absolutely flat out,' I would protest.

'He'll go back to sleep quite easily. The boys want to see him. It won't hurt him, he enjoys it, don't you, Nicky lad?'

'Well, put a blanket round him.'

'I'm not simple. Stop interfering and go back to sleep.'

'Last time he was howling with cold when you brought him back. I had to warm him up beside me, his feet were frozen.'

What I really feared was the fact that Robert was not steady on his feet and his friends 'the boys', a collectivity who sorted themselves out into the nice, the horrible and the faceless, would be in no better shape.

One night I rebelled, tired of being left with a fractious miserable baby in the middle of the night. I appeared in my grubby nightie, frayed lace hanging like a trail of lichen off one shoulder, just in time to see a visiting Gaelic bard bouncing my child around on his knees in accompaniment to some ballad with a keening chorus in which the rest joined raggedly.

'Stop that!'

Six pairs of eyes focussed, to the extent that they still connected to their nerve centres, on the doorway where I was standing. If I'd been carrying my head tucked under my arm they couldn't have looked more aghast. I walked over and picked my son out of the bard's grasp. Robert half rose.

'Carla – you're not – '

'Not what?' I walked over to him, the shoulder of my nightie slipping down further.

'You're not decent!'

The idea of decency in the middle of this boozy sprawl struck me as incredibly funny. Would it matter if I were stark naked? I'd stopped thinking of myself as a woman. I carried coal and cleared out ashes and cleaned up messes and fried food, a dingy drudge replacing the pampered princess I'd been. And yet – I could see the men's eyes were moving up and down, a little furtively. Nicky on my arm hid one breast. The other was, I suppose, fairly exposed.

'Get back to bed,' he urged but not very masterfully. I stood my ground.

'Not till you get this mob out of here. I'm fed up with the noise. I'm fed up of this sickening mess. And I *will not* put up with you treating my child like a stuffed toy to play with. *You* don't get up at 5.30 to feed him.'

One or two of the men rose uneasily.

'I'm – I'm sorry, Carla. We got a bit carried away – '

John Graham, kind, failed and forty, with a single book of poems to his name and a tendency to get worked up about eternal verities when he was drunk, put a gentle unsteady hand on my wrist. 'I'm sorry, lass,' he repeated.

I don't think anyone else apologised, but that night they did recognise that it was my turn to call the tune. Why did I not do it more often? Assert myself, I mean?

They filed out meekly, all five of them, looking stupid and pathetic. And Robert, left alone with me and Nick, tried futilely to pick up some of the beer bottles and only succeeded in knocking over an ashtray piled with cigarette ends onto our apology for a carpet. And he too was defeated and pathetic and helpless. And I stood there feeling such a rushing misery of alone-ness, realising the hollowness of their strength, that I must have decided it was less desolate to be pushed around and at least keep the semblance of the right and proper order of things. If there was no one stronger than me in my life, if this terrible sense of chaos and frailty was all there was. . . .

I stared at my husband as he lay snoring and sprawled minutes after flopping into bed. Robert, if you knew what you looked like! Stubble shadowing a chin already getting fleshy, flab starting to creep up on the Heathcliff look. For my own sake I should not have stared so clinically at your heaving bulk. I sat up in bed shivering and things were shifting, hopes were vanishing. We had been married for just over a year and I was able to tell myself, quite coldly, 'I hate this man.' Then I locked that discovery away, not knowing that there is no way of preventing hate from seeping out. It never occurred to me to act on it, to use its energy to try and change my life. I simply felt as if I were under the enchantment of a bad spell.

8

I suppose it's from that time that the dreams were born, the bad ones, the gardens with abundant fruit that turns out to be rotten, the jewellery that vanishes, fragile glass objects of mysterious beauty which smash or are given to someone else, sometimes my sister Stella. There are dreams about cars – though Robert and I never owned a car. Driving in the dark without light, speeding towards blind curves.

I dream that he is destroying my children, only they are not real children, they are tiny like large insects but precious beyond belief, and I have large families of them, four, five and six, and Robert is being careless, dropping them, nearly treading on them.

I dream of him drowning, caught by a tide and being battered to pieces against a rock. His hands and feet have gone, but somehow he is making odd terrible gestures of distress and I stand not knowing how to help him. I am haunted by the thought of living with this mutilated man, if he survives.

All these dreams, Marius, and many other monotonously repeating, casting their long shadows, without warning, across the years. It is like being possessed. When they come it's like an annulment of all that I've done, all the changes I've tried to make, all the ways I've discovered of tasting joy if not actually finding happiness. I *want* to be on the side of life but for some reason I am not to be allowed to forget the years I spent in the kingdom of the shades.

I dream about Robert's flat. Sometimes it is simply a re-creation of the actual place. Sometimes it is like a large warehouse with shaking ladders leading to high unsteady ledges that I have to negotiate, a squalid place with dumps of refuse and rags. Other times I find a great set of empty, undiscovered rooms, fine rooms nobly proportioned, but in a state of hopeless decay. The roof has fallen in and grass and moss is coming through the floor. That leaves a feeling of profound desolation, some frightful sense of waste and loss.

It was then, I think, that I lost any capacity to look into the future, I mean after that first year of marriage. The eternal present is supposed to be a blessed state, but don't you believe it. It also has its black version. When I started working on your survey, Marius, I discovered many a kindred spirit among those severely depressed women who couldn't get themselves together even to the extent of envisaging a future that would stretch to the end of a single day. They couldn't accomplish a single day's shopping, but made umpteen little trips to buy sugar, fags, tea, sausages, a loaf. Oh yes, I'd been through very similar routines.

Do you remember our 'interview'? I do, vividly. I sat in your office looking unnaturally neat with my eye make-up well toned down. It seemed an occasion to try and look my age, instead of following the fashion-lead of my art college, crowd, half a generation younger than myself.

'So – Miss – er – '

'Mrs. Carmichael. Carla Carmichael.'

'Yes, quite. You say in your letter that although you have no experience of interviewing and you have no psychological background, you think you would be suitable for this job. By the way, how did you come to hear about it?'

'Through one of your students, Mona Andrews, she's a friend of mine. *She* has a part-time job modelling at the art college, where I'm working. So you see there is a certain amount of overlap between the two areas already.'

You smiled, but immediately said, 'If you're working at the Art College I doubt if you'll have time for this. From all I hear, lecturers there put in a lot of evening work, don't they?'

'Oh, I'm not a lecturer, I'm simply a student. And we also

have to work very hard. But I badly need the cash. I have two sons to bring up.'

That's when you started to look at me much more curiously and closely. Your voice became 'unofficial' for a moment.

'You're a brave woman.'

'I love it,' I said simply, and smiled.

I don't think I'd smiled until that point. You went on looking at me. I didn't mind. I was thinking, 'This is the first man I've met in years that I feel like trusting. And what an extraordinary colour his hair is, grey or blonde? I can't make it out.'

'What I want to do in this, um, stage of my project, is to get as much informal material as possible from women who have been diagnosed as depressed. From this I hope to design a questionnaire which will give a much more precise diagnosis about the seriousness of a depression, when it's likely to lead to suicidal attempts or other acts of desperation – '

'Won't you try and find out the causes of depression?'

'Well – ' you laughed slightly, 'that's quite a tall order. We can't do more than hope to establish a few correlations.'

This was Greek to me. I had yet to enter, very slightly, into the realms of the social sciences and discover that 'causes' were quite out of fashion, as was 'meaning', because of the need to become an exact science. Personally, I found it nothing more than the highly developed art of circumlocution – with statistical tables, of course. Perhaps it's just as well I didn't know that at our interview.

You were staring rather hard at me, with a tiny drift of the eyes towards my legs.

'What makes you think you would be suitable for this job?' It was quite kindly asked. 'Do you think you would manage to get through to severely depressed women? It's not easy, you know. They can be almost totally withdrawn. And the interviews themselves, they would only have the minimum of structure. It would be up to you to work out some way of covering certain areas which I would brief you on, and then get as much information as possible on anything you considered important.'

'I think I could manage,' I said, totally confident of my

57

ability to get through to severely depressed women. 'I've served my apprenticeship.'

Some look from the black years must have come across my face, for your expression changed suddenly, you looked at me very gravely and sweetly, a curiously delicate look of compassion and I – I remember stretching myself in an extraordinary way, exposing all the side of my body like an animal relaxing. It wasn't meant to be provocative. It was just that my guard suddenly dropped and I felt a sense of extraordinary trustfulness.

'Well, then, perhaps we can arrange a time to discuss things properly – '

The interviewing job was coming my way. I sat there basking in something that felt like sunshine, and then remembered I hadn't yet asked about rates of pay. They were not very good.

'I'm sorry,' you said. 'It's all I can afford from a very tight budget. Perhaps you want to reconsider?'

I paused for pride's sake.

'No,' I said slowly, 'I'd like to go ahead with it.'

'Oh good! That's settled then.'

We arranged to meet the following week in the evening.

'How much longer at Art College?' you asked as we walked towards the main door.

'Another couple of years. It won't seem long. There's so much to be fitted in.'

'What are you good at?'

'Drawing. Painting, engraving. I'm hopeless at pottery and less than inspired at sculpture. Oh, and I make things out of bits and pieces of material.'

'Collages?'

'That sort of thing.'

'Perhaps you'll show me sometime?'

'Oh yes, if you're interested.'

We paused at the door. You seemed anxious to extend the conversation. Or perhaps you simply didn't know how to end it.

'What are you going to do when you finish?'

I shrugged.

'I have no idea. I'm very bad at planning. I'll wait till I see what the gods offer.'

'That's not a very good policy, particularly if you have any ambition. I'm always telling my students they must have a strategy if they want to get on. Perhaps you should think about a strategy.'

I smiled. 'Perhaps I should. Anyway, I'll see you next week. It's been nice meeting you.'

'Yes,' you said, and put out your hand, a nice long lean hand with decent finger-nails. 'It's been nice meeting you too.'

Career strategy, the long-term view, anticipating things, planning – those were not my line. As far as all those things went, I was very kin to those women I interviewed, those women who cobbled each day together as best they could and certainly never looked into the future for fear of seeing an infinity of such days. No amount of being popular and doing well at college, no amount of rehabilitating fun with the boys at Alma Crescent, could make up for that apprenticeship of grimy haphazard days when I mismanaged, and ran out of things and overspent and worried myself sick.

'Why, may I ask, can't you pull yourself together? Why do you lead such a *messy* little life?' Stella once asked in exasperation after I'd told her what I'd hoped was a funny story about starting out to make a cake and having to turn it into shortbread because I'd forgotten to buy eggs. She was not amused. She also believed in organisation and planning. In her kitchen there was a large memo board with a cute wipe-clean surface and a special pen attached by a pom-pom. She labelled it with the days of the week against which were scribbled items like, 'Pick up theatre tickets', 'Hair appt. 2.30', 'Church Guild meeting' and 'Fitting for evening dress'. Beside it was another smaller board on which she jotted down items that would shortly need replenishing. That day she was in danger of running out of French mustard, martini, tall candles and washing-powder. Somehow, her kind of organisation didn't seem suited to my needs. Just the same I do believe that Stella, in my position, would have managed differently, more efficiently. She had a neat mind, and a tough one.

No, the person I should have turned to for instruction was Robert's mother. Only between us yawned a great gap of cautious, courteous strangeness. She was a rather grim-faced little woman, dark like her son, with stunted legs of an extraordinary shape which, it only occurred to me years after, might have been the result of malnutrition. Robert's whole family was small. How he came to be the lone giant, comparatively, I don't know. He said his mother fed him extra because he was the clever one and that she did without.

By the time I appeared on the scene the worst was in the past. They were all in work and they lived on a council estate on the outskirts of Glasgow. Robert's younger brother Tom, slender and brown-haired, and without the family scowl, lived with his wife nearby. The family scowl ranged from Robert's full-blown version to an unstirring mask of sourness that had settled on his father's face. Even his much younger sister, Mattie, a lumpy girl heavily made up, had a certain forbidding set about her mouth and eyebrows. By contrast, Tom was lively and so was his sense of humour. Perhaps his militancy made him cheerful. And contrary to Robert's sinister warning at our wedding, Tom did not behave as if I were the class enemy. We took a liking to each other straight away, it was all very simple and friendly between him and me. I used to pray that he would be there on the rare occasions we paid a Sunday visit. He felt almost like an ally.

Not that the rest of Robert's family was unfriendly or openly hostile, just very, very wary. Had Robert been living at home when he got married I imagine there would have been much stronger feelings about the kind of woman he'd chosen. But being remote and uncommunicative and living at a distance, he accounted to his family as little as to anyone else for his actions. In that sense my acceptance was made easier. We need not strive too hard, any of us, to overcome the strangeness.

It was my first real contact with hardship, life at the bottom of the heap, even though things were rosy compared to how they had been. Even so it was there, plain to see, in every detail of meagreness, the minimum of everything, curtains that did not shut properly, rooms furnished with only the basics, and the strange smell that hangs round the dwellings of the clean poor, the smell of constant washing of floors and clothes and bedclothes. It was there in Mrs. Carmichael's relentless pre-occupation with thrift – she talked of almost nothing except the how's and where's of penny-saving bargains. Above all, in the expressions on their faces there was the mark of the depression and the dole, the terrible 'thirties. Something that my lot had done to them and people like them.

I had, I think, always felt I was lucky not to have been born poor. I didn't believe I had a right to what I had, simply that I was lucky. It never occurred to me that I was guilty, nor, worse still, that the very creature I thought of as 'myself' could be seen – and dismissed – as a kind of puppet nonentity fabricated from privilege and luxury. Robert encouraged that view when he was feeling savage, but I got the message as powerfully for myself, just sitting in his family home among the members of his family.

Yes, I knew in some sense that they were more real than me, because they had been through the worst and survived. Survived, yes – but not triumphed! That's what frightened me, repelled me. It seemed to me that this partial victory over circumstance was a Pyrrhic victory, leaving the strugglers morose and threadbare, and their lives forever browned by the long immersion in overpowering poverty. I wish I had had the compassion, the generosity, simply the sense of social justice, to feel outrage and nothing but outrage. I didn't. I felt menaced in my turn by flood-waters of drabness. I longed for the safety of that well-cushioned dry patch which my family inhabited. Only that too was not what it had been and neither were they. I was starting to see them in part through Robert's eyes. I saw that the people I loved were not perfect, they could even be seen as ignorant and narrow-minded and self-righteous. It was a bit like losing one's faith.

Sundays at the Carmichaels', kept to a minimum at Robert's insistence, consisted of a glass of sticky sherry followed by dinner (lunch) eaten mostly in silence except for comments about Nicky, a safe subject for us all to focus on, followed by clearing up, followed by cups of tea.

The old man (who wasn't old but looked it) had something

of his elder son's gift for sewing discord, only he did it in sly, polite ways.

'Sit down, sit down,' he would say to me, taking Nicky onto his own lap. 'What's for dinner, mam? Boiled mutton? Sorry we've no roast pheasant, Carla, and I'm afraid we're out of caviar this week, but ye're welcome to share our wee bit dinner.'

'Och, quit it, father!' This brusquely from Mattie, who had heard it before, as I had, the last time we came.

Mrs. Carmichael put a big plateful down in front of me.

'Dinna tak' any notice o' the auld fool,' she said, and her tight little mouth gave me a wry half-grin. She patted my shoulder, a nice gesture of female solidarity, but the thought did cross my mind that I would not like to receive anything stronger than a pat from her hard little fingers.

I wanted to say it was a better meal than we usually had, Robert and I, but that would have been very indiscreet. We were supposed to be 'doing well'. No one had visited the flat, no one had any desire to come over to Edinburgh, so the fiction could be maintained. If Mrs. Carmichael had seen it she would have been as horrified as Stella. The reek of cigarettes and stale beer would have been enough to have sent her raving, for she knew nothing about Robert's liking for the bevvy, and prided herself on having kept her family off the substance that had destroyed so many. The sweet sherry was a gesture for a special occasion, it didn't count as alcohol, it was simply a 'refreshment'.

Once on the train back to Edinburgh I said to Robert, 'I wish your father would stop making that crack about roast pheasant and caviare. It's getting a bit monotonous.'

'Oh, let him have his little joke. He has to do something, for God's sake. You wipe us out every time you open your mouth.'

'That's rubbish – I never say anything that might – '

'It's not what you say. It's your voice.'

'Well, what do you expect me to do? Start faking broad Scots to keep you happy? Then you'd accuse me of mocking you.'

'I don't understand,' I went on. 'You're surrounded by

62

voices like mine. Why did you apply for a university job if you don't want to hear educated voices? Why didn't you stay with your family, like Tom?'

'It's not a question of educated voices,' said Robert, turning to fix his full hostile gaze on me. He was always at his worst after family visits. 'It's the unthinking *arrogance* of you and your sort. It's there – every time you open your mouth. You've taught me to be ashamed of my family.'

'That is a blazing lie. You're always telling me how wonderful they are, how they have a spirit that can't be broken etc. etc. If *you* happen to find it difficult to get on with them –'

At this point the train drew into Waverley and we bundled crossly out with Nicky half asleep and weighing like a lump of lead. Actually, I'm not sure whether I said that or whether it's one of the many retorts I fantasised and yearned for the audacity to say out loud.

As for Stella and her remark about my 'messy little life', I did protest. I asked her how she'd like to try and make ends meet on the sum Robert gave me?

Her face went completely blank.

'The man must be mad – it's impossible for two people, plus a kid, to live on that.'

'He says his mother managed to feed five of them on it, and that's always the end of the conversation.'

'These damned self-righteous working-class types,' said Stella abruptly, though I wondered what others she'd met besides Robert. 'They think they have some kind of eternal moral superiority because they've lived hard lives.'

Well, I knew what she meant. I was getting very sick of the ever-honed cutting edge of the chip on the shoulder. On the other hand, I had learned something of the conditions that produced it, and Stella hadn't.

'You simply *must* insist on getting more,' she said, piling tea-cups onto the tray beside the remains of the currant cake we'd been eating. This was one of my rather rare visits to her house. To begin with, I tried to press for more frequent meetings, but Stella didn't sound very encouraging, and her busy social life often rescued her with a ready-made excuse. She never, never came to the flat.

'Yes,' I said. 'I must.' But I knew I'd be too frightened to do so, and I was too frightened to tell Stella that I was frightened, and all in all I was really frightened of most things, not least the appalling rages that boiled up silent and scalding inside me.

9

Later that year Robert had another book of poems accepted. The publisher's letter actually caused our breakfast silence to be broken for once, a double rarity, for breakfast was a meal which Robert honoured more in the breach than by the observance.

'Oh great!' he said suddenly over his mug of tea.

I couldn't believe my ears.

'What's great?'

'This – here, read the letter.' And he pushed a piece of paper over to me.

'Oh yes! That is great, it's terrific!' I was about to get up and give him a kiss, but he turned his head away. 'I didn't know you'd been writing. Where do you do it?'

'Here and there. In my room at college. In pubs.'

'I wish you'd told me,' I said wistfully. 'You know I'm interested in poetry, in your poetry.'

'Well, you've got other things to think about.'

I considered that. Things went round and round in my head, but it was hardly thought.

'No, I haven't,' I said suddenly. 'I haven't got anything to think about, except whether the supper'll keep if you're late. My mind's rotting. You used to say I was your brightest student but I couldn't write a school precis now if I tried.'

'Well, you don't need to. You're a wife-and-mother, aren't you?' This was the man who had worried, at least once, for a few minutes, about the fate of my intellectual development.

'I can't concentrate,' I said desperately. 'I can't even read a newspaper article.'

'Look, do you *have* to spoil one of the few days that's started with a bit of good news?'

'I don't want to spoil anything, I'm just saying – help me, Robert, please help me.'

'What the hell do you expect me to do?' He sounded startled, almost alarmed.

'Let me share something in your life, anything. Couldn't I help correct some of the first-year essays – or – or – simply talk about what you're teaching, the way we used to do? After all, I did study – '

'You can help correct the proofs of the book. Will that satisfy you?'

'But that won't be for months yet!'

'Good God, woman, what's wrong with you? Why do you keep on with all this talk of *sharing*? I don't want to talk about my teaching, it's the last thing I want to talk about – '

'But you're a good teacher, or you were!'

'Well, it's by accident. If I could pack it in tomorrow I would.'

That was certainly the end of that subject.

'Anyway,' he added, 'We share a bed, don't we?'

I shivered.

'We don't talk in bed.'

'No, I've never been one for chatting while I fuck,' he agreed sarcastically.

I got up and removed Nicky's empty porridge bowl and gave him some milk. Then I refilled our mugs with tea.

'If you want to know, I think I'm going crazy. Crazy with loneliness. I never see anyone except Nick and Mrs. H., day after day.' I took a scalding gulp of tea to try and deal with the lump in my throat.

But Robert was a great deal less moved than I was. 'You should go out more. Go and visit your girl-friends. Or get them to come here.'

'I haven't got any.'

'You're kidding. You used to know half the student population.'

'That was eighteen months ago. They're still at university, I'm not. They're all studying for finals. I'm minding a baby. It makes a difference. And anyway, I did try to keep up for a bit. I used to ask them to come and visit, but they didn't much like coming here – '

'No?'

'No. Word gets around, you know. Do you not remember telling my friend Annie Mathieson that you were going to burn the present she'd brought for Nicky? "No fluffy white rabbits, for *my* son" you said. "Those are toys for upper-class morons". And the place, it's such a tip, who would want to come here?'

'My friends do.'

'Yes, but they never bring their wives or their girlfriends, your friends. No woman ever comes here.'

Robert chuckled.

'Of course not. It's their bolt-hole. They come here to get away from all that.' He stopped laughing. 'Do you think men want to live in their wives' pockets like scented hankies? Do you think we want to play dolls' houses? Do you think we are even faintly bothered about the curtains matching the carpet or the soap matching the toilet paper? It's an insult to life, that sort of thing. An insult to creative force, to *manhood*!' He started pacing around restlessly. 'And I suppose that's the sort of place you're pining to live in – '

Nicky offered him a crust but it was ignored.

'I don't want to live in a doll's house. I never said I did. I just want somewhere that's half decent. And even your manly friends occasionally talk about putting a lick of paint on their houses, or helping their wives choose a new piece of furniture – just occasionally.'

'Maybe their wives have got the jump on them in some way.' Robert did not sound interested. 'Maybe the poor fools even wanted to get married. Not everyone acquires a child-bride the way I did. Never mind, I'm helping them out, keeping the banner flying – '

'What banner?'

'Oh, don't let the bitches grind you down – ' He grinned quite cheerfully, picked up the publisher's letter and put it in his pocket. 'What's the time? I'd better be off. Bye-bye, Nicky boy, give us a kiss. Shit, you little bastard, you've put jam all over me.'

He rumpled Nick's hair fondly, wiped off his face with the dishcloth, picked up his battered briefcase, and looking like some travesty of professional man with uneven hair, frayed collar and muddy shoes, set off for his first lecture of the day.

This, believe it or not, was one of the longest conversations we had had since we were married. It wasn't simply that we 'failed to communicate' (to borrow the well-worn cliché of later decades), we literally did not talk. A pall of silence had descended when we returned from our honeymoon. It was for both of us the moment when the long-lasting truth of our situation hit. To face each other at close quarters day after day. . . .

Robert tried, for the first few weeks to be a conventional fireside husband, no pals, no drink. Also no talk. His powers of withdrawal were phenomenal, totally proof against my attempts to charm him into some kind of animation. I soon gave up. Besides, in spite of my vexation, I knew it was something worse than a fit of the sulks. I was watching someone silently growing crazy and I didn't know what to do. But Robert did it for himself. One evening he suddenly announced with an air of incredulous re-discovery, 'I'm off to the pub!' And like a man reprieved he was out and off and never looked back. The bevvy was thereafter part of the scene and all that goes with it.

I continued to commute between the frying pan and the fire. I was not much good at managing either. Things seemed to be forever burning in the one and failing completely to burn in the other. I can see that beastly grate still, smoking away and mysteriously creating mountains of ash with never a flame showing and seldom a proper glow, a sullen smoulder all that my life-denying ineptitude could achieve.

But by the time the publisher's letter arrived I had at last mastered some of the minor arts of running a home, and that morning, once Nicky was down for his mid-day nap, I sat myself down in reasonable warmth with a mug of coffee and tried to sort out my thoughts. 'Don't let the bitches grind you down!' . . . 'Not everyone acquires a child–bride the way I did.' I knew, how could I not, that Robert had married under duress. I also knew that because of this marriage he'd missed the chance of a travelling fellowship to America. Certainly I'd been nothing but a liability on his fortunes. Yet somehow it had never so far occurred to me that this life of drenching boredom, isolation, incompetent worry and largely hostile silence was not necessarily typical. I suddenly felt the full weight of Robert's ten years of seniority and how much I did feel like a child, an unwanted child who bungled and got in the way. The only faint credit mark that might be ascribed to me was that Nicky was a boy, a fine burly boy in the image of his father. The only person in the world, it seemed, who was unequivocally on my side was Mrs. Habib, but of her more anon.

It didn't add up to very much, on my side of the ledger. And yet, in the weird way that happens to people who have lost all confidence, I didn't even trust myself to know how bad was bad? I needed to find out.

'But surely,' I can hear your quiet astonished voice, 'you must have realised that your marriage wasn't *normal?*'

What's normal? I don't know, you don't know. You had a good marriage, Marius. I did not. Whose was more typical? But I know what you mean. Only, my dear love, what could I know about marriage? Not many people have much to go on. I had even less than the average. My father was a widower from the time before my memory, and home life was built round a housekeeper. Even when he married Mary, it didn't make all that much difference. In a sense, she may have supplied a model for my role as Robert's wife. Under infinitely more sordid circumstances I became his housekeeper, certainly his chattel. But that's also part of a good Scots tradition.

What about Stella? Well yes, there was Stella and her marriage. Before my own it was a matter of supremely little interest. I never cared much for that overclean Henry of hers. I should think having sex with him smelled of soap and after-shave.

After my marriage two things happened. First, I consigned

her house (where the lavatory paper did match the soap and the bath salts as well), her expensive clothes and her baby daughter, born a couple of years before Nicky and intended by nature to be frilly and sweet, to the exalted level of things which I had forfeited by my recklessness. I had betrayed my class, therefore no goodies. And this rough justice I seemed to accept all too well. In actual fact, I didn't want a frilly daughter but I would have liked a son who had not inherited or acquired his father's compulsive need to prove how tough he was. Yes – even at the age of eighteen months.

Secondly, it became more and more difficult to get back to any kind of natural intimacy with my sister. During my visits, which were well spaced out, Stella would chatter on comfortably about her friends and their children; she would discuss the pros and the cons of sending daughter Imogen to St. George's or St. Margaret's; she would complain of the awful price of domestic help. I really don't know whether she thought it was a kindness to pretend that all these matters were also part of my life, or whether she was simply determined to keep off any subject that might become dangerous. Her health was another great stand-by. She had a little fund of minor ailments, a touch of exzema, occasional sick headaches, bouts of sciatica, and, more humiliatingly, attacks of piles. These too afforded safe conversational ground.

And yet it was to Stella that I decided to go that day that I first asked myself whether by any chance my lot was markedly worse than other women's? Whether it was 'normal' to spend so much time gasping with a kind of airless anger that ended up in crushing gloom? After all, she was my sister, my older sister, and I was very fond of her. And anyway, who else was there?

It was stupid of me not to 'phone first as I usually did. Somehow, that afternoon I couldn't face the whole business of asking Mrs. H. if I might use her 'phone, then timidly asking Stella if I could come round, that is, if she wasn't too busy, and waiting with a beating heart to hear whether she'd say 'yes' or whether her voice would go a little tinny and she'd say: 'Sorry, not this afternoon, I have to go down town' or 'we've got people coming in and I'm up to my eyes – '. I'd got into the way of feeling it was a great favour to be allowed round to my sister's house.

That afternoon I couldn't risk having the favour refused. I left Nick in the care of Mrs. H. and set off across town. It wasn't until I was getting off the bus and walking up the road that led to the charming garden-bordered street where Stella lived that I realised I had absolutely no idea what I was going to say.

There was a long delay after I'd rung the door-bell. My heart sank. I should have 'phoned first. She was out – no, at last there were steps coming across the hall and the door opened. Stella stood there in a sort of housecoat, flowered and quilted, with wide ceremonial sleeves and her hair was rumpled.

'What on earth are you doing here?'

She sounded sleepy and not pleased to see me.

'I – I thought I'd just drop in. I wanted to see you.'

She looked at me more kindly, perhaps realising how brusque she'd been.

'I'm sorry, I'm not properly awake yet. I was just having a lie-down. Come in. D'you mind coming up to the bedroom? I don't feel like getting up yet.'

'You're not ill, are you?'

'No, no. Just tired out. We had a big dinner-party last night. I thought they would never go. The men, of course. I said to Henry, really, why ever did you offer yet *another* round of brandies, couldn't you see that half the women were dozing off and obviously dying to be in their beds – ' She laughed. 'Still, I suppose it's better than everybody eating up and galloping off. At least you know it was a *success*.'

We went upstairs and into her big warm bedroom.

'D'you mind?' she said again, clambering onto the double bed and pulling the quilt over her. She yawned and looked cross again. 'Look, I don't mean to sound unfriendly, but please don't just – *arrive*, out of the blue, again. I like to know where I am.'

'I'm sorry.'

A thought occurred to her.

'Are *you* all right?'

71

My nerve failed.

'More or less.'

There was silence.

Then I said, 'Shall I make some tea and bring it up? Would you like that?'

Yes, Stella would like that. After fifteen minutes of dithering round her kitchen, wondering which of various teasets to use, I got a tray together and brought it up. Stella had by this time fetched her embroidery, finest needle-point, from the couch where it was lying and was plying her needle.

'I do like to keep occupied,' she said. 'Look, don't you think it's coming on nicely?' She held up her pretty work, an intricate design of foliage in many different shades of blue, for me to admire. I took the fabric in my hands. 'Why don't you take up something like that? It's a lovely hobby. I can tell you where to write off for designs – Carla, you're not listening – '

I passed the work back to her and the words suddenly rushed out.

'I can't go on, Stella. I feel like an old woman. I feel as if my life is completely over but it'll be years and years and years before I die. I feel as if I'm going to live out my dying years forever.'

Stella's head shot up. For a minute her eyes were wide and shocked. 'Now I've done it' I thought, and my pulse fluttered and raced. I had taken the first step into thin air.

'What nonsense – ' Stella's voice was not completely firm. She started again. 'What nonsense is this you're talking? *Honestly*, Carla – ' That's better. That's caught the indignant tone of our nursery days. 'You haven't changed a bit, it was always the end of the world whenever anything went wrong. Anyway, what *is* wrong?' She looked instantly as if she regretted asking such a direct question. 'I mean, are things any different from usual?'

I shook my head.

'No. No different. Just that I want to walk under a bus. I would, if it weren't for Nick.'

'Now that is enough. That is really *wallowing* in self-pity. It won't do, you know.'

She took my face between her hands and rubbed my cheeks

briskly, another nursery habit, half-scolding, half-petting. She looked at me again, anxiously. I wasn't responding to treatment. I sat there with all the life and fight drained into a ball of lead somewhere in my stomach.

'You know, you're not the only one who finds life hard going.' The pep-talk continued, but in a very gentle voice. 'You mustn't just give in. And you mustn't make the mistake of thinking that just because one - um – lives in – er – comfortable surroundings, life is nothing but bliss. It isn't. I have a lot on my mind, who doesn't? And I don't have a perfect husband. Henry can be irritating and bloody-minded and thoughtless with the best of them. I told you about last night – '

'Oh but that's nothing, Stella.' I spoke very quietly.

There was silence, helpless silence.

Stella took up her sewing again. It allowed her to keep her eyes safely lowered. 'My guess is that you're run down,' she said eventually. 'Why don't you go and get a check-up from Fergus? You're certainly looking rather pasty. Here, let's see your tongue. Go on, put it out. Good God – it's yellow! No wonder you're feeling low. You're probably bilious.'

'Next thing you'll be saying my blood needs purifying with sulphur,' I joked drearily. 'Or that I need a good dose of Spirit of Pigs.' Stella laughed, probably with relief. The ground seemed relatively safe once more.

'How's father?' I didn't see him very often.

'Oh, well enough. Busy, as always. They're putting some new fruit trees in the back garden.'

'That should be nice.'

She went on sewing and telling me further snippets of home news, if the years-old saga of the squabble between father and his senile neighbour over upkeep of the intervening garden wall could be called news. After another half hour or so, she said she'd better get up and dress. The au pair would be back with Imogen any minute now.

'Well, I'd better be going.'

I knew that nothing would change, nothing would be achieved by staying on. Still I felt a sinking dread at having to leave.

When we got to the front door, she hesitated a moment before seeing me out.

'You know, I didn't mean to sound unsympathetic up there.' We looked at each other warily. 'I know life is pretty rough for you. I do realise that.' She paused and I waited breathlessly. 'Only there really is nothing much that can be done. Is there?'

'No, I suppose not.'

'I mean, any idea of – it's quite unthinkable. There's never been any breath of scandal in the family until – We all stood by you when things went wrong, didn't we? It wasn't easy. But I don't think any of us said a word that might make you feel – guilty, or ashamed. You would say that we behaved well, wouldn't you, Carla?' She sounded almost pleading.

'Yes, yes, you behaved marvellously. Only it's not the end of the story. I still exist, though I wish I didn't – '

'Now don't start that again. This is very distasteful but I'd better spell it out, once and for all. If you came here this afternoon with any idea that I might encourage you or help you to – to run away, you've got another thing coming. In our family we simply don't *have* separations or divorces. Father, as you very well know, is one of the most respected men in his profession, think what it would be like for him. Not to mention his church work.' Stella had gone pale at the spectre of scandal re-emerging, even in imagination. 'There is such a thing as enough.'

'That' I said, suddenly roused, 'is one of the cruellest things you could say. As far as you're concerned, I can be neatly brushed under the carpet and forgotten, because there is such a thing as enough. Suppose I also feel that there is such a thing as enough? Have you thought of that?'

But Stella simply looked cold and flustered. 'I'm sorry if we're going to end up squabbling. It doesn't help anything. I've told you, I'm sorry things aren't better for you. But it was your mistake and your marriage. And now you've got to live with it.'

'Good-bye.' I opened the door and made down the steps quickly before Stella could see that I was crying.

'Come round next week! Give me a ring!' Stella called after

74

me urgently. I didn't take any notice, only walked savagely away from her house with angry tears lashing down my face. Each side of me, from the neat gardens, shone blurred yellow gleams of forsythia, aconites, crocusses, a premature spring rebellion of yellowness which meant nothing, for there would still be endless weeks of this wind and slanting sleet driving the blood from your face and your fingertips. There was a sort of agony in the sight of them.

A woman padded past me, splay-footed, dog on lead, hat on head, expressionless. 'She has a face like a coffin,' I thought. 'Everything happy or sad, good or evil that has ever happened in her life has been shut up inside that face, that coffin.'

That's what Stella was telling me to become. Containment is all. One day I would burst with containment. Meanwhile, I had had a sort of answer to my queries. I had discovered from my own startling outburst that bad was indeed very bad, and I had also discovered that it didn't matter to a soul except me.

A nearby church clock struck six. Good Lord! I must hurry back. Esther will start to think I really have gone under a bus.

10

Esther was our neighbour across the landing at the top of the stair. I first met her over a mop and bucket as I sluiced soapy water around in an attempt to carry out the startling commandment which someone overnight had hung on our front door on a large card with very black lettering – 'It is YOUR turn to wash down the stair'.

'Not like that, ducks,' she said, rounding the corner and meeting a little rivulet of dusty water running inexorably down reminding me of the dribble marks which ruined watercolours at school and the art mistress would say sternly, 'Too much water on the brush'. The problem was the same, only the paint-brush was now a mop.

'You've got it too wet, luv' said Esther picking her way past the little cascade. 'Squeeze it out a bit. Haven't you got a proper mop-bucket? Hang on. You can borrow mine.'

I straightened up, and she saw my shape (it was before Nick was born).

'Hang on,' she said again, and disappeared behind her front door. When she came out again she was carrying her mop-bucket. She had also taken off her overcoat and was wearing a brilliantly flowered though frayed overall.

'Here, give us that.' She took the mop out of my hands, poured the hot water from my bucket into hers. 'Now just go and put yer feet up. I'll do it for you. And any other time till the baby's born.'

I started to protest. After all, she looked at least sixty.

'No arguing,' she said, 'just do as you're told.'

And from then on I knew Esther was on my side — not against Robert, they'd been friendly for years, the only person on the stair he had a good word for — but against the world. That of course included aspects of Robert though they were in some sense depersonalised, part of the way things were.

Esther was on my side. She helped when the baby arrived. She offered to baby-sit, only Robert rarely wanted to go out with me. When Nick got bigger, Esther took him for walks and outings, an amazing strength still there in her large battered presence. In short, without Esther (or Mrs. H. as I called her for a long time in my mind) I could not have made out.

She and Nick are waiting for me when I get back from Stella's, windblown and apologetic for being so late. Esther has got the fire going and Nick's little pyjamas in front of it, warming up. This pleasant little scene casts a mild human glow over the bleak clutter of my home and mercifully takes some of the edge off my bitter sense of abandonment.

Esther is putting on the kettle, she is telling me Nick has been a good boy today, a very good boy, and she smiles over to him where he's playing noisily with his cars. She makes me a cup of tea but won't have one herself.

'I can't stay, Carla. I got a few things to see to — 'phone calls to make.' She makes it sound mysterious and important. 'But come over later, when the wee chap's asleep. If you feel like it.' She smiles her broad toothy smile, says 'Ta-ra Nick' and lets herself out.

I could, I suppose, just as well describe her smile as toothless, for there are almost as many gaps as survivors, but the effect is nonetheless showy.

Mrs. H's 'phone, very useful since we do not have one, is a surprising object to find in her otherwise sparse and shabby home, almost as sparse and shabby as ours, though the style is different. The 'phone is in some way connected with her husband, that is to say, her ex-husband for he had left her long before I appeared on the scene in circumstances which make it surprising to me that his photograph still adorns the walnut veneer sideboard on the side where the veneer has not started to buckle with damp.

Mrs. H's kitchen-living-room is an amalgam of functions and styles. There is the sideboard, for example, but there is also a shaky kitchen table of plywood covered with a thin layer of lemon-yellow formica. Beside the gas cooker is a cupboard without doors containing cooking pots and a frying pan resting on stained newspaper. On the mantelpiece are one or two carved wooden boxes, a vase of fretted bazaar-type silver work with a bunch of bright paper flowers, and a photo of Mr. and Mrs. H. in a mother-of-pearl and ebony frame. An embroidered tarbush hangs on the wall on one side of the mantelpiece, on the other a frightful simpering child clutching a teddy-bear taken from the cover of a mail-order firm's Christmas catalogue. There are no real 'treasures' (Mrs. H. is too poor for that) but there are curiosities, a few, among the stacks of papers and photographs in the sideboard drawers.

'I've never thrown anything out,' Mrs. H. would say, adding sadly, 'but I've had to sell a few things. The decent stuff.'

Her attitude to her ex-husband I find inexplicable. She is not a woman to let the world walk over her. Yet she talks of him more as though he were the dear departed than the *salaud* who walked out on her for a girl in the summer-show chorus at Rothesay. For Mrs. H. has had a stage career, of sorts.

'I was never a beauty,' she would say thoughtfully, 'but I had plenty of oomph. They don't know the meaning of the word, those little girls that show their bums and think they're being sexy. Cheap, that's all it is. Now *I* had personality. I didn't need to show my bum. And I had a voice too – before I wrecked it. Oh yes – ' she would drag lovingly at one of her eternal Capstain – 'I know I did for myself. Forty a day. You can't expect the old lungs to work miracles, can you?'

Since her ex-husband is an Algerian, and Mrs. H. has spent much of her adult life in different parts of the French Empire, she calls him a *salaud* when she is in the mood to bad-word him. French abuse comes to her more naturally than English, although her speech has retained much of its original Lancashire. I love this peculiar hybrid of ee-bah-gum and Gallic cadence. They blend surprisingly well, sharing perhaps a

78

similar shrugging detachment about the follies of this *cirque*, this *comedie* of life, one warm and amused, the other cynical and amused.

I need it, I need Esther's funny half-world of shrewd good sense and extravagent reminiscene. I need it particularly tonight to take away the taste of that too, too solid world wherein Stella can think her crisp thoughts and make judgments that have the neat finality of press-studs snapping shut. Later on that evening I go across the landing, and although I've done it many times before, tonight it feels different, like making a declaration of solidarity, finally joining the league of those who live on the periphery of all systems and consequently see squint.

'I hope Nicky wasn't too much of a handful,' I say anxiously after Esther has sat me down in front of the fire. 'I didn't expect to be away so long.'

'No, no. He was fine. On his best behaviour.'

I can relax back in my chair. Sometimes the conduct report is not so rosy. Sometimes Esther hands Nick back to me, on days that she's feeling low or he has been particularly difficult, wheezing reproachfully, 'He's getting too much for me, Carla. Little devil. He should get a hard smack for some of the things he gets up to –' at which point my fragile spirits fall into a terrible abyss. Mrs. H. is my one hope for some respite from Nick.

Stella had him once for a day but the offer was never repeated. Father was not an enthusiastic grandfather. In fairness I have to say that he was as fastidiously uneasy with Stella's Imogen, bubble curls and all, although it's possible that Nick's status as child-of-shame together with his rebel personality did compound the difficulties. But basically father's neat dandified personality rejected anything but a child modelled on a church elder – grave, obedient and noiseless. Father, you see, was an ardent Presbyterian. *His* defiance of an Italian mother, who by her own admission had made a serious mistake in marrying a Scot, was to discard Rome for Geneva. Opportunism probably played its part – his career as a lawyer in Edinburgh was less handicapped. As a sop to his mother, he gave his daughters Italian names. Stella was originally 'Estella' but she cut off the initial E at some point in her emergence towards selfhood.

'Had a good time at your sister's?' asks Mrs. H.

'No, not really.'

She looks surprised.

'Why's that?'

'Oh, silly stuff. We don't really see eye to eye about things any more. Her life's very different.'

I was not prepared to say more, and hoped she hadn't noticed a slight quiver of my lips.

'Ah well. Ways part, don't they? And talking of that, guess who 'phoned this evening?'

'Who?'

'Ahmed.' Ah! the *salaud* of a husband. I prick up my ears, for I have a kind of obsessional interest in her stories of this man. It is not so much for the stories as for her attitude. I am utterly perplexed why he should be enshrined in the manner of a dead hero, in spite of being very much alive and often reneging on aliment payments.

'Yes, he's had a bit of good luck. Sold his house for double what he paid. He says he's going to send me a present. I said just make it what you owe me, mon vieux, and I'll be quite happy.' She laughs quietly. 'It's not like him to 'phone mid-week. Sunday is the day he 'phones. It was always his low day.'

I understand now why that expensive telephone has been retained.

'I know he's still got a soft spot for me.' Mrs. H. is going to the sideboard to get out the photograph albums. She likes showing them to me. It is part of our 'cosy' set up, Nick asleep, Robert not yet returned and probably out for the evening and I more and more often taking the risk of his coming back with or without companions and actually finding I'm not there to make tea or produce food.

'Got any candles, Carla?' Mrs. H. is bringing the albums over to the table. I smile. This means we're really getting down to it, really entering into the spirit of things, just what I need this evening.

'Yes, I think so. I'll be back in a second.'

When I return with two plain white wax candles, there on the table is a half bottle of sweet port and two tiny pale green glasses with stems set out between two cheap brass candlesticks of rearing cobras twisted round in spirals. I know, because by now the ritual is well established, that those are Mrs. H.'s only two 'good' glasses, the rest being Woolworth's tumblers. Sherry or port usually only appears if Mr. H. has paid up the aliment, but presumably Esther is gambling on the expectation of plenty, or at least something, after that 'phone call, and we must celebrate.

She pours us out two thimblefuls. I light up the candles. We sit down side by side with the albums and boxes in front of us, and I wait like a child impatient for the curtain to go up.

'Cheers!' she says, and we raise our glasses and sip. One of the candles flares, making a little overflow of grease which slides down and dribbles onto the cobra's outspread made-in-Birmingham hood.

With a flourish she lays them out, the old photos of stage shows and parties in the nightclubs of Algiers, Tangier, and moving further east, Hongkong, Bangkok and Singapore. I've seen them before but it's like going back to see a favourite film again and again.

'That's Elsie – the one in the black, remember I told you, she ran off with a sailor, stupid bitch, 'cos of course he dumped her soon as he'd had enough and by the grace of God we found her before she'd actually had to take to the streets. But the place she was working in! We hardly recognised her, she'd really lost her looks, poor old Elsie . . . that's Esteban who *said* he was a Spanish count, but I'd like to know how come a Spanish count couldn't sign his own name? Still, you got to hand it to him, he had the looks. And he did a very nice act, acrobatics mainly. Very classy. Look, that's him in his sequin trunks. What a body, eh?'

Yes, I quite fancied Esteban, but it is Ahmed who dominates the photo-call for me. Ahmed Habib, Esther's man, who seems to have been forgiven unspeakable wrongs. I have to admit he is a honey, is Ahmed, with twinkling eyes, crimpy black hair, arched eyebrows and a pert confident smile showing very white teeth, negroid vitality combined with zestful sharp detail of French physiognomy. Of course, it is a publicity photo I am looking at, no doubt carefully posed and carefully chosen to go on the bill-boards alongside an extremely glamorous Esther looking like Ouija with bandeau low on her brow, ear-rings like chandeliers and a great deal of kohl on the eyelids.

Ahmed conjured and danced demonstration ballroom and a few 'fancy numbers', like the 'apache' number. Esther sang, danced as Ahmed's partner, and very reluctantly, when no other assistant was available, allowed herself to be sawn in half or hold the hat out of which chickens or mice were produced.

'Not rabbits?' I asked. She laughed.

'You don't get rabbits in the Far East.'

Mrs. H. did not much approve of the conjuring. It lowered standards. But, as she said, 'it brought in the money, and we couldn't often forget about that.'

She liked to show me the informal snaps, the parties, the picnics, the scenes of marital bliss arm-in-arm with Ahmed, the bungalow they rented for a whole season in Tangier, the hotel in Singapore, a kind of poor-whites version of Raffles, I suppose, where nevertheless they had a private servant and a private masseur.

I wanted to see the professional photos, the tangoing couple, the fox-trotting team, the 'apache' number with a discreetly dishevelled Esther bent in a bow over the arm of Ahmed, brigand-like and beautiful in a costume which owed something to the Ballets Russes. However, on the anecdotal side I am always hoping for further revelations about Esther herself, for I cannot help feeling that so far I have only been presented with the acceptable side of her life and career. I cannot believe that her buccaneering charisma has been acquired solely by bending in stately backbends over Mr. Habib's arm. What about that 'oomph'?

This evening, over the candles – and we have to be sure not to get through the port too fast or the party will fall flat before the past has thoroughly bloomed again – she seems ready to be expansive, mellowed perhaps by that mid-week 'phone-call.

'Of course, Ahmed had his difficult side – '

We are gazing at one of the frozen moments of happiness,

Ahmed kissing Mrs. H.'s hand with gallantry at a supper table crowded with flowers and glasses. The couple look suspiciously young. 'Actually, this was when we was courting, but he stayed that way right till the end – ' a touch of defiance here, knowing I find that hard to square up with the walk-out. 'Only when he got jealous – ' There is a pause for effect, immediately successful.

'Jealous?'

'Yeh – when he got jealous he was a fiend, a *fiend*, I tell you. Sulking, suspicious, mean-minded. He'd take it out on me on stage too. That's what I really minded. Not partnering properly, making me look clumsy. Oh what a man – '

She shook her head, defeated by the complexities of Ahmed.

'But why should he be jealous?'

'Ah well – ' Mrs. H. gives me a funny look. 'Well, for one thing, as a singer I had what you might call a following. I got some lovely presents. They've gone, of course. A long time ago. Otherwise I'd show you them. I like showing you things – ' she suddenly put her hand on mine.

We seldom touched, a matter almost as potent in our relationship, delicately balanced between intimacy and formality, as between man and woman. Don't misunderstand me. There was nothing sexual about our liking for each other. It was far more profound than a matter of attraction. Sympathy, need, admiration (on my side), all sorts of feelings were engaged that must not be made too specific. Above all, there was the delicacy of giving each other value knowing ourselves to have none in the eyes of the world. Fallen aristos, I imagine, may develop the same kind of bond and similarly invoke the past, taking careful liberties with it, having decided there is no more to come. I was too young to have a past. Having no visible future it really seemed quite enviable to have this evidence of life having been lived.

'Tell me about the presents,' I say, turning my palm to hers and squeezing her hand briefly before releasing it.

'Well, there was those ear-rings – ' she points to the familiar publicity photos. 'Paste of course, I wasn't in the diamond class, but very good paste. Set in hand-worked gold. I had to pretend to Mr. Habib that I'd bought them from a bankrupt widow who'd gambled away what her husband had left her. But actually, they came in a bouquet – which was sent to me after a certain night in a certain gentleman's country villa – '

'But where was Mr. Habib?'

Mrs. H.'s eyes roam, as they always do when she's making some kind of calculation about how much to let on. They roamed like that before she told me about the chorus-girl in Rothesay.

'Mr. Habib – had a little business, as well as the theatrical side. He had – um – lots of contacts all over North Africa and the Far East. We never bothered with the bits in between, Turkey, Egypt, those sorts of places weren't our line at all. We liked the real good-going colonies, French *or* British – ' she sits up, prepared to defend an unpopular cause. 'I know it's all out of fashion now, but the Empire was *good*, good for everybody. All this independence nonsense! What do you and me and the man in the street care about independence? We want to know the score, we want to know that things are going to be run properly. All right, there's a lot of kow-towing and arse-licking – sorry, luv, excuse the language – '

'I don't mind.'

'It doesn't do any harm,' she says wearily, 'provided you know it's all going to go on the way you're used to.'

I have nothing to say. That's Robert's business, to argue Mrs. H.'s fervent conviction that predictable 'serfdom' (his term) is preferable to unpredictable liberty.

I tend to get the personal and the global rather confused. If I think of imperial power as Robert, then I can understand every insurrection, every struggle for independence and cheer them on. If I think of it as father, then brass and leather-bound kindness laced with severity seem so heart-breakingly desirable I wonder to myself why they ever wanted to trade it in for anything else. Following my own experience, is it not possible that these prematurely born nations may have fallen victim to a terrible mistake, not knowing where they will land up when they break the bonds of orderly despotism? I am out of my depth, and in any case far more interested in Mrs. H.'s paste ear-rings and Ahmed's mysterious absences.

'What was his business?'

Mrs. H. starts, her mind has obviously been elsewhere.

'Whose business?'

'Ahmed's – Mr. Habib's business. You were telling me he had lots of contacts.'

'Oh that – ' Her eyes roam again but she seems to decide that I am not a child any longer. Or perhaps the port has removed a few restraints. 'He was a pimp.'

I look puzzled. Mrs. H. sighs, having overestimated my worldly intelligence. I am desperate not to lose contact.

'Just explain, and I'll understand,' I say eagerly.

'Well, the girls in our show, we always chose pretty ones but we couldn't pay them much. So Ahmed said, if they liked to earn a bit more, he could put them in touch with – um – menfriends who would like to be entertained. In private.'

'Oh, I *see*.' There is a pause. I am quite happy that Ahmed's business has been so plausibly explained. It fits.

'Aren't you shocked?'

'No. Should I be?'

'Yes, I think you should. You come from a good background.'

'Maybe. But I've moved from my good background, haven't I?' My mind clouds bitterly again, remembering the events of the afternoon. Fat lot of good my background is doing me now. 'Anyway, don't you know how I landed up *there*?' I nod in the direction of the flat across the landing. For the first time it dawns on me she does not. Did I suppose it was written in my smudged eyes and the frown-lines which are starting to appear?

'No. You've never told me a thing about yourself, except that your dad's a lawyer.'

I think for a moment. My story. I'm afraid it may spoil our little party, as it may well spoil your recollection of me, Marius. As I feared for years it would spoil any fun or frivolity I might try to take part in.

'There's nothing very interesting to tell. It's simply that Robert and I had to get married. It's not a good way to begin.'

We look at each other. Esther's expression is sad. For a moment I'm reminded of Mrs. Crawford, our honeymoon manageress, who would have had a fit if she knew she was being paired up with Esther Habib. But, unlike so many older women who seemed to keep going only by fuelling themselves with moral outrage, they shared the same rare quality of tolerance for which I loved them.

Esther puts her hand on mine again.

'I'm sorry, luv, I didn't know. But it's easy done, that's for sure. And a long time living it through.'

I lower my head to hide the fact that I'm starting to get sorry for myself over the port.

'Let's talk about you,' I say. 'Tell me about the champagne supper in the Dutchman's garden, when the bushes caught fire from the fireworks. . . .'

Esther smiles and tops up our glasses just a little. Artist that she is, she knows how to make the most of nostalgia, how one must take care never to pour out confessionally, always dramatise, relive, re-invent. She knows that nostalgia must be used as a repertoire, never as catharsis. There must be a performance and applause even from an audience of one. I have the good sense to realise that I have not yet lived long enough to be able to turn my experiences (such as they are) into theatre so I keep my revelations to a minimum. Besides there is the additional disadvantage that I'm still living them, whereas Mrs. H. can safely touch up her memories with hyperbole. The past is glorious. Not only that, in some subtle way she allows me into it. I become more than listener. We wander together in the arms of gentlemen-lovers who prevail upon our sense of the social order to be discreet. It is not quite upstairs-downstairs, but we are emphatically clandestine, improper, beyond the pale, dubiously glamorous.

'Oh yes, those were good times,' Esther sighs.

'Would you like to have become really respectable? I mean, to have married the man with the lovely villa? Did you love him more than Ahmed?'

'I don't know, ducks. It was the grand passion all right, but then Ahmed and me, we'd been together for years and it was like a business really, you know, planning our programme and thinking up new acts and all that. I couldn't have given up all that. The work and all. No, the answer's no, I never wanted to be what you call "really respectable".'

I look at her with envy and admiration.

'Mind you, if I'd known it was all going to end up like this – ' Esther makes a funny face and gestures towards the damp discolouring one wall. 'Well, but never mind, it was fun while it lasted. And that's a lot more than most people can say.'

She sounds defiant, but she has no need to be on my account. I need no convincing. Esther has *lived*. Most people that I know have inched their way cautiously along a path of unenterprising virtue, while I have fallen into some kind of bramble-patch. I look silly from both angles, thrashing around in my thorns. I am neither having fun nor saving up credit slips for heaven.

'D'you know what became of him?'

'Who?'

'Your lover, the one who sent the ear-rings.'

'Yes, I do. He died in a Japanese prisoner-of-war camp.'

I am aghast, shocked. This man, merely part of the iridescent fairy-tale of Esther's past, has suddenly become real. He died. He died presumably in a terrible manner, from illness or starvation or brutality. I feel suddenly cold as if I'd been walking arm-in-arm with a ghost. How stupid! How stupid to forget that even in nostalgia's fancy haze one cannot remain safe from the dark.

11

It was the war of course that put an end to the good life. They were in Singapore, Esther and Ahmed, when it broke out, a distant matter which to begin with showed little sign of disrupting their lives. But then at the end of 1941 came signs of sinister change, air-raids, news of Japanese landings up country, the sinking of the *Prince of Wales* and the *Repulse*. Sooner than most, Esther started to feel twitchy.

'I've always been scared of Japs,' she said. 'Really scared. We'd see them when we were working in Hong Kong, the business men all polite and neat, and then we'd hear the kind of things they got up to with the call girls. Made you sick. And they weren't fussy, those girls. So I wasn't for hanging around. I said to Ahmed, "Time we were out of here", so we got moving and got ourselves onto a ship going to Bombay. And then we cooled our heels for a few months doing a bit here and there, we had no contacts and there was no night-life to speak of, not our kind, so I started to try and figure out ways of getting us back home. I found out about a ship leaving with chaps being invalided out and at the last minute two nurses had gone too sick to travel. So I said I'd had nursing experience – you got to bluff in a tight corner – and to cut a long story short I wangled us both on board. By the time they discovered I didn't know one end of an enema from the other it was too late, wasn't it? Anyway, I made myself pretty useful, one way and another, and Ahmed, he did conjuring and cheered them up a bit. So it was OK until we got home. Back to Lancashire.'

She rolled her eyes. 'My God, you should have seen their faces! I'll never forgive them!'

'Who? Why?'

'My family. They wouldn't talk to him. My own family, mother, brothers, sisters, would not talk to my husband. 'Cos he was a wog. That's what they called him. To my face. They said he was to move on, they didn't want to be disgraced. "Thanks very much" I said. "That's the last you'll see of *me*." And I walked out and I've never been back to this day.'

She looked across at me triumphantly. My admiration deepened.

'And then what?'

'Well then, ducks, it was very tough. Not much work and not much cash and then Ahmed, who's hardly spoken a civil word to me since we got back, takes off with a scrawny young blonde in bloody Rothesay. Summer season it was. Miserable. Poor-class stuff, tap routines and high-kicking. And we was down to one number and billed in small print.' She pauses. 'I don't blame him for breaking out, not now. Not looking back. He wasn't a small-town sort of man. And he just hated UK in wartime. After all, we'd lived pretty well, most of the time.'

'But I just don't understand,' I said in bewilderment, as I'd said before. 'I don't understand how you can be so *nice* about it.'

Esther smiled.

'I wasn't nice at the time. I was flaming. When I found out for certain. . . .'

Yes, I knew what she did when she found out for certain. She slashed his costume and she wrecked his make-up box and then she locked him out of their bedroom and howled so loudly that the people in the next door room thumped on the wall. And when Ahmed came to the door she wouldn't let him in, so of course he went back to his blonde.

And yet somehow Esther had managed to forgive him and was glad to get his 'phone calls. He was running a theatrical agency in London by this time, and seemed to be doing quite well. It was all quite beyond me. I did not understand the first thing about forgiveness. Instead I felt graven with various

89

humiliations. Esther sometimes tried to suggest that a bit of shrugging and ignoring wouldn't go amiss, but on the whole she didn't offer advice. This was partly out of delicacy, partly because she really preferred talking about herself.

'. . . you see, he's a few years younger than me. It never made a bit of difference – never' – she stressed the word defiantly – 'until I got so pulled down by the war and this bloody country and jobs so hard to find. They wouldn't have us in ENSA. Said I was too old.' There was outrage in her voice. 'When I *think* of some of the cows that got behind those mikes – of course, me own voice had gone a bit by then, *un peu rauque*, you might say. But Ahmed was loyal, right to the end. "They don't appreciate your style" he'd say. "You're a *diseuse*, in the French tradition. We should have gone to France, Esther." "And work for *les boches*?" Well, from his point of view it made better sense. He wasn't all that fussed who he worked for. And ninety per cent of the French weren't either.' She paused. 'Now I'm nothing great as a patriot, Carla, but that I could not do. Go over to the enemy. Mind you, sometimes I ask myself, where's loyalty got me? Nowhere. Nowhere except a cheap flat in a mucky street in bloody Edinburgh – '

'Why did you settle in Edinburgh? Glasgow would probably be more your place if you have to live in Scotland.'

'I don't *have* to, but I'm buggered if I'll go back to the family, not after the way they behaved – ' (well, I was relieved that all things don't get forgiven) 'and this is where I happened to be when it came to looking for a flat.'

'Robert says we've all got one foot in the grave here, from birth.'

'Well, what's *he* doing here, then?' countered Esther sharply.

She thought Robert was just fine until he started in on the middle classes. That she could not stand. It was the difference between the exotic and the political outcast, the *demi-mondaine* and the (would-be) revolutionary. One recognises dependence on the the bourgeoisie, symbiotic dependence, the other does not. But in fact it was comical. There was Robert, for all his anger, ensconced in a university, bellowing his hatred and cursing compromise – but didn't he whiten with fear and give in to marrying me? And there was Esther, whose dream so she said, was a nice little semi-detached in suburbia, but she would perish of misery in such a place, of that I was sure.

For all her tory loyalties, it was she who was the true iconoclast for *she* knew that nothing endures, that life has to be improvised again and again, that all political systems are against the individual life-force, that they are powerless to prevent the things that really cut deep, like Ahmed defecting for a younger woman, or being billed small on a poster, or losing your voice. Actually, did she know all that? Perhaps not. What she certainly did know was how to cast shadow pictures on fact and create illusion. As I've already said, Esther was my salvation. She moved through the mirage-waters of the past with such skill that there was hardly a jolt as we beached again on the unpromising shores of the present. All we needed was a fairly modest amount of alcoholic stimulant, and we tripped as high and as beautifully as opium-eaters. Perhaps without the 'phone calls from her Ahmed it wouldn't have worked.

I hoped, I hoped to God Esther was not living on the greatest illusion of all. I knew in my bones he wouldn't be back. And I couldn't bear the thought of her debonair courage being ripped apart by such a realisation. I steered very clear of her ideas about the future. Perhaps like me she had lost the capacity to have one.

Meanwhile he 'phoned most Sundays and sometimes paid aliment.

It was all quite beyond me. I only knew that sometimes Esther was on her uppers. She had a tiny annuity, a little bit of savings and what the newborn welfare state supplied. There were times when she came to me to borrow tea, and times when I measured it out in careful teaspoonfuls. Robert's life-style was expensive. I still had not cracked the problem of how to make the housekeeping last out. I had sold all my jewellery except one gold locket and Robert's ring. When we went to the Faculty May ball I had to wear the locket on a black velvet ribbon. Its chain, like a gold bracelet, two brooches and a pair of amethyst ear-rings, had been turned into basic groceries.

91

To make up for the lack of a gold chain I wore a costume of amazing splendour, created by Esther and me – but I should not have introduced the subject of the Faculty ball quite so casually. For events like that, you must realise, were as rare as Cinderella's famous outing in my particular version of banishment. That I did not cope with my transformation in quite the manner she did is another matter. I'll return to that. But the ball, the very fact of it, was the startling thing.

It was purest chance that it came my way, but you have to be in the mood to snatch at chances. I was. I suspect it was the paper poppies that lit the fuse, Esther's paper poppies sitting in a two pound jam jar at one end of her kitchen mantelpiece. She used to make the artificial flowers for her own and the dancers' costumes and she still made them in tissue paper – 'to brighten things up a bit'. On this particular evening they were balanced with another blazon of red, fresh tulips at the other end of the mantelpiece.

'Oh, look!' I had come in as I often did once Nicky was safely asleep. 'You've gone wild. Buying tulips!'

'I didn't buy them,' said Esther proudly. 'They were given to me. Stolen into the bargain.' She winked at me. 'I have an admirer.'

It turned out to be the park attendant where she and Nicky went for walks. That afternoon, full of fine spring sunshine, he had declared his ardour to the extent of telling her she was a fine-looking woman, gallantly kissing her hand and picking her a bunch of forbidden flowers. I couldn't believe my ears. A park attendant in an Edinburgh park? Then it turned out he was an elderly Pole, and it all made sense.

'D'you think he's going to propose?'

'No.' Esther made a face of regret. 'He's married. But it's the gesture, isn't it? Makes you feel you're still a woman – '

'You'll always be a woman.'

'Bless you, luv. Most days I feel like an old battered dustbin.'

'Yes,' I said feelingly. 'I know what you mean.'

'You?' Esther turned on me accusingly. 'What are *you* talking about? Ye're young enough to be my grand-daughter, near as anything. And look at you, with your frilly skirt.

You're a treat, my girl, a smasher, and don't forget it.' I had for once climbed out of my indescribable winter tweed and into a cotton skirt with a frill round the edge, a hangover from my student days. 'Here – hold still a minute.' Esther picked out one of her paper poppies, then came over and fumbled with the clasp that held back my hair till she had managed to stick it in. She stood back to gauge the effect. 'Oh yes, you'll do all right. We'll take you on, dear.' We laughed and she poured out sherry and said 'Cheers!'

I raised my glass.

'To stolen tulips!'

'To indiscretion!'

'To indiscretion!'

I should not have been drinking that particular toast. You have to have a talent for it, like Esther. I had no talent. Witness my predicament. Still, I drank with relish, delighted to find Esther in such gay humour. There were times when she could be formidably gloomy.

'You look like a proper dancer, with that flower and the skirt and all,' she said suddenly. 'Come on, get up. On yer feet. I'll swear you can dance with legs like that, and look at those long bony feet. Go on, stretch them, one at a time. No, not like *that*, here –' she bent down and yanked my foot round with her hand. 'That's better. Now, let's see what you can do. After all, I've taken you on, haven't I? Y'er in me troupe now, you've got to work for it.'

She started humming *Begin the Beguine*, put her hand on my hips and twisted them in time to the tune. 'Left foot back.' She kicked my foot gently in the direction she wanted and before I knew it I was staggering through one of her age-old dance routines, guided as God knows how many terrified little show-girls had been guided through their paces by a pro who knew that the first way to get people moving was to move them.

I felt like a fish returned to water. Movement, rhythm, stretch and swing – it was all coming back with an ache and a tingle, the forgotten joys of dancing. We did a tango, rather stylishly, though I came to grief on the back-bend, then a rumba with many a fancy extra which I picked up so quickly that Esther protested I'd soon be upstaging her. Then she tried me with a simple tap routine but just as I was starting to get the hang of it the neighbours from down below started knocking on the ceiling. Finally she started singing one of her smoochy old numbers and left me to weave my way round the kitchen table feeling torrid and seductive. By this time she'd flung an old cotton lace shawl round me. It smelled dreadful, of damp and mothballs and ancient unwashedness, but who cared? It was bright red like my poppy, it was my colour of hope. She let me borrow it for a few days, for when eleven o'clock came and I thought it was time I got back to my own place I couldn't bear to be parted from it. I wanted to take something back from the party.

So you see, Marius, that past of mine that so intrigued you, that made you suspect I had 'lived' in some way which you had missed out on, that you envied a little? – well, much of it, the best in fact, was nothing more than kicking my heels with a brave old woman minus most of her teeth who had nothing to live for except 'phone calls. And perhaps Nick and Robert and me.

12

Robert was in when I got back. He looked at me as if I'd gone mad.

'Where've you been?' he asked sharply.

'Nowhere, just at Esther's.'

I cautiously opened the door into Nick's tiny room. All quiet. That was all right.

'Have you been having a party or something?'

'I suppose you might call it that.'

The roles were for once reversed. Robert was fairly sober, having spent the evening correcting essays. I was ever so slightly tipsy. I had a paper poppy nodding against my left ear and an old scarlet shawl with a fringe draped over my shoulders. I waltzed round the room with my arms stretched out and collapsed giggling quietly into the old mock-leather armchair with the stuffing coming through its multiple cracks and splits.

My husband is looking a trifle embarrassed. 'Where did you get that tatty shawl?'

'It's not a tatty shawl! It's part of Esther's gipsy outfit. I think it's gorgeous.' I arrange its fringe carefully over my bosom and shrug my shoulder at Robert. 'What's more, I think I'm gorgeous too.' My words take me completely by surprise. 'We spent the evening dancing, if you want to know. Esther says I'm a natural.'

'Natural what?'

'Oh very funny – '

I'm feeling reckless and provocative, in both senses of the

word. I get up and go over to Robert, and whether it's the sherry or the shawl, I'm suddenly very aware that I'm tall and straight and strong with inspiring legs and long lively feet that haven't felt the ground as they did this evening since I gave up fencing. I'm spoiling for something, I'm not quite sure what.

Robert is holding a large gilt-edged card in his hand.

'What's that?' I ask, peering over his shoulder. 'Oh look! It's an invitation! For us.'

'Don't get excited,' he says wearily. 'It's just a faculty jamboree. Routine issue to staff members. The ritual promenade of zombies and zombettes.'

'It's a dance – it's an invitation to a dance! And it goes on till 3 a.m. – with two bands! Oh, don't tear it up, Robert, I want to go!'

'You must be joking. They're deadly, these functions. I got inveigled once and that was enough. You'll be bored silly, I can tell you.'

'You may be bored silly. I won't be. I want to dress up. I haven't worn a long dress since I was a student. I've hardly been to anything, for that matter. I've almost forgotten what it's like to be out after dark.'

'Do you really want to go?'

Robert's usually lethal weapon of ridicule is slightly blunted by astonishment plus a certain unease.

'Yes I do. I want to go very much.'

I clutch my shawl round me like fairy armour, like a mantle of power. It is Robert's turn to shrug, not as a flirt, but as a man giving in to the incalculable absurdity of womankind.

'All right. If you're so set on it, we'll go. You fix up baby-sitting and borrow a dinner-jacket that'll fit me, and we'll go. Though it's a crying waste of money.'

Now although half of me said under my breath, you sod, Robert, you miserable sod, you're not going to lift a finger to help and you can't even let me have my way this once with a bit of grace, the other half knew that it had scored a singular victory. And it also had a vague idea that, flattering though it might be to think it was all to do with being irresistible in a red shawl, his unexpected giving in might just be connected to the *débacle* of our last outing, which had been to Stella's not very many weeks before. It might just be that he felt a little act of restitution was in order.

Stella's invitation to dinner was, I'm sure, intended as a gesture of good will, for it came not very long after that visit when I'd left in tears. 'I can't throw you a lifeline' I imagined she was saying, 'but I can give you bits of cake from time to time.' And I suppose it just goes to show that I must have shared her belief, insulting at one level, that cake would somehow help for I was always glad to receive offers of cake.

We were invited to dinner in order to meet a client of Henry's who actually knew and liked Robert's poetry, and at first seemed prepared to like Robert as well for they stood in a corner near the drinks and appeared to be enjoying themselves. Unfortunately he had a wife, who soon sailed over to join them. His wife was deeply involved in art appreciation and indeed ran a small circle of appreciators and even more unfortunately she had decided that poets like to be quizzed about their Muse by ladies with fluttering eyelashes and an air of expectancy. From across the drawing-room my pre-dinner drink was spoiled by a sense of trouble looming. Robert was starting to look very large and restless. He was also starting to help himself to Henry's whisky. I could only pray that he and the relentless lady would be well separated at the dinner table, but as luck would have it she was directly opposite him and returned insistently to the subject of art appreciation, about which she had missionary views. The 'less fortunate classes', she felt, would benefit enormously from learning to appreciate art. It was indeed wrong and foolish to think that art was the prerogative of an educated elite. And the poor woman looked extremely pleased with herself for having such liberal thoughts.

'What makes you think art is for appreciation?' asked Robert suddenly, leaning forward with his chin raised, a gesture I dreaded. 'What do you know about art anyway? You think it means attending evening classes in pottery, don't you? Or flower-arranging. Or genuflecting in front of the Old

97

Masters on a guided tour of the National Art Gallery. Well, you can keep yer art and its appreciation. The "less fortunate classes", by which I take it you mean the workers, will get on just fine without it.' He paused and I hoped and prayed that he had finished but he hadn't. 'And now I'll let you into a little secret.' He stared wickedly across at the dumbfounded woman. '"Appreciation" is a word that makes me puke. I don't write poetry to be *appreciated*. I write to sing to yer guts, or tear you apart, to smash through the crust. . . . *Appreciation*, my dear, has about as much significance as picking yer nose gracefully and admiring the snot. You should get yourself a group of artistic nose-pickers.'

Perhaps if the woman had had a different sort of complexion the situation might, by some fearsome acrobatics of diplomacy, have been saved. But as it was she started to blush, and she blushed and she blushed, deeper and deeper, while we all sat mesmerized by this rising tide of blood. And it was so cruelly exposing that all of a sudden her husband got up with a scrape of his chair and said, 'Come on, my dear, I don't think we need to stay here any longer', and swept her out of the room, followed by Stella who by contrast had gone a furious chalky white. So ended the possibilities of patronage for Robert and of our presence, ever again, at Stella's and Henry's dinner table.

'I'm sorry, Carla', Stella said, hardly able to speak to me as I helped her make coffee for the uneasy remainder of her party. 'I simply cannot cope with such unpleasantness. I can't risk such a thing happening again. I mean, does he *have* to be so grotesquely offensive with his ideas?'

At the dinner table I had wanted to disappear, quietly and forever. Now I felt like raking my nails down my sister's smooth cheek. I wanted to shout, 'Well, wouldn't *you* get mad if some ignorant bitch condescended to you all evening?' But I only managed to mutter, 'Perhaps it's better to have offensive ideas than no ideas at all', and I doubt whether Stella heard me.

Unfortunately, unlike Esther, my loyalties were sadly split. I told Robert he had behaved like a boor, that he had sabotaged my relations with my family and that it wasn't surprising 'decent people' didn't want him in their houses.

'Oh spare me your decent people,' he said angrily. 'Do you really care about having dinner with Henry Johnson and that crowd of strangled half-wits he calls his friends?'

'They're my family. Stella and Henry are part of my family.'

'Well, what of it? You go on about your family as if they'd been born with holy writ coming out of their mouths. Why don't you see them for what they are? Just very ordinary, narrow-minded, useless people.'

'They're not! They're not narrow-minded and useless. And even if they are, it doesn't matter. They're all I have. The only people who care about me.'

Confronting Robert, I conveniently ignored my own painful conviction that they didn't care nearly enough. He looked suddenly anxious.

'Is that what you really feel?'

'Yes, it is.'

'That's silly.' He turned away from me. 'You know I care.'

'How do I know you care?'

'*How*? Because I do, that's how.'

'It never shows.'

He glanced over at me, then out of the window again.

'I'm not the gushing type. Surely you know that by now?'

'I don't want gush. I want some help around the house, with Nick. I want to go out sometimes. I want – ' my voice shook and undid it all. Robert whirled round.

'Now for God's sake, stop all this bloody self-pity.'

I was immediately dry-eyed and steady-voice. Robert's horror of tears had that effect, a withering one. Tears seemed to be, for him, a kind of blasphemy of the human spirit, a maudlin collapse into degradation. It was one thing he shared, probably without knowing, with the stiff-upper-lip brigade.

'So,' he said, looking at me as if he were on one island in the middle of a large ocean and I was on another quite some distance away. His was larger and craggier. 'What is it you want?'

'I want you to show that you care for me. If you do.'

My voice sounded parroty and child-like, very contemptible.

I would have been contemptuous if someone spoke to me like that. He looked out of the window again. Then suddenly he slammed down his fist violently on the windowsill.

'I make love to you, don't I? Isn't that "showing" it, as you call it?'

I was instantly made strong by that beating-down fist. He was not entirely at ease with himself.

'You don't make love,' I said calmly. 'You fuck.'

'Well, fuck you!' he said quietly and bitterly, and we both emerged from that encounter shoddier by a good deal.

But it was true, he didn't make love, he didn't know how. He fucked. Perhaps I had a rather particular interpretation of that word. For me it summed up exactly the quality of his sexuality, his impersonal violence – oh I don't mean anything horrific, just that he was rough, impatient, and totally unaware of his own strength. Poet he might be and sometimes a good one, but artist of the flesh he was not. It was the assertive male robot, the creature of mechanical lust, that got into bed beside me, that woke me up in the small hours and if not too drunk to sustain his erection pumped routine emissions into my sleepy body.

But wait. There was once, and only once that I can remember, when something quite different happened. Yes, Robert was ill, a very rare thing, running a high temperature, his lungs and throat inflamed. And he was scared, the only time I ever knew him to be physically afraid. By the time I joined him in bed I was tired out with running after him and wanted only to turn my back on him and plummet into sleep. But he clung to me, silently asking for reassurance. He was being like Nick with a bruised knee, so I held him and stroked him and hoped it would soothe him off to sleep. And then to my amazement I felt him stroking me, exploring my body slowly, his hand uncertainly lingering on my breasts, my stomach, my thighs, no hurry to get straight into my cleft, for once. I could feel his delight, I knew he was entranced, that my skin was the finest thing he'd touched, that I was long and smooth and delicious to him. I felt him shaping me and making me flow, a land discovered with amazement, a land flowing with rivers, not only the liquid of sex but all sorts of flowing, the draining plentiful sweetness of genuine desire.

Yes, I'd conveniently forgotten that. How, long before you and I, Marius, discovered the roots of bliss in each other, I had had one taste of ecstasy. We soared that night, Robert's overheated body and unarmed mind carrying me high out of myself. We gave in totally, lost boundaries. I did not know until that night the meaning of 'one flesh'.

But it never happened again. We pushed away this curious gift, this discovery, not brave enough to acknowledge the existence of a hidden spring for fear of what it would do to the ugly homestead we'd constructed on top of it, the pattern of bickering and irritation, the resentment which had already set hard. A terrible denial, I agree. But how *could* this sudden flowering of sexual joy co-exist with the roles we'd set for ourselves?

There is a way of dealing with these things, and that is to leave them disconnected, an odd thing that happened, fancy that. . . . When we finally separated that night, Robert, having sweated profusely and probably brought his temperature down, had already collected his sleepy wits.

'That nearly killed me, Carla pet. Are you okay?' He sounded wry, earthy, as if he'd survived some taxing work-out in a gym. Nothing need be disturbed. I took a little longer to forget, certainly my body did. Next time we made love I felt that delicious draining fullness starting up again, but Robert's desire was once more shut away in its usual quality of mechanical thrust. We were back to normal.

Well, that was not scheduled as a memory, indeed it was not. I need time to recover. When did it happen? In the early days? Later on? I simply can't remember. I can only remember it happened. Oh Marius, why such confusion? Why such desperate confusion? I wish I had not remembered that incident. It is nothing so straightforward as love denied, only a reminder of passion, intensity between us, something that crackled painfully, fed by the wrong fuel. I don't even know what lit it in the first place. Perhaps nothing more profound than reckless curiosity, emotional arson. Strike a match and see what happens. Ah, but Robert wasn't your normal tinder. He didn't burn easily, he grudged every moment of his burning. Passion is not, as people so often like to think, the great bright bonfire of easy love. It is always something dark and resisted, at least among Scots. His poetry was burnt out of him with his teeth clenched until he could resist no more. His love for me – well, I don't suppose that ever truly existed. Only something did, that's the mystery. Something did.

13

'Hullo, Carla.'

Stella's voice sounded high-pitched and guarded over the 'phone. It was the first time we'd spoken since Robert was shown the door.

'I'm wondering if – '

My own voice squeaked away huskily. I was really very nervous.

'If what?'

'Well, we're going to a ball, at least I hope we are, and I was wondering if – '

'Do you want to borrow something to wear?'

'Not exactly. Not me, it's really – for Robert. You see, he hasn't any dress clothes and I just thought perhaps Henry had an old – you know, an old dinner jacket that he doesn't wear – '

There was a very long pause at the other end of the 'phone.

'Look, I know it's terrible cheek to ask after – um – what happened.' I couldn't stand the suspense any longer. 'But I do so want to go. It's a faculty ball. And Lord and Lady Strathaillie are going to be there, as guests of honour,' I added, hoping to impress.

My 'phone call was the result of desperation. I had 'phoned Moss Bros. and realised there was no way we could pay for a hired suit. Esther and I had looked at one of Ahmed's old conjuring outfits but it was, for many reasons including odour, cut and size, quite out of the question. By this time the dance was only ten days away.

'*Please*, Stella. I haven't been dancing since I was a student.'

'Good Lord.' Stella was all cool astonishment. 'Well then you'd better go, hadn't you, before you forget how.' Having managed to convey her sense of the barbarism of my life she suddenly dropped her guard and sounded like her normal sisterly self. 'And what are *you* going to wear?'

'Me? Oh, I'm going to try and furbish up my old striped dress. It's the only one that doesn't look hopelessly girlish.'

'No, you can't wear that,' she said seriously. 'Not if it's a proper dinner and dance. Maybe I can lend you something of mine . . . look, come over, we'll have a dressing-up session.' She sounded friendly and excited. Reluctantly I brought her back to the main subject of the call.

'And – um do you think – *does* Henry have an old dinner jacket that Robert could wear? I think they might be about the same size, or near enough – ' and if you replace flesh by muscle, I wanted to add. Robert already carried too much weight but never let it be said that he was flabby like Henry.

'Yes, yes,' said Stella impatiently. 'Don't worry, I'll find something for him. When are you coming?'

I had a quick consultation with Esther about looking after Nicky.

'Tomorrow after lunch?'

'Yes, that's fine. See you then.'

We spent the afternoon in Stella's bedroom playing at fine ladies, as we used to do when we were kids. There was only one bad moment when my bra came into sight, limp, stringy and utterly useless. In fact my breasts, remarkably unaffected by one round of child-bearing, were actually holding it up rather than the other way round. I don't know why I bothered to wear it, except that not to do so would have felt almost as naughty as going without knickers. (We had no thoughts then of symbolic acts of arson.)

Stella said in a rather taut voice that I must wear a strapless bra because most of her frocks were low-cut, and started looking in her lingerie drawers.

'We used to be much the same size, didn't we?'

104

But with the passage of years I seemed to have got rather fuller in the bust, or Stella to have shrunk a bit. Her various bodices made me bulge over the top.

'Oh heavens, that won't do!' She giggled with dismay. 'You look as if you're going to play the French chambermaid in a restoration comedy. What are we going to do?'

'Choose a frock with a boned bodice and I'll manage without.'

'Well – ' She sounded dubious.

We looked along her row of evening dresses. They were dauntingly correct, white brocade, lilac brocade, beige chiffon –

'I thought that might do,' said Stella, pausing at the beige chiffon. 'It's got this lovely trailing scarf.'

Yes, I could see it rippling out behind her as she took her place graciously at the top table of some civic banquet. On me, the beige chiffon looked like a grubby shroud. I quickly took it off, and went back to searching through the row of dresses. I was starting to feel depressed. Then my eye caught a gleam of colour at the back of the wardrobe.

'What's this?'

My hand closed on ruby-red slipper satin. I tugged it forward.

'That? Oh, it's only an old skirt. I'd forgotten about it, I haven't worn it in years.'

I pulled it out. It was lovely, cut in a way that would lie smooth on the hips and swirl out at the bottom.

'I remember this. You used to wear it to go dancing with your Greek. With a black lace blouse – you haven't still got that, by any chance, have you?' I suddenly saw myself in ruby-red and black lace. Stella shook her head.

'No, it's gone.'

'Oh – ' I could have wept.

'Well, but wait a minute.'

She rummaged among the dresses again and pulled out something black and lacy. I fingered the material critically. Yes, it was right.

'You can try getting a blouse out of this if you like. You may find enough good material. But it's torn in several places,

105

that's why it's at the back there. Finished. I really must have a clear-out one of these days.'

'I haven't got a sewing machine,' I said.

Stella turned to me, exasperated.

'Right. You can borrow my old hand machine. Henry's just given me an electric one that's got so many gadgets I'm scared to use it. However, this will make me face up to the beast. Now, *are* you equipped for this blessed dance? No, you are not. A bra you must get if you're going to wear flimsy black lace, and I'd better give you the money for it, hadn't I? There – and here's some for a taxi to take you and one sewing machine and two dresses back home. Oh yes, and of course a dinner jacket and trousers for Robert. I was forgetting.'

She disappeared into a room I took to be Henry's dressing-room and came back with black clothes over her arm.

'You've given me an awful lot.'

I was looking at the notes in my hand.

'Well, get yourself some eye-liner or perfume or whatever you like. You might as well make it an occasion.'

Stella had never slipped me a couple of pounds or anything else to help out with necessities, and probably that was right, but for luxuries she suddenly had an open purse and a generous heart. I was extremely touched, and determined in honour bound not to spend the extra at the corner shop.

Esther helped me with the blouse. It may not have had couturier finish but it had what was more important in my eyes, a theatrical style. It had wide bat sleeves and a large loose frill of a collar round a deep décolleté. Out of an old white silk petticoat we made a beautiful romantic floppy rose with a gold lamé-covered button from one of Esther's stage waist-coats for a centre, and we placed it, slightly offset, above my cleavage. Fortunately there was enough black lace to make a frill for the edge of the skirt, for I was taller than Stella. To complete the effect, Esther decreed that I should wear my hair piled up in a chignon and adorned with a wreath of white flowers. So while I machined away at the blouse she twisted and wound fragments of white silk round wire and made my wreath.

I had by this time almost lost sight of the end point of all this preparation. It was the costume that engrossed me, all those lovely textures, improvising something exciting out of scraps and cast-offs. Long before we got to the ball I was slightly drunk on red satin and white silk and liable to see cascades of black lace whenever I shut my eyes. It was a new and curious hunger. When Esther showed me her costumes stacked away in an old cabin trunk, I felt an itch like a miser after gold. I fingered old fading velvet and crumpled silk and jingled bazaar ornaments as if they were an 'open sesame' into a magic world, of brilliance and the free flight of make-believe. I don't know why I fell in love with what was worn and tinselly and vulgar, but it grabbed my imagination as no fresh crisp material or real valuable jewellery ever did. Perhaps I had lost faith in the latter, seeing it melt like snow into a few short-lived pounds. Nevertheless, in honour of the occasion, I did wear my gold locket on my black velvet ribbon to the ball.

'Doesn't she look *queenly*?'

Esther was quite overcome by my appearance. We had gone over to her flat to show ourselves off and see that Nicky, who was spending the night with her, was safely settled down. I felt three inches taller than usual (I've never been abashed by my height) and quite enchanted by the fall of red shimmering material from my waist, the white wreath round my stately chignon, and the smell of perfume which fairly buzzed round me. As Robert remarked acidly, but with a bit of a smile, as we were getting ready, 'You've fairly eclipsed my after-shave.'

'Well, will we do, Esther?' he said abruptly. 'I feel about as relaxed as a bear on its hindlegs in this outfit. I can't wait to get out of it. But Lady Muck here said she wanted to go dancing, so there's nothing for it, is there?'

'Listen, *mon vieux*.' Esther went and stood very close to Robert, her hands on her hips. 'We haven't put in a week's hard work on that costume for *you* to pour bloody cold water over everything. If it wouldn't actually kill you, suppose you tell her how she looks? Suppose you actually let on that you think she's smashing? You do, don't you?'

Robert drew in a deep breath. he looked straight at Esther.

'Yes,' he said. 'I do.'

It was too much for him. In the taxi he sat in the corner far away from me and kept his eyes firmly on the streets while I thought, self-engrossed, what a pity it was I had had to wear an everyday jacket over all this finery. However, that piece of drabness could be left behind in the Ladies' Room. I sailed into the big reception room with its giant chandeliers and looked around for someone to appreciate me. Eventually someone did, though perhaps 'appreciation' is not quite the right word. He was a man called Joaquin Lefèvre.

14

Joaquin had a nickname in the faculty. He was known as the 'solitary stud' but that I did not know when I first met him at the May ball. He had a longish face, rather pale and waxy, fabulous dark eyes and a romantic haircut with a full curling fringe of dark hair and a lot more round the ears than was considered in good taste. Robert's hair was also longer and shaggier than the norm, but he merely got me to clip it with scissors from time to time, whereas it was clear that Joaquin knew of an idiosyncratic hair-dresser who understood what 'Byronic' meant in terms of coiffure.

It was his mouth that really gave the game away, a mouth that was too fresh and red, startlingly so, against his sallow skin. It was a greedy mouth, a pampered mouth, and set in that long waxy face with its slightly weak chin, suggested some kind of invasive lifeform with a will of its own, a victorious parasite. The whole effect was odd, a curious botched beauty as if something originally fine had melted and slithered out of form.

Hardly an appealing portrait, is it? And looked at dispassionately neither was he. But there was more to him than his face. There was his body which was marvellous, long-legged, taut, straight-backed. And he moved with an arrogance and dash which distracted from the unpleasing qualities of his drooping mouth and boneless cheeks.

He was wearing a frilled shirt with his dinner jacket. That, together with the hairstyle and the large wrought gold ring on his little finger made me wonder for a moment whether he was queer, but then I decided no, not with that glance that skimmed over women's breasts and then looked lazily at their faces.

Slouched elegantly on a bar stool with one leg perched on the rung and the other extended almost like a dancer, he stuck out from the parade of academics in their best like a feline amongst a crowd of penguins. I stuck out by virtue of my operetta black-and-scarlet and, so he said later, 'other qualities'.

We eyed each other from opposite ends of the bar. I was feeling agitated, excited, suspecting that I still knew how to be at a party, after all – except that so far there had been no party. There had been a mediocre dinner served at tables of sixes and eights, followed by ineffably tedious speeches. Was it for this that Esther and I had worked away at my costume, that I had coiled up my hair with such care, shaved under my arms, and bought expensive scent?

There were two dance floors with two bands, one for Scottish country dancing, the other for ballroom.

'Aren't we going to dance?' I asked Robert, who certainly did look uncomfortable and slightly trussed up in his brother-in-law's suit. But he had himself propped against the bar and had found a buddy, a thin mathematician with glasses who was expounding on Bertrand Russell's theory of numbers, a subject that seemed to offer more than a twirl on the dance floor. It was clear I might yawn away unnoticed for hours to come.

Joaquin moved up slightly from his end of the bar. I swopped places with Robert, a natural enough move since the argument about Russell's theories was going on across my face.

'May I perhaps get you something to drink?' Joaquin was exquisitely polite, and his accent curious and rather pleasant.

'Thank you,' I smiled at him, grateful for the rescue.

'I'm drinking a rather good brandy. Would you like that, do you think?'

I said yes. He bought me a double. Very discreetly his large eyes roamed over my neck and breasts. I started to feel ill at ease, but he quickly paid me a gallant conventional compliment.

'Let me drink to the belle of the ball!'

I laughed.

'But where is the ball?'

'Ah! That you might well ask.' He made a face and rolled his eyes. 'We two appear to be the only people here who look as if they have come to enjoy themselves. I make the same mistake every time. I flatter myself that mostly I am, let us say, acclimatised. I have grasped the fundamentals of the Scottish culture. But every time I come to a party or a dance I am shocked. The men go on talking amongst themselves as though there were not a woman in sight. Extraordinary!'

His head swivelled in a motion completely automatic as a young woman in green taffeta passed us.

'Who's she?' I asked innocently.

'I've no idea.' He sounded suddenly annoyed.

'I know very few people here.' I felt I had to excuse myself in some way.

'Ah.' He drank some more brandy and looked carefully past me. 'Which gentleman is your husband?'

'The large one. He's a poet. He's in the department of English Literature, but he is two hundred per cent Scottish. Perhaps you've seen him around the university?'

Joaquin shrugged as if the matter didn't merit certainty one way or the other, but he continued to stare at Robert's back thoughtfully, while I stared more openly at Joaquin. 'A lounge-lizard, that's what you are. A slimy, handsome lounge-lizard.' I felt happy and protected, having got this clear to myself. I could now enjoy him in a deriding sort of way. Just the same, his physique was superb, streamlined, built for speed, fast movement.

'Are you a fencer, by any chance?'

He looked pleased.

'Yes, as a matter of fact I am. Epée and foil. What makes you ask?'

'It takes one to spot one,' I said smiling.

'Aha!' He lifted my hand to his lips. 'So you are a fighter. A beautiful fighter.'

'Well, not any longer, I'm afraid.' Suddenly I realised how much I missed it, how my body used to feel keyed up and

111

strong, how one's wits danced aggressively in feet and wrist and eyes. 'I have a little boy now, and it's not possible to go regularly to the club, so I don't go at all.'

Joaquin's face took on the blank look that signals switch-off when a woman is clumsy enough to introduce a domestic element into the game of seduction.

'Naturally, that makes for difficulties.'

He returned a flat ball. There was a bored lull, and his eyes roamed again. But returned.

'That is a very dramatic outfit you are wearing – may I congratulate you? You are the only woman here with – how do you put it – flare?'

That went straight to my heart, but I resisted the impulse to tell him naively the true story of my dress, seeing how he had reacted to mention of Nicky, and merely thanked him, saying I had a great weakness for things with a Spanish flavour.

'Why then, we are excellently suited! I am, as it happens, half Spanish.'

'Really? And what is the other half?'

He made a face.

'Belge. My father makes money in Brussels. My mother makes love in Madrid.' We both laughed. 'I take after mama.'

His long lashes drooped with sly innocence, a kind of slow-motion double wink. 'You are absurd' I thought. 'But I'd love to dance with you.' Out loud I asked him what he was doing here at the university.

It turned out he had a two-year appointment in the Department of Spanish, which was nearly at an end.

'And then what?'

'Well, I don't know – back to Madrid, I suppose. But I shall resign my post in the university.'

'Why?' I asked.

'Because – you know, perhaps I have been a little corrupted by life over here – '

'*Corrupted*?'

How could this playboy have been corrupted by anything in Edinburgh University?

'Yes,' he said, and his voice changed. He looked at me quite differently, a cool unflirtatious look. 'I am far from being a

Republican, but to go back to that atmosphere of dogma and repetition – It is probably good in everyday life that there are authorities and police and so forth, to keep order, but in intellectual life – You simply do not know how lucky you are here. You can argue, you can question, nobody is going to report you if you disagree with your professor. No, I don't think I can go back to that. Perhaps I will go abroad again, Paris perhaps.' He shrugged. 'It is not very interesting. Tell me – ' his voice changed again, 'what is your name?'

'Carla Carmichael.'

'And mine is Joaquin Lefèvre, ardently at your service. Do you know something? We are wasting time, standing here. We should be dancing, should we not? These gentlemen will no doubt keep the bar from falling down.'

I tapped Robert on the shoulder.

'I'm going to have a dance. Is that all right?'

I think he said yes. In any case he didn't show much interest. He and the mathematician were now onto problems of Cartesian duality and were locked in happy strife.

Joaquin cupped his hand under my elbow and we glided through to the dance floor where as luck would have it the band was playing a tango.

'That's my favourite dance,' I said happily, remembering the crash course of Latin American dance in Esther's kitchen. This is more like it, I thought, as Joaquin moved me smoothly into the dip and sway and pause of that luscious rhythm. Oh yes, I'm starting to fly! He danced superbly, holding me close till we moved as one creature, then releasing me to stand back and admire me boldly while my scarlet skirt spun out. Then he bought champagne to drink as we sat out a boring fox-trot at a dark corner table, and I drank a private toast to old Singapore, a long continuous toast spanning several glasses. Then more dancing – rumbas, sambas, tangoes. Joaquin had had a word with the band-leader and the Latin American numbers came up again and again. We danced every one and I thought 'I haven't been as happy as this since I got married'. Then the band went off for a break and Joaquin appeared with two more enormous brandies.

I drank mine too fast, careless by this time, leaning back in my corner and letting my dashing admirer be gallant. He edged closer to me and put his arm round my waist while I looked mistily at the lights beyond the darkened dance floor and realised they had flowered into opalescent moons with aureoles. I let my head slip for a moment onto his shoulder, feeling peace in the middle of my excitement, aware of his steady heartbeat and his breathing close to my face. I felt, little fool that I was, for a moment protected.

Then all of a sudden my right breast stiffened in its discreet casing of black net. Joaquin's hand was caressing it gently and expertly. With horror – because that breast had apparently acquired a life of its own and was flooding me with frightful sharp pleadings of desire – I tried to push his hand away but he caught and held it, and there we were with our clasped hands still pressed against my breast.

'You mustn't – ' I said feebly, pushing again.

'No, don't do that,' he said in a low voice. 'You are beautiful and passionate. Don't expect me to treat you like a woman of stone.'

No, I was most certainly not a woman of stone, I was a woman suddenly standing naked within her clothes, very soft and strong and hungry, but also shivering with fear.

'Let's get out of here,' murmured Joaquin in my ear, 'let's go for a drive.'

'Oh *no*, I can't possibly do that! What if my husband sees us? Besides – ' The dizzy lights swum more dizzily. Joaquin's hand was now stroking my neck, delicately, beautifully.

'Look – it's nothing. Just a little drive to get some fresh air after all that dancing. We will stroll to the door and of course if he – or anyone else sees us, we shall simply turn back with no drama. Believe me, I have no wish to face *un écossais enragé*.'

We met no one. They were all either drinking or dancing. Joaquin ran a long-bonneted saloon of some kind. I don't know what make it was, but it was foreign and expensive with leather upholstery and a quiet powerful engine. Ahead of us its headlights threw out two long confident beams.

It must have been very late, the small hours of the morning, for already the dark was getting thin and silhouettes sharpening. Arthur's Seat lumped black before us as we headed for the

114

park, the street lights rushing past like flickering beads carelessly discarded. Joaquin parked high up beside the loch, and switched off the engine. There was a moment of intense quiet. Then he leant over and kissed me full on the lips with his greedy mouth, and there was no romance about it, only appropriation.

'Get into the back,' he commanded softly.

I was shivering and shivering partly from cold but more from excitement. However, I also realised as I tried to say something that I was very drunk.

'It's no good – ' I managed to get out.

I think I was actually talking to myself. I think I was trying to tell myself that although, by an almighty effort, I might overcome this brandy-laden inertia, this agony of need, I might even manage to fight off this seducing bully – I wasn't going to try. Giving in was too sweet. Not to struggle was delightful. I was fed up with struggling.

But Joaquin misunderstood me.

'Shut up,' he said unpleasantly. 'We are past that stage. Get into the back.'

There was no more caressing, no more courtesy. I'm sorry to say I didn't even mind. I was too randy by this time to mind anything, even the fact that he swore as he tried to cope with the tangle of suspenders and pants under my beautiful slipper-satin skirt, now wrenched up round my waist.

'Get these things off,' he said, giving up on the pants. And somehow I did. Then he hooked one of my legs over the front seat, pushed my skirt practically over my face and I felt him come into me, deep and sudden, while one of us gave a great 'ah-h' of preliminary satisfaction. Then we were off, chased by desire, chasing desire, a raw business of gripping and panting and flinging ourselves onward in great leaps, and then suddenly there was a juddering as though we were, together, a boat stopped by a great wave and vibrating uncontrollably with the shock.

We lay for a minute or two in the jumble of clothes and flesh in a kind of swoon of sudden-ness. And my God! how quickly it passes, the life-bursting moment with all its whirling crescendo! One minute before and all the tangoes, the brandies, the expanding lights, and my sense of crazy flight had massed together, swamping even the degradation of those carelessly pulled-apart legs and the look of total self-absorption on Joaquin's face. And then – crash goes the wave and there it lies, the smashed moment with its flotsam and debris to be gathered up. Pants to be found and fumbled on, fly-buttons refastened, skirt straightened, blouse to be tucked in. My white wreath is lying on the back seat of the car, a silent reproach that I have let my finery be mucked around in this graceless fashion. I try to pin it back and recoil my hair. The dawn is a few degrees nearer and in its colour-blind light we look dishevelled and ugly. At least Joaquin does and I feel it.

'Get me back,' I say, cold with panic. Robert by this time is sure to be looking for me. I have done something dreadful and I don't know whether I can carry it off. In the mirror set in the sun-visor I check that my make-up is not all over my face, that my hair is not too tousled.

Joaquin simply says, 'Yes, of course.'

We drive in silence as though we were strangers.

Robert was looking for me, that is to say he was alone pacing up and down in the foyer of the hotel and there seemed to be very little of the party left. His face, when I appeared with Joaquin, went white.

'Where in hell have you been?'

There was a locked, quiet quality in his voice. It was so menacing there was only one thing I could do, simply walk right into the danger zone and pretend like mad.

'Sorry – have we kept you waiting?' I spoke with a calm and jaunty deceitfulness I didn't know I possessed although I felt sick with drink and fear. 'Joaquin took me for a spin round the town. It got so stuffy in there, I just had to get a bit of air. I got more than I bargained for,' I added laughing, sailing close to the wind, as if I'd known all my life that this was the best way to unnerve a person not entirely sure he wanted the truth. 'He's got a car that goes like a rocket and drives like a maniac. But thanks all the same.'

I smiled pleasantly at Joaquin, who was watching me with some amazement. He merely nodded and said,

'It was a pleasure. Shall I fetch your coat?'

'Don't bother,' said Robert unpleasantly, 'I have it here.' He pointed to one of the settees.

'Well, can I give you a lift home?'

'No – thanks. We'll pick up a taxi.'

Fortunately there was a rank close by, for after that almighty effort of situation-saving alcohol took over again, and I could hardly keep my feet going in front of me. Yet, through the whirling fragments of my mind (I don't think I had ever been so drunk before), there persisted a feeling of pure, clear astonishment. How had I got away with it? Why had Robert not smashed in Joaquin's face? Or mine? Or was that still to come? After all, would someone like Joaquin *ever* take a young woman out in a car without intending to remove her pants?

Crouched in my corner of the taxi, I watched my husband. He looked gaunt and tired and sunk in depression. The anger was gone. Somehow I had picked up quite accurately that he was by no means certain he wanted the truth, that when it came to the possibility of a real showdown he was on some kind of unsure ground. How strange. Was it possible that the careless ruler of my life did not feel quite so sublimely justified as I had thought?

He sighed deeply. 'What are you thinking?' I wondered, as I seldom did. A lot of hysterical feelings started up. I wanted to say I'm sorry, I'm sorry, I've done something stupid, something I shouldn't, and it may hurt you. Please forgive me. I wanted to say, too, you've driven me to it, you've made me so unhappy. But you're unhappy too, what is it? What is it? Can't you let me come anywhere near you, to comfort you? I must have been very far gone to let any idea of Robert's unhappiness take shape.

When we reached the street door I was still too drunk to get upstairs without help. For the second time that evening, I gave over. Robert half-carried, half-propelled me up the stairs. He was aghast, disgusted.

'You mustn't get yourself into a state like this!'

I staggered across to the bedroom. My limbs had melted down but my speech had not. I turned round and stared at him.

117

'*You* tell me that? You have the nerve? Well, take a look – take a good look. This is what I see, time and time again. I have to watch you become limbless, or listen to you throwing up –'

'Oh, leave off, Carla!' he begged. 'I can't take any more tonight. I took you out to this damned dance, didn't I? Because you wanted to go. Do you have to end up the evening sounding like a bitter old bag who can't live without carping or preaching – '

'Well, that's just what I am! A bitter old bag in her mid-fifties, that's what I feel like!'

'No, don't say things like that – '

'But I will! I will say it. What else do you expect? Living with a revolutionary genius the world won't recognise? You take every one of your disappointments out on me. I'm the enemy, I'm the whipping boy for all your bloody blighted hopes. Well, what about *my* blighted hopes?'

I had him licked. He sat down in the dreadful leaking armchair and covered his face with his hands.

'Oh God,' he said, 'do we have to go on living like this?' I didn't know whether he was referring to the human condition or just us two. 'What's happened to joy? What's happened to light-heartedness? What's happened to my living self?'

I stood uncertainly by the bedroom door. If he had looked up, would I have gone to him? I think so. But he did not, he stayed there hunched round his own hopelessness. 'You poor sod,' I thought, 'You're as lost as I am.' Then my interest faded and very soon after so did consciousness.

Anyway, it changed nothing, those few moments of dim pity. When I woke up next morning, queasy but sober, all I wished most devoutly was to get life back onto its normal tracks as fast as possible. Security, God damn it, is what you're used to.

15

Joaquin reappeared, to my horror, a week after the ball. There was a knock on the front door and when I went to open it there he was, holding a large and costly bouquet of flowers. My first thought was how to get rid of them, not him.

'May I come in?'

He smiled at me confidently, assuming the right to enter.

I led him into the living room where he gave me my bouquet with a flourish. At the same time I could see his eyes make a fast casual scan of me and my surroundings. Behind his air of courteous detachment there was a slightly baffled look which I thoroughly understood. I was wearing my everyday outfit, a checked shirt-blouse and a dull blue skirt. My legs were bare and I had on a pair of well-scuffed sandals. Sun was pouring into the room cruelly exposing every threadbare patch and tear, as well as the layer of dust I half-heartedly removed from time to time but had not done for weeks. Even a man of such all-purpose *sang-froid* as Joaquin must have been somewhat jolted after the Carmen-apparition at the ball.

He looked round him again and I imagined that he had sold off the entire contents for a few shillings and made a few mental readjustments accordingly.

'You look well, my dear.' He kissed my hand rather disdainfully. 'It is such a beautiful day I thought I would stroll this way and pay a call on the lady who likes things with a Spanish flavour. How did I find you? Well, the university diary has its uses.'

I meant to ask him to sit down, to say I would make coffee if he liked, in short, to behave as a proper hostess, but all I managed to blurt out with extreme awkwardness was, 'I wish you'd go away.'

'Oh come.' He was not at all put out. 'Surely not. I do hope not. Maybe I have taken you by surprise. I apologise, but in the circumstances it is difficult to give you warning, isn't it?' He had come right up to me. I found it difficult to meet his eyes. 'Do you really want me to go away?'

He made his voice sound, mockingly, sad and hurt. I raised my eyes.

'Yes, I do.'

'Oh dear.'

He smiled and put his hand up to cup my neck for a moment, then slid it quickly down to touch my breast. I should have slapped his face, but I didn't. I wanted him, and he saw it.

'Come on,' he said quietly.

'You can't stay long.'

I was trying to think how soon Esther would be back with Nicky. I should have taken him out myself, it was such a beautiful day. I was handing him over too often, and if I'd taken him out, well, then *this* wouldn't be happening. . . .

Joaquin was undressing methodically at Robert's side of the bed, his long brown body coming gracefully into view. He folded his clothes carefully and laid them on the chair. This was not a matter of tangled heaps. And I, just as methodically, went into the bathroom to put in my diaphragm. I didn't know yet if I'd got away with that awful piece of rashness up behind Arthur's Seat, but I was taking no further chances. Quite without conviction, I looked at myself in the mirror above the basin and said quietly, 'Carla Carmichael, why on earth are you doing this?' It was interrogation for form's sake, something to point up the numbness, the blessed numbness, I felt as to morals or consequences. In no other way was I numb. I ran moist with anticipation. I couldn't wait for Joaquin's body.

He was there waiting for me in the frowsy bed Robert and I shared, and within minutes we had had the same hectic explosive experience as in his car, preceded this time by enough tender foreplay for me to think, wildly, for a split-second 'He's in love with me!' No, he wasn't. And it still makes me ashamed that not only on that occasion but a few others as well, his loverly skill tricked me briefly into ideas of tenderness, the persistent childish hope of being cared for as well as given pleasure.

After it was over Joaquin reached for cigarettes. I took one. We shared the battered metal ashtray, souvenir of some pub foray, which was always at Robert's side of the bed. I made a note to empty it and remove incriminating stubs. Washed with physical relief, I felt also relieved that the worst had been revealed. I didn't care now what Joaquin thought of the poky room with its one north-facing window, the array of my shabby clothes half revealed by a wall-cupboard whose door had been replaced by a limp curtain. I'd hoped it would look nicer than the door besides taking up less room. It didn't. It simply added to the number of things that drooped or sagged. Some of the rings had come detached and I hadn't bothered to fix them. He could see me now as I lived, feckless and incompetent.

'You have a marvellous body.' Joaquin spoke with a funny tinge of formality which under the circumstances seemed slightly kinky. His hand passed down my side. 'Long and supple and smooth. And strong. I like women with strong bodies.'

'I could say the same of yours.' If only your face were different, I wanted to add.

'We are perfectly matched.'

He stubbed out his cigarette and turned round to kiss me. He kissed seldom, part of a peculiar parsimony as if every gesture was an investment in arousal.

'In body, perhaps,' I gasped, realising to my amazement that it was going to happen all over again.

'That's all that matters.'

. He was making me shiver by circling my nipples lightly with his thumb.

'For you, yes.'

He stopped suddenly, his expression full of distaste.

'Please – '

121

'What?'

'We are adults. We don't need to play sentimental games.'

'No, of course not – ' I lied in my teeth. 'Just don't think – you fill all my needs.'

He was so smug, so arrogant, this man who had so completely the measure of my sexual starvation, I had to try and put him down somehow.

It was a feeble and unsuccessful attempt. He laughed and as if to demonstrate how feeble, pulled my willing body on top of him.

'This is the need that matters, isn't it?'

Yes, at that moment it was. It was all that mattered for another ten minutes of gasping pleasure. Afterwards, a hasty scramble into our clothes. Esther and Nick would be back any minute now.

'I dislike planning,' said Joaquin rather loftily, as we stood in the living room again. His flowers were wilting in the sun. 'But clearly if we are to continue meeting, given our various commitments, we must make some kind of plan.' He consulted his diary. 'Can you arrange to be free on Tuesday afternoons, do you think? I have no lectures or tutorials.'

'I don't know – I'll have to think.'

I was trying to buy time, to give my agreement at least the appearance of a decision, and also there were the practical arrangements to be worked out. (So I had already agreed? I don't know. But do you think that after mature reflection I would have returned a virtuous negative to this great serpent's fruit of pleasure that had so unexpectedly been thrown my way? I doubt it, but there is just the possibility that I might have returned a scared negative.)

Anyway, there is no time to consider now. Esther and Nick are knocking at the door. Joaquin and I stiffen up slightly, re-establishing ourselves as strangers, as I go to open it.

'Here we are, then,' Esther comes in breezily, but is clearly taken aback at the sight of a strange male figure. She stops, looks shy, and pushes Nick forward while she retreats towards the threshold.

'Come in, Esther.' Nick is now holding my thighs in an already paralysing grip, which is his way of showing that he wants to be carried. With rather bad grace I pick him up. He is very heavy.

'This is Monsieur Lefèvre – ' I've no idea whether Joaquin calls himself 'monsieur' but it sounds suitably formal – 'who's interested in the possibility of translating some of Robert's poems.' As a cover-up, it's pathetic – I've never been remotely connected with Robert's work. But Esther is not the sort of person who automatically probes statements to see if they'll hold up.

'And this is Mrs. Habib, my next-door neighbour.'

Reluctantly they shake hands. Then Esther, who is obviously feeling self-conscious at being 'seen' by a stranger when she has no stockings on to hide her varicose veins, insists that she must get back to her own flat.

'I'll see you later,' she says to me.

I'm left with Nick and Joaquin. The latter gives me his card.

'Why not make an arrangement with your good neighbour?' he says casually. 'And drop me a note.'

'Oh, I can't involve her!'

'My dear, the choice is yours.'

The words carry a kind of challenge as well as the suggestion of a handsome offer – the choice between a squashed cabbage leaf and a woman of spirit and potential independence, someone who can call her body, if not her life, her own. By giving it to another man? Well, that's an odd one. And so is the idea that Joaquin is offering anything at all, except gigolo services. But I am not in any state to cope with the ironic commentator who has already learned to deliver a few parries and thrusts on the edges of my consciousness.

Meanwhile Joaquin reaches across and rumples Nicky's black curls.

'You're a splendid young man, aren't you?'

To my astonishment Nick smiles back. He usually bristles like a little animal at endearments and pats from strangers.

I want to say, 'Oh no, Nick! don't be taken in! He's not a friend, he's the enemy.' At the same time I feel like crying, for suddenly flashes before me the scene that should be taking place, a real lover tearing himself away, a real tender lover, loving me and also my child, not this arrogant poised stranger who has casually said good-bye and banged the front door behind him.

I have never known such clear and passionate envy of anyone as I had of Joaquin, able to walk away from that shut door, walk towards the next thing, his life in his pocket, so to speak, not fragmented and in hock to people betrayed. Silently I took off Nick's jacket and got out his box of toys. I helped him build a tower to be knocked flying when it had reached a certain height. He was patient and let it grow till the smash should be worthwhile. Then we would start all over again. Brick by brick, and my thoughts on adultery, the red-letter sin, the terrible fate of women taken in adultery, while my body still throbbed gently from its recent pleasuring. I was panic-struck not only because of Robert and the things they did in Muslim countries, but because of the unstoppable nature of the beast. I would not find the strength to say 'no' to Joaquin, that lordly apostle of hedonism. He – it – was too persuasive. I – I had need. In the middle of this clamped-down apology for a life, I had *need*. The word had a screeching sound. I suddenly had a vision of my sister's face, shocked, were I to screech out that word in front of her.

Oh, I could imagine her consternation! I could see her pretty face go cold with fright and disgust. It was the fright which frightened me so much. I had seen it already, that awful mixture of disgust and panic, when I told her I was pregnant. There it had lain between us, the fact of my sexuality, like a great naked deformity. We, two women who had grown up together, unashamed and intrigued by our bodies, in the days before men, could not meet each other's eyes over this extraordinary terror. Sexuality was terror. Not only because it was formless and anarchic but because it signalled pleasure, appetite, shameless and animal. A carnal gutsiness which had no place in pastel-coloured air-freshened lives.

And now I had done it again, the dreaded thing. Given the chance of one evening of innocent social fun, I had made straight for tainted meat and had wolfed it down like some starving animal.

Yes, that was the way I thought of my sexuality, Marius, in the bad old days. By the time you met me I had made some progress. I was no longer ashamed of pleasure. But it remained for you to show me – to discover, perhaps? – that one can after all have the best of all possible worlds. For we loved in a way that was gutsy and profound and beautiful and earthy, all things at once, full of appetite and poetry, full of laughter and awe. There were no contradictions, no incompatibles.

I put it down as much to that big-hearted house as to anything within our own two selves for it was never quite like that at your place, your elegant flat with its sparse furniture and spot-lights and well-chosen modern paintings. It seemed to need the disorder of Alma Crescent, the vibrant disorder – all caused by people doing things, Louis whittling and hammering away, Nick working out his amplifying system, myself racing to complete assignments for my course – before we could abandon ourselves completely to that great hurling benign force of love.

Why did you want to change it, Marius? Why did you want to change my house? Could you not see that that way serious trouble lay? It had served us so beautifully as lovers. You stayed there night after night in spite of the disorder. You cooked us such splendid meals in the kitchen you described as a glorified outhouse. We lay, you and I, often enough soaking and gossiping in the big old bath tub with its lion paws. And yet when the talk veered towards that state that we both called cautiously 'something more permanent', suddenly struck with unnatural wariness and caution when we approached that area, the question you always brought up was: What to do about the house? as if, as it stood, it was too old-fashioned, shabby, somehow not worthy. But since it was large and we were both not rich (your Patrick's boarding-school fees ate up your salary) the practical solution, you maintained, was to 'do it up'.

I don't suppose you could possibly guess at just what depth that house was planted in me, or I in it. Interfere with it and you meddled with my soul, my person-hood. It was the one place in my life, lived or symbolic, that I could call my own, entirely my own. I should have told you plainly. I should have said, 'If we are serious then we must start again, in another house, not carve up this totally precious place. I will leave it if I must but I will not change it.' And I should have told you – oh of course I should – that your meddling, your innocent suggestions about kitchens, bathrooms, knocking down walls and fitting central heating, were stirring up a busy bad phantom in the night, someone who once said: 'Do you think we want to play dolls' houses? It's an insult to life, to creativity. . . .' To think that I, all those years later, should be the defender of an idea once used to keep me in my lowly place! That was a clever phantom, that was, rousing old and new furies with one thrust.

16

Joaquin always appeared punctually for our Tuesday after-noon appointments. They merit no better term than that, for they were kept within a strict time-limit and an even stricter limit of emotional range, transactions rather than amorous encounters. Joaquin was better at that aspect of things than I was. I knew perfectly well that 'love' didn't come into it, on either side, but I wanted at least a spice of romance to make all this grind of deceitfulness and anxiety worthwhile. I was not allowed my spice.

I tried once or twice to make our bleakly casual leave-takings a little more affectionate, putting my arms round Joaquin, even stroking his cheek. Alas for me! It wasn't only romance seeking a little expressive relief but, in spite of the nature of the man, a horrible need to cling, to be shown fondness.

He stood it once or twice and then politely removed my arms from his neck.

'We're not in love, you know.'

His tone was gentle but frightfully reasonable.

'No, I know. But just the same – it is *strong*, what we feel. It must be. Otherwise it wouldn't be the way it is. And is it so extraordinary to want to hug someone you've just been in bed with?'

He patted my cheek, smiling. It was not a romantic gesture, professional perhaps.

'No, not extraordinary, just childish. But we are adults, Carla, you and I. And we do feel something powerful, a powerful physical infatuation.' He must have seen disappointment or mutiny in my face. 'Oh Carla! Isn't that enough? But my dear, it has to be. You know very well that it is your body, your superb body, that attracts me. Not your good sharp mind and certainly not your feelings.' There was a pause to let this sink in. 'You should be flattered. Unlike most women you have a rare capacity for sheer pleasure. Don't distort it with cheap daydreams. That, you know, is a sort of pornography. Pleasure is clean, honest, with no hidden games.'

I was easily mesmerised. I set to work to be adult, to turn my values upside down. I tried hard to feel as Joaquin decreed, or rather, not to feel at all. I tried to accept the philosophy of the pleasure principle, its purity and freedom from the disease of romantic illusion, but it was no good. I craved and I craved – for some little bit of personal tenderness to humanise this damned skillful pleasure he and I were so good at. After he had left I would swear nothing would make me repeat this abominable cycle of lust and anticipation which ended always with such an ache of loneliness. Yet by Monday I was already counting the hours to his coming.

It was a curious business, he in his way as lonely a person as myself. Perhaps pleasure-seekers are always lonely. Certainly he was not a man with many friends. The 'solitary stud'. How did I get to know his nickname? I seem to remember it was one of Robert's buddies at a drinking session in our flat. Occasionally I was part of these now, more used to them, accepting that if social life was only this, then this I had better share.

I remember my face getting hot as I was teased about the heavy pass the 'stud' had made at me on the night of the May ball.

'Don't have anything to do with him,' I was warned. 'He's the worst kind of womaniser. A pro. He probably keeps count. I've never seen him out with the same girl twice.'

I smiled and laughed over Joaquin's absurdities. Yes of course, there was nothing more ridiculous than a chap who collects women like trophies. Perhaps I should have been flattered, then, by his weekly visits. Instead I was secretly rabid with jealousy over all these hordes of women that he was supposed to chase. They would be picked up in his long-bonneted car, taken out to dinner, there would be all the lovely trimmings of moneyed seduction, candles and wine and flowers. They could even spend the night together. Surely even Joaquin could not remain completely aloof under such circumstances?

For me, none of that. We pleasured each other in full day-light without trimmings or illusions. After the first visit he never brought flowers. Once he brought wine but I was afraid it might smell on my breath so he drank alone, a somewhat bleak and one-sided celebration of our particular sport. Very occasionally he would consent to have a cup of coffee – if we had got up in time.

You will have realised from all this that Esther had been persuaded to play ball. I approached her after Joaquin's first visit with many misgivings, and obliquely. I suggested that since she so often took Nick out I felt I should pay her a little something, and also perhaps we might fix on regular times, say, Tuesday and Friday afternoons? She looked so hurt that for a moment I thought I'd shattered our friendship for ever.

'Why should I want your *money* after all this time?'

'I don't think you want my money, Esther. It's just that I feel I may be taking advantage of you.'

'Ducky, we're both more or less on our uppers. Unless Robert's given you a rise in the housekeeping – ' She paused, quite bewildered. 'And you know I like taking the little fellow out.'

'When he behaves himself,' I put in, smiling.

'You can't afford to pay me,' Esther repeated. 'Look, come in a minute. There's something I don't understand.' We went into her kitchen. 'You've really upset me.'

She walked distractedly over to the window and back again, limping a little from the arthritis in her ankle. I put on the kettle to make tea, as much at home in her place as my own, bitterly regretting my clumsy attempt at being devious. It shocked me to see how easily she could be reduced to this state of agitation, this sturdy friend who might slap me down, even sulk when she was in one of her moods, but who always returned in the end to her jaunty defiance of quiet desperation. I looked on her as a kind of store of human warmth, someone I

129

could huddle against, metaphorically, and be thawed out. As she ambled distractedly round the room I saw pain – inflicted by me, the first sign of change wrought by the coming of Joaquin, the alien. Her expression was like a child's, like Nicky's, when I shook him for some naughtiness he didn't understand.

'Here, have some tea.'

I filled a mug and pushed it towards her and spooned sugar into my own.

'It's not like you, Carla, to suggest what you suggested. As if you wanted to lower me in some way.'

'*Lower* you? Good heavens, it's nothing like that – ' But wasn't it? Without the inspiration, if such it could be called, of Joaquin's seigneurial tones – 'your good neighbour' – 'an arrangement' – 'my dear, the choice is yours' – would I ever have dreamt of turning Esther's freely offered help into a cash transaction? The whole thing, anyway, was ludicrous. I had some vague resentful idea of getting the money from Joaquin. If he refused, what then?

'We're friends, aren't we?' Esther asked the question abruptly, wary of definition where none had been needed before. 'Ready to help each other out? Not getting in each others' hair?'

'Of *course* – '

'Well then – ' She had recovered a bit and was looking at me, demanding an explanation, the first time ever. For as I think I've made clear ours was not a relationship of bleeding out our lives to each other. Esther knew just how unhappy I was without being told.

'What's up, Carla?'

I tried to tell her to forget the whole thing, I mustn't stay long, Nick was only just asleep. But she was having none of it.

'Why d'you want me to take Nick out more regular? I will – and no question of payment, thank you very much. But I think friends should be straight with each other. Not twisting things round with stories of "taking advantage".'

Did she have any idea of what was coming next? I didn't even have the words to explain it, not to myself, let alone anyone else.

'Monsieur Lefèvre – '

'Where d'you meet him?'

'At the dance. He wants to – keep in touch with me.'

'And is that what you want?'

Good question. I paused.

'Yes.' I looked full across at Esther. 'I do. Or rather, it's what I need so badly I haven't the strength to decide whether I want it or not.'

She hesitated.

'You mean – a gentleman friend?'

'Yes.'

I hoped she might think there would be some little trimmings and courtesies involved, the kind of thing that at least in her fantasies she associated with gentlemen-friends. I knew perfectly well that there would be neither. It was the way he'd summed me up, the way I lived and the way I dressed. There would be no perfume of exotic naughtiness. That had come and gone, oh so briefly, with the champagne at the ball.

Esther was deeply silent. Surely she wasn't going to turn disapproving – not after all our tangoing down memory lane? She must have had her mind on the same images.

'I feel it's my fault in some way,' she said at last.

'What do you mean?'

'I've been a bad influence. Told you things I ought to have kept quiet about. After all, you're a well brought-up girl.'

'Yes, I know. Came from a good home and all that. But I don't have a good home now. And nobody in either home takes much interest in me, do they?'

'Well, I know – Robert's not an easy man. But you ought to think twice before – I mean – well, to put it straight, my dear, he's a strong man with a nasty temper when it runs away with him. Not that he's all bad, your Robert. I like him, I always have – ' She looked so distressed I wonder how I had the heart to persist in splitting her loyalties. 'I know he's not easy on you,' she repeated. 'But he's struggling, always struggling with himself, is Robert.'

'Oh?' It came out sarcastic, incredulous.

'Oh yes. He says being a poet is like being only half a man.

131

He says he sometimes wishes he were down the mines or in the shipyards, no doubt about who he is or what he stands for.'

'But he's proud of being a poet!'

'Only half. Only half. The other half's saying, "What's a great sturdy fellow like yourself doing scribbling on little bits of paper?" It's not a country for poets, this, Carla. If you ask me, it's not a country for much except hating yourself.'

I was silent. Yes, it was quite a national pastime. People quite often seemed to go out of their way to do things for which they would afterwards hate themselves.

'And you know, Robert does – mind about things,' Esther went on. 'Oh, I know it doesn't help *you* much, but there've been times when he's come in to me to sober up. "I can't face her", he says, "I can't face being despised, not to-night, Esther." And then another thing he said once, kind of desperate: "I've dragged her down, Esther, I know I have. And I can't stop doing it." If only – well, it's a shame he's so locked away in himself.'

'Yes,' I said uneasily, wishing we had not got onto the subject of Robert. 'I didn't know he confided in you so much. I'll quite understand if you don't want to be mixed up in – what we were talking about. Though maybe it's not so very different from you and Ahmed in the old days, going your separate ways. You said what the eye didn't see – '

I was being devious again, playing on Esther's fears that she had seeded an idea or two in my mind. Also, love Robert as she might, she loved me, if not more, then more frequently. I think quite simply Esther was dead scared of losing me.

'I'll help you,' she said, 'but there's something you don't understand. Ahmed and I, we shared a lot. We worked together, we had good times and hard times together. We could afford to turn a blind eye now and then.'

'You mean it's better to deceive someone you love than someone you don't?'

'I don't know about "better" – less risky, that's all. Oh, don't think I blame you, luv. I don't, not at all. You got to have *some* sparkle in your life. Why d'you think I went on the stage? Just so as I *wouldn't* end up like my sisters and my girlfriends. And you, you're like me – ' Believe it or not, I was tremendously flattered. 'You're not cut out for home and hearth and all that. You need some excitement, a bit of silly madness. . . .'

Esther – I recognised the change of voice when she started letting her fantasy wander – was busy talking herself into a drama of which she could approve, if only for picturesque reasons. I think, I suspect, that a cold deliberate piece of adultery was as much against her ethics (for different reasons) as it was against my sister Stella's. So, knowing the likely terms of my liaison with Joaquin, I was deceiving her as well as Robert.

Still I went ahead. Later that evening I ran out and posted a note to the address on Joaquin's card which I then tore into pieces the size of confetti and threw down the grating in the gutter.

17

I spent the rest of that evening sitting by the window, one of the hidden legion of lace-curtain watchers, except that we had no lace curtains. Robert stayed out a lot these days. There weren't so many drinking parties at the flat, they tended to go in phases. On balance I preferred it this way although it made the idea of being Robert's wife ever more puzzling and hollow. I still had not fully accepted the fact that as a companion I apparently rated zero. I didn't know the world was full of women sitting alone at home.

But this evening, tired out, I was glad enough to sit quiet and watch the life behind the windows on the opposite side of the street as the early summer light slowly changed and faded. A man, stripped to his vest, washed his face and neck in a sink. A woman hung out children's pants and bright little shorts on a three-sided washing line fixed to the window frame. Another woman watered her window-box, a rare splash of colour on the blackened front of the tenements.

The sight of those children's clothes roused me. They suggested buckets and sand, a family outing. 'I must take Nick down to the beach,' I thought, 'as a change from the park and the canal bank.' I didn't really enjoy taking Nick out. It made me feel sorry for myself, sorry for both of us. For Nick had a mistaken idea of being friendly. He would go eagerly up to other children who promptly shied away from him because he pushed and barged to be first on the chute or the swings, because he didn't know his own strength and sent the frail peaceful darlings flying. My heart was always twisting into the oddest shapes, maddened by his determination, full of hurt for his look of bewilderment when children ran howling back to indignant consoling mothers. Some were moved to say strong things about my son and his need for a good hiding, but more often they would gather up child, push-chair and shopping bags and make off with ruffled feathers and re-proachful looks.

We were outcasts. It felt more obvious in those public places. Things went better when we were out with Esther, who anyway had a quietening effect on Nick. We could, the three of us, feed ducks without his setting them off in quacking panic. We could gaze at the animals at the zoo, each of us holding one small strong hand, and there was no fear that he would create hysteria among the captive beasts by yam-mering at the bars or the wire mesh. He was a child that needed a regiment of minders. Even Robert, who occasionally took him out at the week-end, admitted, though with a certain pride, that he was a 'battling lad'.

Mercifully he was a sound sleeper. In the evenings I had peace to cultivate the pastime of brooding, that deep burrow-ing into the warm snug blackness of depression. In point of fact, it isn't warm and snug at all, it is a place of torment. Still, it is a wallow, a submersion, a giving in and a giving up. Until I started making curious embroidered pictures (a more positive legacy of the May ball than Joaquin, but less immediate) that was how my evenings were mostly spent, either at Esther's or sitting motionless, mesmerised by the hopeless muddle of my existence.

I found myself many times over when I worked for you, Marius. I interviewed women who dreaded going out of the house because they were transparent and all the world would see right through to their desperate sense of worthlessness. (They were not all living on social security or abandoned by their husbands, these women. Some wrung their hands and berated themselves in interiors like my sister Stella's, though most had their backs to the wall in survival terms.) I found women who took the same pains as I had done to stack the odds against themselves, who found it easier to stick obstin-ately to the view that life had it in for them, they were bound to lose; it was less painful to expect nothing except the worst, easier to give up hope and determination. I found women teetering on the brink of chaos, thought and action frozen into rituals of repetition. One woman was scared to move in case she fell to pieces. She would edge her way across the room as though she were on a tightrope. The world is a dangerous place for women who have lost their nerve, or had it broken.

I came across women who thought they had reached the end of the line, and one or two who actually had – and *they* were too far gone to be bothered with melodrama or self-pity which among the rest (and I include my earlier self) wound in and out of the punishments inflicted by real life and inner tormentors. When they said 'I want to die' or 'I wish it was all over' they meant it. They weren't bothered about the effect.

I don't know whether your questionnaire (or 'inventory' as you preferred to call it once you started giving conference papers on the subject) succeeded in sorting out the truly defeated from those who had at some level opted for defeat, although that seems to me a crucial distinction. I lost interest in it, I'm afraid, since it ignored all that I believed was important – fantasies, dreams, specific fears and their ingenious interweaving. Instead it was all ranking and rating – 'Rank the following in order of importance: financial security, good family relations, good sexual relations, etc etc. . . .' Now rate your present satisfaction with each from 1 to 10. Where would you place yourself on a "worry scale" from 1 to 10?'

What banality! What intolerable banality! When I saw what you did with all my data, those fully typed-up interviews which you raved about for their thoroughness and insight, when I saw that they were all filed away as 'background' for some hazy book you were going to write, I lost interest. You assured me, as you proudly showed me the draft of the questionnaire that it had been 'informed' by my interviews. If so, I couldn't see it. I was so embarrassed, it was like being handed a string of sausages and asked to admire it. Because I can tell you now, Marius, what I couldn't then, being already halfway in love with you and ready to pardon anything, that I think your questionnaire was a bloody insult to any woman who had to answer it, I really do.

136

I never did understand that split in you. As a private individual you were well-read, imaginative, apparently interested in the wider issues of the human condition. In your work there was not a trace of it. You were obsessed with measuring things. You, who talked with all the fluency of a natural lover of words, docked your prose style to produce barbarous pomposities and cautious 'value-free' statements as informative as old bus-tickets.

Well, I suppose you were ambitious. That sort of writing got published.

And so you continued to manipulate your statistics and boil up figures and there emerged, not information about people, but factors – the 'hostility factor' and the 'self-aggression factor' and the 'stringency factor' (translated as 'perceived material hardship') and the 'mourning factor' (not bad, that, the one spark of imagination, that set of questions on what women felt they had lost in life). And you got very excited over your figures and factors and were sure you were contributing significantly to knowledge about female depression. Only by this time there was not a woman in sight, just factors, and the fact that depression is a living response to experience had likewise disappeared. Above all, above all, Marius my love, you could ignore the enemy within, the mind with its passion for making its prison high security, adding walls and fortifications, patrolling it with savage sentries, planting mines on the perimeter.

And something else you overlooked – the courting of dark places in the soul, the prayer for oblivion, the pre-occupation with death, not so much as an event, but as a place in which to lie quiet and hidden, death-in-life. The lure of Thanatos. I did suggest that you should look into the Thanatos factor, but you looked uneasy and said it was not really a very useful concept. I said the Greeks had found it pretty useful and so had Freud. 'Not a bit of it,' you said, 'he was forever changing his mind about what it represented.' Well, so he might. Deathly matters come in many guises.

But I don't want to argue with you now. I am telling you about my own wandering in the shades, my own experience of Thanatos, my own bad dreams, lived and dreamt, all the

137

things your survey women were given no chance to say, all the things I chose not to tell you in case you would love me less.

So, back to the window where I stared and brooded, telling myself the rosary of my wrongs. I no longer thought about actual escape. Instead I fantasised, swinging from drab anger up into ephemeral daydreams and back down into the slough of despond.

My fantasies were naive and crudely fashioned, like toys for backward children yielding colour and pleasure as simply as possible. Sometimes I was back on the fencing piste again, fighting and winning against impossible odds, world-famous men. Sometimes I was a gipsy, the beautiful deserted lover in the *Dances of Galanta*, ever to haunt and make wretched the man who had left me to marry the peasant girl. But sometimes I took *her* part, and was sweet and pure and simple. Sometimes I was cool and *soignée*, sometimes I roamed the world. Sometimes I had a lover; quite often I did not.

But my favourite fantasy was really very simple. We had run away, Nick and I – he was always part of this favourite day-dream which is strange for I never thought of myself as a very devoted mother. And we lived in a whitewashed villa which blazed with flowers and whispered with crickets when the sun went down. It smelt delicious, of lemon and jasmine and herbs, and I was always dressed in brilliant silky garmets and always the centre of a crowd of lively, brilliant people, musicians and painters and writers, and they all loved me very much. It wasn't altogether clear whether I too was an artist or simply a charismatic woman. It didn't matter. What was important was the ease and generosity of it all. I kept open house and open heart. I was surrounded by colour and love.

As for Robert, I didn't even bother to dispose of him. He didn't exist, he had vanished. The ideal state was that he had never existed at all. I could not even bring myself to make him the reason for my flight. No, it was Edinburgh I was running away from, Edinburgh that became the symbol of things hated. I was running away from its hideous cold, its judgmental grimness, its air of apprehensive dignity which hid the splinter of ice in its heart. Edinburgh was not my town. It belonged to my elders, my oppressive forefathers, the horde of frock-coated men who figured in my dreams from time to time as 'The Ancestors'. They were a curious collection, dressed with the formal and terrible propriety of undertakers and frowning with the learned puissance of Victorian men of letters. I suppose I got them from old family photographs, this gang of punitive archetypes, the churchmen and lawyers and medical men who filled up the family tree on both sides except for that thin line stretching back to a Calabrian farmhouse.

To dream of them was to dream of death. They were all old and all male and all dressed in black. In one dream of peculiar menace, one of them steps forward to rebuke me for not sufficiently respecting my ancestors. Did I not know that the founder of my family had written the greatest text of all time? It was called the *Moral Pathology of the Living and the Dead* and it listed the judgments made on every human being who had ever existed. This overawed and terrified me, carrying some notion that my 'ancestor' was that logically impossible creature, all-knowing and all-powerful, super-God.

The Male Principle. I feared and venerated and hated it – before or after Robert? I don't know, for here is a paradox. In some way he and The Ancestors were linked, certainly over the question of my punishment. I see him as a kind of crazy inversion of that wrathful mob, a savage attacker of that propriety which they cherished, a defiler and blasphemer in the church of correction and correctness, but nonetheless like them black and harsh and judgmental. His humour was either foul or cruel. His poems – ah well, here is something of a mystery. For in between his tracts of violent political rhetoric (some of his worst) and his brilliant restless evocations of cityscapes and characters there occasionally appeared poems, usually short, of amazing lyrical tranquillity, as if this heavy-breathing appetitive man had suddenly been stopped and taken unawares by a calm and lucid moment, his inner eye focusing suddenly on some humble form of beauty which had moved him to write a song of praise. I never, or almost never, witnessed his tranquil lucid moments, so I'm left uneasy, having to accept that what gentleness was in him he could not bring himself to share with me.

So who was harsh and who was hurtful? And how did I figure in Robert's dreams? Did I have brass feathers and steel claws and a venomous head hissing from side to side? Did I pursue him like a vengeful fury? Was he, too, afraid in the night, in the pit of sleep?

Mercifully I shall never know.

18

My liaison with Joaquin came to an abrupt end one day when he broke his own rules and started asking personal questions. I don't really think it had much to do with affection. I think it was mainly curiosity and the strange wish that cold men sometimes have to play benefactor.

We were sitting in the sun, smoking and drinking coffee, after a rather perfunctory attempt at making love. The chill was starting to get to me. I was starting to lose interest and desire, and possibly Joaquin felt challenged to engage me in other ways, for suddenly out of the blue he said, 'Tell me, Carla, how do you come to be in this place living this life?'

I looked at him and thought: 'What business is it of yours?' Out loud I said, 'I made a mistake, that's all. It happens very easily. And then you're stuck with it.'

'Not necessarily. Mistakes aren't like boxes, to shut you in forever.'

'No?'

'No. Not unless you give them that power.' There was silence again. 'I can't help feeling' he went on, 'that there is something oddly *wrong* about your situation.' For a self-proclaimed nihilist that was a very lax statement. 'Why do you accept it so passively?'

I frowned.

'There's not a great deal I can do.'

'Oh come. One can always do something.'

'I wonder.'

'Well for one thing, forgive me, but you could at least clean this place. You keep yourself and the child quite properly so you obviously have some standards. I do not know how you can live in this – ' he did not articulate the word of his choice but simply passed his finger down the grimy windowpane and glanced at the unsavoury dishtowel lying abandoned on the back of the chair. 'Of course, it's not the essential. The essential is for you to get out.'

'Look here – ' I wanted to tell him to shut up, what right had he to pass judgment on me, my situation? But his bluntness left me floundering.

'I am not saying this through any personal interest, you understand – ' Yes, I understood perfectly. 'It is simply that you seem to live in a *negative state* which is a little, shall we say, disquieting to see.' He paused and drew in smoke. 'Could it be by any chance that you are lazy? Lazy and obstinate?'

'Possibly,' I muttered, feeling a threat which had nothing to do with grimy windows or dirty dishcloths but had much to do with the fatalistic lure of those brooding sessions in the evenings. Easier, much easier, to swim with the downward vortex of calamitous thoughts than to struggle against everything, circumstance, the world outside, the exquisite consistent logic of damnation. However, there was more to it than that. 'It's also a question of fear,' I said, looking straight at Joaquin.

'Fear? Of what?'

'Many things. I have no money, no way of earning a living.' This took me by surprise. I was talking as though the idea of 'getting out' was constantly in my mind, but it was not. After the day I so foolishly bared my unhappiness to Stella the idea perished. Unless, of course, you count those fantasies about a villa in the sun.

'Myself' said Joaquin, 'I believe that fear without a concrete threat is simply a form of laziness.'

'Wouldn't you call my husband a concrete threat?'

'You are afraid of him?'

'Yes. I am. Very afraid.'

Joaquin smiled.

'You amaze me. For a woman so afraid of her husband you took a very big risk the night of the dance. And you carried it off superbly. You do not lack courage in certain situations.'

'So?'

'So – clearly you *can* overcome this fear, when the motivation is strong.'

'Well, that's it, you see. I don't think I do have the motivation, to change my life, I mean. I just don't see anything *out there* – ' I pointed towards the window 'or feel anything *in here* – ' I pointed towards my own diaphragm – 'that seems worth making an almighty struggle of will. I'm too tired. It all seems pointless. I thought you would understand that. Isn't that something like nihilism? Not finding anything worthwhile?'

Joaquin's eyes blacked over as though ink had been added to their original darkness. For some obscure reason I had made him very angry.

'No,' he said softly, 'it is not. It is nothing like nihilism. Nihilism is not "throwing up the sponge", as you say here. It is a point reached through much experience and much tough analysis of that experience. You think it is some refuge for non-starters? How wrong, how stupidly wrong you are. On the contrary, it is out on the other side of a total crisis.'

He drew in his breath sharply, nostrils pinched, and I had a sudden intimation, a sense as vivid as a smell, of chaotic violence. Joaquin's face was white, his eyes still black with fury, but he was a thousand miles away. Uneasily I watched him and wondered what had been his total crisis, what he had seen, experienced? I fumbled with fragments of Spanish history. The Civil War? Where had he been? How old was he? Thirteen, fourteen?

I didn't know what to say. 'Sorry' is limp and stupid if you have carelessly touched on something frightful.

But the look was gone. He was back again though still angry.

'How dare you live your life in this state of collapse! This childish sulking for lost toys! You, with your youth and your health and your good sharp mind. In the name of dignity, if nothing else, get yourself out of here. This place suits you about as well as a pig's mask. It is outrageous to bury your life in this squalor.'

I was on my feet, blazing.

'My life is none of your business! You've said it often enough and cruelly enough. So don't ever criticise me again, in the name of dignity or anything else. You have no right!'

Joaquin also got up. He stood straight and formal and then bowed to me as a fencer would to his adversary. For once he looked slightly disconcerted.

'I suppose you want me to go?'

'Yes.'

'And not come back?'

'That's right.'

He stood uncertainly in front of me. Then he put his hand on my arm. I shook it off.

'Carla. Are you very angry?'

'Yes, very angry.'

'That distresses me.'

'You don't know the meaning of the word. Stop playing games, Joaquin. Or stick to the ones we've already played. You know, no feelings. You made that rule, not me.'

'I am sorry. I see I have hurt you quite badly.' He took my hand. 'Well, let me say this. There is no question of love. Don't take it personally, I promise you the word has no meaning for me. But this I do feel, yes, feel for you. A kind of comradeship, if you like. There is something about you almost like a boy, something vigorous and masculine – in your character, I mean, although you do your best to ignore it. I like the fighter in you, yes, even when I am the one who gets hit. That's what I am trying to encourage. Why smother all that good fighting capacity? You are not really this sad, sullen creature, are you?'

I sat down again and put my head in my hands. My hair fell forwards hiding my face.

'Do you think it helps to be told about my good fighting capacities? I don't want to fight, I just want – '

My favourite day-dream rose in front of me. In it I was never a fighting character. I was smiling and lovable, domi-nating through charm, not the sword, not even the foil.

'What is it you want, then?'

I looked up. My throat ached with the effort to stay dry-eyed and detached.

'I want all those things you despise so much. I want love and appreciation. I want to be spoiled and petted and looked after.'

'In other words, you want to be a little girl?'

'Why not? Why not?'

'That's escapism.'

'Some women manage it.'

Joaquin sighed.

'Not all their lives. Sometimes it's better to lose all that early rather than late. At least time is on your side.'

'I want to start again. Right from the beginning. From the time before men.'

'That's impossible.'

'I know it's impossible. It doesn't stop me wanting it.'

'Are men really so hateful?'

I looked at him, stared at him hard, then shut my eyes.

'I don't know many men, but from the evidence so far – ' I opened my eyes again – 'yes, they are. Hateful.' I felt like adding, 'And that's what you get if you start rousing my fighting capacities.'

Joaquin turned away and took something out of his pocket. Then he leant over the table and I saw that he was writing. Moreover I saw that he was writing a cheque.

'Whatever are you doing?'

He straightened up and handed the cheque to me. It was for £200 and made out in my name.

'Are you completely crazy? What is this? Some kind of squaring up for services rendered?' I was practically choking with anger. 'Is this the final insult? The final rich man's insult – '

'It is not an insult. I am not trying to pay you for anything. I am offering you this in all sincerity, in case you should ever find the courage to walk through that door and not come back. It may help – to start again, though not from the beginning.'

I stood there, pulled apart by remorse and suspicion and bewilderment. Was Joaquin the cynic, the nihilist, really to be believed capable of an act of pure generosity? What was I to say? What words must I eat? He was picking up his briefcase, his jacket. He was going.

He turned to me and held out his hand.

'Good-bye,' he said. 'And good luck. It has been an interesting friendship.'

'Yes,' I whispered. 'I'm sorry, about some of the things I said.'

'No need. Adios.'

He walked down the little corridor to the front door, and I think his hand was almost on the handle when there was the sound of a key turning in the lock. The door opened towards him. Robert and Joaquin stood face to face with a half-open door between them staring at each other like burglars caught in the beam of each others' torches.

19

There was a moment of intense obliterating silence, broken only by the sound, deafening to my ears, of crumpling paper as I screwed up the cheque in my hand. I was aware of sun hurting my eyes, of the air being full of dust motes shining celestially, glittering with terror.

My voice had gone. I tried to say something that would unfreeze the moment but nothing came out. Robert pushed past the door and past Joaquin and came towards me.

'What the fuck's *he* doing here?'

It was still more astonishment than rage. Not for long.

'He – '

Joaquin had come back into the room.

'I came to pay my respects – to Mrs. Carmichael,' he said coolly, 'and to apologise for the fact that I cannot get hold of a book I had promised to lend her. A translation of Lorca's poems. It appears to be out of print.'

'Indeed.' Robert was slowly looking him up and down as if he were some surprising piece of offal. 'Well, get this straight. No one lends books of poetry to my wife, not unless I know all about it. Now get out, you filthy prick, and leave us alone while I explain to my wife that she really must not go in for literary friendship behind my back. It is a very silly thing to do.' His voice rose menacingly.

'Are you proposing to beat her up?' asked Joaquin contemptuously, eyeing Robert's clenched fists. 'That is stupid. She has done nothing wrong. In any case, does it *really* give such satisfaction to hit a creature so much weaker than yourself? Do people like you have no pride?'

'Oh go *away*, Joaquin,' I begged. 'This is not your business. I shall be all right. Robert's simply taken by surprise, aren't you, Robert? There's no question of – ' my throat closed – 'I mean, you won't, will you? I haven't – I didn't know it would annoy you so much, just a chance visit – Joaquin, will you please go away. Now.'

He went, tall and relaxed as ever, the ghost of a shrug his only farewell. An extraordinary man, a solitary randy feline with some troubling past expunged by that total crisis that led to nihilism. But meanwhile here was Robert and here was I with my crumpled cheque in my hand and my prayers that I had pulled the bed back into order and my heart banging against my ribs.

Robert came right up to me. He caught hold of my left arm by the wrist and bent it up. Fortunately the cheque was in my other hand. I closed my eyes.

'I don't want to know' he hissed into my face. 'I don't want to know. If I ever find out you've been screwing with that olive-oil bastard I swear I'll bust you up good and proper.' He bent my arm further back. It was starting to hurt badly. 'So – get this straight' – still this passionate hissing whisper – 'I do not want to know.' He was breathing like an engine, holding himself back with difficulty. He knew all right. I suppose he too was afraid. Of the take-over by violence.

'There's nothing to know' I said through lips of paper. 'Please, let go of my arm.'

He did and threw himself down into a chair. He was sweating with fury. Then he sprang up again and started marching across the room scattering things as he went. He kicked the dresser so hard the crockery inside gave a great rattling noise and something fell over and probably smashed.

'Oh don't!' I begged. 'Don't bust the place up! Nick'll be upset. And it's not worth it, Robert, really it isn't! I won't see another soul without your permission, I promise you. Just – calm down, please, please. Look, here they are now. I hear them at the door.'

And indeed there were Esther's familiar three bangs on the

door, a sound of such sweet sanity in the middle of this chaos that I wanted to put my head on her shoulder and weep. I didn't, of course, but she saw something was far amiss. For one thing Robert wasn't usually around at this time. For another the room looked tornado-struck. He was around, it turned out later, because for once he'd been moved by a desire to play father and had intended taking Nicky to the swing park. And this rare homing impulse had brought him in at the tail-end of my ridiculous affair.

Five minutes difference in timing and there would have been none of this, none of this terror, partly on my own account, the sheer smelly fear of being badly hurt, partly the revelation of this raw red anarchy of a raging man tossing into futility the match-stick houses and the poor little webs of 'decency' we set up to try and contain it. I saw in the glare of it just what Robert meant when he said domesticity was an insult to his manhood. Certainly, if this was his manhood, he needed a cave and a wilderness and a woman in skins. Not me. Not me.

'Can I do anything, ducks?' Esther asked anxiously.

'No, I don't think so. But thanks just the same.'

'Remember, I'm just across the way if you need me – '

'Yes, yes. It'll be all right, though.' I tried to smile. I loved Esther from the bottom of my heart at that moment. 'Come on, Nick. Soon be supper time and then bath.' I took my son by his sticky little hand and shut the door, and the mirage of the ordinary disappeared.

I couldn't immediately carry on.

'Please, take Nick for a minute, will you?' Robert had by this time calmed down enough to open himself a bottle of beer and perch his packet of fags on the window-sill as he always did. Nick made for his father with all his usual ecstasy and swarmed onto his knee as I turned into the bedroom, looked for any signs of Joaquin's presence, tore the cheque into tiny pieces and stuffed them deep in my handbag, then made for the bathroom where I hung my head over the pan and vomited exhaustingly.

It all came up, the immediate terror and the futility of guilt for a stupid cause. I purged myself of the past few weeks, of

Joaquin and his clinical lust and my own salt-water-drinking desire and the wretched ridiculous loneliness of it all. I didn't purge myself of my fear of Robert, that was too deeply rooted, but at least the animal panic was temporarily gone and in some sense I felt I had survived, would survive. I think the sheer relief felt something like hope.

I was tired to the point of reeling. I gave Nick his supper and bathed him in a fog of exhaustion, letting him fill the tub with cars, bricks, cotton-reels, farm animals, only drawing the line at picture books. It was one of our regular battles, this wish he had to dunk all his possessions in water. I don't know why I bothered to fight. He was blissfully happy and afterwards went fast asleep, flat out, without stories or fuss.

As I came through to the front the first peals of thunder broke, the sultry finale to a brilliant summer day. We sat in silence, Robert drinking his beer, gazing out at the forked lightening squiggling evilly across massed clouds. Then with a hiss and a sigh the rain came down, curtains of it, flooding gutters, making people dash for shelter. I felt as if I were somewhere fathoms under the sea, as if I'd sunk like a stone straight to the bottom. I could feel the cushiony wavy pressure of water mass on my limbs when I tried to move.

'Are you all right?' Robert asked. 'You're staggering like a drunk.'

'I'm just tired. Terribly tired. I think some coffee would help.'

He got up.

'Sit down. I'll make it.'

This was not usual. He came back shortly with two mugs of black coffee.

'The milk's gone sour.'

'Oh. So it's true about thunder. I always thought that was an old wife's tale.' I took one of the mugs from him. 'Thanks.'

He looked at me. 'Yes, you're tired out. It was the fright, wasn't it? I gave you a fright.'

I said nothing. I couldn't make out what he was getting at, whether he was pleased with himself or sorry for me.

'Well, we'd better go on from there.' He went over to the window and fished two cigarettes out of his packet. The poor

150

flowers in the window-box opposite had taken a terrible battering from the rain. 'D'you want one?' I took one of the cigarettes and he lighted up for both of us.

'How long have we been together?' he asked.

'Three years this autumn.'

'And it doesn't get any better, does it?' Robert leaned forward and stared at me. For the first time I saw that his eyes had a lot more hazel than mine. It surprised me. I'd always thought our colouring was almost the same except for my browner skin. In the early days he used to tease me and say I was half wog with that skin. 'Do you want to go on like this?'

'No, not really, but I don't see – '

'Well, I think I've had about enough. Enough of your nagging and your bitching and your everlasting complaints, and now I find you messing around with Spanish playboys – see here, Carla, I think it's time you went.'

Was he drunk? Was he joking? Was this my punishment? Was he perhaps serious? I stared down into my coffee mug and wondered why I wanted to cry. I should have been running through that door, shouldn't I? A prisoner released. Yes, straight into the ranks of The Ancestors. I see them pointing their long fingers. I see their frowns, the grave orgy of their digust which will have me grovelling on the ground, the adulteress, the failed wife. Oh, save me from that! This place is my miserable uncomfortable raft, the only thing I have to float on in an ocean of uncertain being. Don't push me off, Robert. . . .

And anyway, how dare you? After all the neglect and carelessness and swiping sarcasm of the past three years? What's a bit of infidelity compared to *that*?

'You've never given me a chance,' I said at last. 'Not the faintest chance. I've been here on sufferance since day one. I don't believe I'm even a human being in your eyes. They say,' I continued bitterly, 'that serfdom went out in the eighteenth century. Well, they're wrong, the historians. Serfdom is still flourishing – in every dingy little household where the man sits back and snaps his fingers for food. Not only dingy ones. Mary's a serf. Stella's a serf in spite of her pretty dresses. We're all serfs – '

151

'My mother isn't a serf,' Robert interrupted sharply. 'She does all the work and a damn sight better than you do, but there's nothing serf-like about her. She's got her pride and her dignity – '

'Oh spare me your mother! How can I ever match up to a woman who brought up her family on the dole? And why, tell me why, should I? You've said yourself her life was terrible, more than any woman should go through, yet all you do is make *my* life as tough and joyless as you possibly can. O.K. Let's split up. I'm tired of being the scapegoat for your terrible youth, that terrible childhood of yours. And anyway, you love it. You'd be lost without it.'

'You bitch! You bleeding senseless bitch! How can you say things like that? How d'you expect me to forget the things that have cut into my soul?' He thrust his face towards me at the word 'soul'. 'I am what I am because of the things I've been through.'

'And so am I. I'm a victim of circumstances too. Only mine were good and yours were awful. But somehow I'm to blame. I'm very handy. Out there the going may be tough, you can't get into the middle-class club – '

'And do you think I want to?'

'Well, it riles you that you can't. But back here, Robert Carmichael, you've got it all sewn up. You've been so deeply wronged by something I represent you can treat me any way you like – '

'No, no, it's not like that. I'm not doing that. Oh, don't you understand? You're so ignorant. How can I *share* anything with you? You don't care about my folk, my background – '

'I did try. Before we were married. I used to ask you all sorts of things. We used to talk about poverty and capitalism and things. I was thinking of chucking my degree course to take up social work – '

'Oh, humble thanks, Lady Muck! Just what the working class doesn't need.'

'Well, does it want hung-over revolutionaries? Alcoholic Lenins, the lot of you! Pub massacres, pub insurrections, pub triumph of the proletariat – but all you ever do is stagger home and take it out on the serf. And why is it that your brother

Tom, who really is a revolutionary, or so you tell me, doesn't apparently need to get pig drunk *or* push his wife around? Answer me that one.'

'Simple. He didn't have to marry her.'

'You've brought that up once too often!' I shouted furiously. 'Don't worry. I shall leave. You don't have to throw me out. I should have done it long ago when I first thought of it. On our honeymoon.'

'On our *honeymoon*?'

'Yes. The day I was ill.'

'But that was the day I bought you the ring! I was sorry I'd upset you.'

'Well, while you were buying the ring, I was packing my bags. Funny, isn't it?'

'No, it's not funny.' He was terribly hurt. 'It's not at all funny. I thought I'd really done something that pleased you. Was it all just a big act, then?'

'No, it wasn't.' I was suddenly made miserable by his distress. 'By the time you came back I'd changed my mind. Or rather, the manageress changed it for me. She said every woman hated the first six months of marriage. And she also said men were basically kind, or "had a kind streak in them". Do you think she was right?'

I didn't expect an answer. Robert, poor sod, was still oddly devastated, staring emptily in front of him. At last he looked at me.

'Have you still got it? I never see you wearing it. Come to think of it, you never wear any of your jewellery nowadays. You used to wear ear-rings and bangles and things. They were bonny. I liked the colour. It was always the colour I liked about you, all those bright daft things you used to wear when all the other girls were going about drab and sensible. . . .'

I swithered, half-touched by this nostalgia, half-scornful. Then I remembered creeping off to the little second-hand shop with my pretty bits of glitter, and being so scared and embarrassed that I didn't dare argue with the grainy-skinned man of indeterminate age over the price he offered. ('You should have taken me with you', said Esther, shocked and pitying, when I told her what I got for them.) I remember

153

vividly that he had some nasty affliction of the fingernails that had thickened them into ugly yellow hooves, appropriate enough, I felt, caught from the habit of turning and fingering the bright little relics of women's vanity and putting as mean a value on them as he could.

'I've still got your ring. But that's about all. I sold the rest. Because I haven't been brought up in the hard school that made your mother the woman she is, and I didn't know how to manage on the house-keeping you gave me. I still don't. We're thirty quid in debt to to Mr. Fowler at the corner shop.'

Robert put his hands to his eyes and rubbed them hard with the heels of his palms as if he were trying to grind his vision into clarity. Red-eyed he stared into space, a look of hopelessness on his face. I waited for the outburst. Second only to my relationship with Joaquin – and for a lot longer – I dreaded his knowing about that growing debt.

There was no outburst. All he said, with a sigh, was, 'Thirty pounds is a hell of a lot of money.' And so it was in 1956, on a small income.

I got up.

'Well, I'm going.'

'Where to?' asked Robert stupidly.

'To Esther's. I'll stay the night there and then we'll have to work something out in the morning. What are you looking at me like that for? You should be glad. You told me to go, and I'm going. Obedient to the end.'

'Have you any idea what you sound like, Carla? Have you any idea what that tongue of yours is like? It's defeated me, that tongue of yours.'

Now if I had been a real confident shrew, or even a gipsy, I'd have laughed at that and counted it a victory. But – always my anger fizzled out too soon and in its place stood useless things, half-baked remorse, grudging pity and welling self-pity. I hung around, half hoping Robert would say something more. But he didn't. He was busy grinding his eyes again.

'Good-night' I said finally, and went to collect a few things from the bedroom.

Esther looked as if she'd been half expecting me. We drank tea and talked in a subdued way about things.

'Is it for good then?' she asked.

'I don't know,' I said hopelessly. 'I don't know whether he means it.'

'But do you mean it?'

'I don't know, I don't *know*. There's Nick. I can't leave Nick. And I don't know where to go.'

'There's always home. They'd take you in, wouldn't they?'

'Yes.'

Yes, they would, but my gorge rose at the humiliation of it all. 'He's flung me out, father – '

'Is it – ' Esther probed gently, 'on account of it being Tuesday? Has he found out?'

I turned to her.

'Yes, I think so. He arrived as Joa – as the other was leaving. Only it's not out in the open. He says he doesn't want to know.' I coughed nervously, remembering that arm twisting and Robert's face. 'He made me sweat for it. It wasn't worth it, Esther, neither of them were worth it. I'm well out of it.'

But that was adrenalin jauntiness. After a troubled night spent on the couch in Esther's half-furnished front room (it was really a store-room for her old theatrical trunks and boxes) the spirit of defiance was hanging limp. I ached in body and my mind was full of confused dreams, of Nick and some other mysterious child who was pale and ill wandering lost in an Edinburgh devastated by bombs or decay. I suppose I was half expecting the knock on the door and the sound of Robert's voice. This was at about 8.30 in the morning. Esther came through to me.

'He says the little fellow's crying for you.'

'Oh. Well, is he going to treat me decently if I go back?'

'I didn't ask him, ducks, but he sounds pretty subdued. Maybe you should have a word with him?'

And so – I walked back through the door that Joaquin had hoped I would have the courage to close behind me on the outer side. I could not face going out into nothingness dragging the empty skin of a failed wife-and-mother behind me. And, although it chokes me to admit it, I think I must still have wanted to be with Robert, to be wanted by Robert.

20

Do you see, Marius? Do you see now what I brought you as a love-offering? Do you start to have some idea of the Anti-Christ I laid, still living, at your feet, Lucifer with his black smoulder and his sparks of lost grace? You brought me a charming creature, dead and sweet, a plucked rose, your Linda. I brought you Robert, wrapped in my silence like a gagged witness in a cloak, and furtively laid him at your feet in the primitive dark where such encounters take place. And I thought, yes, I thought he had gone up in the flames of love, the bright burning that went on and on all that year, the year that started with the fluttering fireworks of a superb autumn, when we met again after the long break of the summer holidays.

Started when our hands suddenly locked as we wandered round the museum one lunch-hour, gazing at the faces of Indian deities peacefully withdrawn behind smiles of enigmatic bliss. And we looked at each other and went with our locked hands out of the museum, into your car, and drove, idiotically changing the gears together, no moment of contact to be lost, in silence all the way over to Alma Crescent. And only then, in my studio bed-sit reeking of paint and resin, did we let each other go and stood quaking on the brink of a happiness not unlike the fear of death, the self about to be dissolved, whirled out and lost. Even for the promise of ecstasy it was hard to be brave about that threat of disappearance.

But that afternoon it happened. We disappeared and became

like all lovers the first and the most beautiful. We clung to each other still frightened small by the upward plunge, the timeless flight, arrow winging, ball dancing on the top of fountain. And then wide, wide, no shape, spread out on a rocking sea of non-self – and I found it was not the terrifying end, as I'd feared. The infinite is a comfortable place in the arms of love, oh my Marius, all that the mystics and poets have cracked it up to be, and this we found out for ourselves, you and I, two ordinary people very much in love, and thus touched momentarily with profound creative grace.

You didn't go back to work that afternoon. Students must have waited and secretaries fumed, but you never stirred. And so after months of doubt when I didn't know what was happening except that I longed for you, it was in the end very simple, as if it could have been no other way. You became, not my first and not my last lover, but in a sense the only one.

Surely you, my archangel, would put a sword through the hidden bundle at your feet? Demolish the past in ignorance? For months and months I had no dreams of Robert. I believed he was gone for good but he crept back, a shadow behind a curtain at night, the flavour of angst after a too long and too hectic party, then more clearly, the usual round of anger and carelessness and threatened destruction. Of course there was always Nick to trigger these off, Nick so like his father, half-tamed but basically a wild lad with a temper and a will stronger than my own. Only Nick I loved in spite of the dance he led me, and the anger hurt.

Even in the middle of joy, this extraordinary blossoming of life, each day as exciting as a birthday in childhood, the unquietness in me rose and took over from time to time. I had one dream that so upset me I nearly told you. It was simple, bare of the usual shuffling of violent images or those even more dreadful ones of Robert in distress. It was no more than frozen terror that he would come into an empty room where you and I, powerless, were trying to hide from him. I woke from it sweating and nearly hysterical, half-convinced I must tell you, unwrap my bundle, and own up to the long war I still waged to get back all of my life within my own domain.

But your attitude to bad dreams wasn't encouraging. You

157

believed that dreams were merely mental waste, and if they were disturbing then cheese or alcohol or indigestion was the cause. If I woke up beside you in agitation you would hold me close and say lovingly, 'Forget it darling, it's only "noise", your mind getting itself cleared.' Cleared? But I used to go around in a fog, half here, half there, half now, half then for the whole of the day, lethargic, unproductive, after one of those bad nights. A funny kind of 'clearing'.

You said, with some justification, that I had a tendency to hang on to morbid ideas. You were not much in sympathy with morbidity. You'd had your own dark time with Linda's illness and death, then left on your own with a young son to bring up. Morbid ideas overwhelmed you; you had thoughts of suicide but remembered Patrick. You didn't know yourself, you said, you'd never have believed. Now grief seemed to have toned down into something profound but unturbulent, a tragedy lived through and eventually accepted by an optimist, a sweet-natured person, ready to live in the light again.

Your optimistic sweetness was one of the things I loved. Occasionally I wanted to hit you for pretending that every situation could be handled by the right application of flippancy, your English lightness insulting my Scottish intensity. I wanted to shout, 'You know better! Don't pretend!' But on the whole I blessed you for it, blessed you for the relaxing grace of your way of being. It was mighty restful, after that other.

And yet – I had to protect you. Both of you. I know it makes no sort of sense, but I couldn't bear the idea of your quizzical funny eyebrows lifting and your quiet snobbery coming into play. Nor could I bear the idea of *his* appalling scorn, the kind that was roused by any kind of obedient character.

The fact is, Marius, I knew even then in my heart of hearts that you were a slighter man than Robert. Tamer. An engaging schoolboy still, in many ways, in spite of all you'd been through. Why should that have mattered? I loved you, adored you, partly for those very reasons, because you were so wholesome and sweet and had a lovely gift for lightness.

Perhaps after all I don't understand my own feelings about

power, my admiration and my loathing, nor why I need to put it on record that Robert was a bigger man than you, not as big as he thought he was but bigger than you. His ideas were grander, his vision (when he wasn't pissed out of his mind) larger, his fears more jagged and his loves, of which I was never really one (indeed poetry and Scotland were, I think, his only true loves), more searching. Of course like so many talented people in this talent-denying country, he flickered out. He lives in Australia now. Perhaps he is creative and inspiring over there. I wouldn't know. I don't try to know. Nick goes there a lot but it is tacitly understood that he carries no information in either direction.

No, the theme of betrayal makes little sense, not on my side. For you it was a different matter. You had kept your fidelity to Linda when she was alive and barely broken it since her death. You had shrunk away from the jolly promiscuity that was bashing up friends and marriages right, left and centre.

'I sometimes think,' you said into my shoulder one night, 'I'm not yet ready for happiness like this. It makes me want to weep my heart out, when I think of her. She never had it. I never gave her this kind of joy.'

'I expect you gave her quite a lot, love.'

'I hope so. I hope I didn't hold anything back. I just have this feeling that life had hardly started for her, that we were only half-awake, in spite of being happy and in love. I wish I could believe – '

'What?'

'That it would have changed. But I doubt it. I'm not a very venturesome person and neither was she. It's you who've changed things, shaken me awake. Did you know that? I didn't realise how bored I've been most of my life. Since I reached man's estate, anyway – '

'Bored? Why?'

'I suppose because everything seemed so fixed. Comfortably and pleasantly fixed. I think we both wanted it that way. Orderly progression. Me getting on with my career. And Linda – well, I'm not sure about her. She adored Patrick but she didn't want any more children, not after the pregnancy she'd had. She was awfully ill. I don't know if that was some

159

kind of warning – do you know something? When they said she'd got leukaemia it wasn't only shock I felt, and the sense of the very worst, most dreaded thing, it was rage – pure infantile awful rage. It was the first time in my life something quite outside my control had taken over and was going to wreck everything. For about a week after I went around looking for someone to kill. Do you think that's terrible?'

I lay in the dark and stroked your body.

'No, I don't. I think it's very natural.'

'You are lovely. Do you mind me talking like this? Do you mind me talking about Linda?'

'No, talk all you like.' I didn't mind. She didn't threaten me. Rather, I felt vaguely protective, an older sister, a luckier sister. I had the priceless boon of life and second chances. Love helped, of course. It's amazing how generous and tolerant and lovely one can become in love, though even so it's probably just as well you waited a good while before showing me your photographs, that bulging dossier of family happiness.

By that time we must have been lovers for more than a year, a couple in the eyes of our friends, even Stella accommodating to the fact of unwedded bliss because of your mannerly charm – 'your lovely man' she used to call you, nearly driving me round the bend with irritation. Not that I paraded you much in front of my family but Stella was, all things considered, fairly co-operative over the boys now that they were no longer cast in the role of home-bashers, and she saw you a few times at Alma Crescent. And then checked you up and found to her delight that she knew a friend of your mother-in-law and could thus 'place' you. And although clearly puzzled that a man of your antecedents should more or less live in the disreputable, colour-clashing muddle of Alma Crescent, she had no serious ground for disapproval, except that you were a psychologist. 'But of course he'll get a chair eventually, won't he? I'm told he's doing very well.' Chairs apparently made things all right, even trendy modern Chairs.

Enough of Stella – the photographs, you showed me the photographs one wet afternoon when we were for some reason at your place, so seldom the setting for our time together. Yet there we are on your broad studio couch poring

160

over the albums and envelopes full of snaps. I see a charming smiling woman, very pretty, very graceful. Yes, you've prepared me well, she is much as I had imagined she would be. Linda. She looks friendly. I think I would have liked her. She kneels beside her small son, squinting slightly into the sun, no shadow of early death in that face, nothing but health and firmness and vitality. There are photos of picnics with friends, of family groups with parents, yours and hers. For the camera at least you seem to live with your arms round each other. I can't suppress a bit of a pang at the him-and-her snaps, just the two of you, her head always inclined towards you, you looking down at her, the two of you softly triumphant in your union of happiness. The wedding album, however, leaves me cold. Wedding photos are all the same, a bridal bundle of lace and some kind of grinning waxwork in sponge-bag trousers and beetle coat. Even you, my love, look pretty unimpressive. I turn away, the better to stifle a recollection of olive drab. There were no photographs at my wedding.

Back to the family snaps, feeling a kind of uncertain trespasser's awe as I look at the face of a woman younger than myself but vanished, no link between those smiles and her non-presence. I try to say something that would express my sense of mystery and sober privilege to be here, alive, with the man who has his arm round her in the photograph.

'It seems incredible – all that lovely vitality and confidence, just wiped out because her blood cells ran riot.'

'I know' you said. 'It doesn't make sense, does it? Someone dying young – I don't think you ever totally believe in it. You just get used to the fact that it's happened – in time.'

We turned over more snaps. Then you said in a different tone, 'But you know, she wasn't really all that confident.'

'Oh?' I was slightly shocked. Radiant confidence, I'd have said from those snaps, in spite of all her charming air of deferring to you.

'You'd never have guessed of course, if you didn't know her well. She put on a pretty good act.'

Oh God. Those acts. In fear small animals freeze, women act, men fight.

161

'You surprise me. I'd have thought she had everything to be confident about – looks, poise, an adoring husband, adoring parents – '

'Well, that's it, you see. She'd never tested herself. She never had to. It all came so easily. She'd have thought the world of you, you know. She'd have thought you were wonderful.'

'*Me*?'

'Yes. Because you've had to struggle. Because you're independent, and you take risks – '

'Well, I don't know about that – '

'Oh yes. Anyone who does something creative takes risks. But Linda wasn't a risk-taker. I don't suppose I am either, not by nature.'

'I never think of it like that. I'm just doing what I want – at long last. I don't see anything very wonderful in all that. And as for risks, well, there's quite an art in taking the right ones. On the whole I haven't.'

'You mean rushing into marriage? But you were so young, darling.'

That much I had told you. Married at nineteen to a bit of a ne'er do weel. Thus do we trivialise our bogey men.

Your thoughts were still on Linda.

'I don't suppose I gave her much encouragement, to develop herself. At one time she thought about having her voice trained – she had rather a pretty voice, it wasn't such an absurd idea. But I'm afraid I rather pooh-poohed it.'

'Why?'

'Why? I don't really know. Partly selfishness, I expect. Might take up too much of her time. Yes I know, love, don't give me that look. I was an unreformed character then. I promise you it wouldn't be like that if we – ' You broke off, at a loss, then grinned at me. 'I know you wouldn't stand for it.' The shadowy question of marriage which we circled round, uneasy in our separate ways, was once again treated as a kind of hypothetical joke. 'And then, you know, I think I was afraid she'd make a fool of herself.' We were back to Linda. 'I simply cannot stand amateur ladies doing their thing. My mother used to sing sentimental songs excruciatingly badly.'

'But surely that's part of the risk? The creative risk that you admire so much. You may make a total fool of yourself.'

You looked vague and avoided that. 'I don't think she was the type to study something seriously. And really you have to be serious or leave well alone. Particularly in the arts. That's my view.'

'I see.'

I stared down at the photos again, the smiling face and the friendly crinkled-up eyes and, well hidden from me and posterity, uncertainty, a lack of confidence. Well, even the gentlest of double-binds undermines the confidence dreadfully. If Linda took a risk she would be an amateur lady doing her thing and possibly making herself ridiculous. Question. How could Linda ever be seen to be serious? If she'd wanted that?

'You're very quiet,' you said, stroking my hand. 'Does it bother you, seeing these? It's only the past, darling. Don't be afraid of it. I just wanted to share it with you.'

Well, I was upset, but not in the way you delicately hinted. Sure enough, I did envy you (and Linda) all the normal tenderness of your life together but it was not that that made me thoughtful, made me want to get back to Alma Crescent on my own, a matter I was quite firm about from time to time. Besotted I might be, but I needed my occasional nights alone, my times of withdrawal, and this was one.

You were not very pleased. You looked taken aback, rather hurt. I said, 'Oh, it's nothing. Really. You know what I'm like. I need to reassemble myself.'

You rolled your eyes, mock dismay.

'Such a poor little creature! Such a delicate fragile creature who comes to pieces in my hands! Suppose I promise to cook you a special dinner and leave you severely alone until then, curled up here with a drink and a book. How about that?'

Oh very tempting! Your charm, your warmth. Love, concern, to be wanted. I very nearly gave in, but didn't. I really *did* need to go away and be by myself. You gave in with reasonably good grace, but sometimes I have wondered. One always does wonder, when exactly doubt is seeded.

That evening I sat in front of my big gas fire after the boys were in bed and drank whisky, thinking of you and Linda and me and Linda and you and me. We seemed to be dancing a sort of shifting dance, three people, three couples, turning and twisting, smiling at our improvisations, but gradually the different patterns dying down until there was only one couple left, a man and woman. And the measure they were treading was monotonously simple. Advance hands out, clasp, kiss, he leaning down, she stretching up. She little-girlish, he remote, a captain, a father – kind, good, firm. The free flow has vanished.

I poured more whisky thinking glumly of those photos I'd seen, ensnared in them all the kinds of happiness I'd wrung my chapped hands at not having had ten years before.

But I've known other happiness since, with another Marius, a man who brings wine and cooks great festive meals in the shambles of my kitchen, who plays crazy games with my boys and comes with me to my crazy parties, and laughs because life seen through love is a dazzling joke! Only if I marry him I will also marry his twin, that strong man with his arm round his slender wife protecting her from all danger, all disturbance, all fear of risk-taking or becoming serious. That kind man who took all the burden of decision-making. That good man who so clearly ruled the roost.

Egged on by the sharp disinhibiting jabs of the whisky, I pushed myself to see what until then I had refused to see. That you existed prior to being my lover, all but a fraction of you shaped by the mould of your past. The Marius I knew was on vacation. He was celebrating his return to life. It would fade away, order and sobriety would return. The old order. No, no! Change was in the air! These were times of change. And anyway, you knew I'd never be another Linda, you'd said as much.

But did I know? I loved you so much. Wouldn't I do anything, sacrifice anything, to be with you? Didn't I already see myself leaning up against you, head inclined, owned, protected? The burden of independence thankfully shed?

I looked round at my chaotic kingdom. I was a little drunk by now.

'Don't you ever forget,' I said out loud to myself. 'These

have been the best years, the *very best*. Before he came as well as after.'

The room was sorrowfully silent. My half-finished work, in the gloom, looked ragged, without life, doubting itself. Artistic panic plunged me further down. I clung on. One of my paintings and one of my tapestries had been chosen for an exhibition, an outside independent exhibition, nothing to do with the college. Yes, but I did those six months ago. Maybe the spark's died. Maybe I've given it all to Marius.

'Linda,' I asked passionately, 'would you really have envied me? Am I really what you would like to have been? Swung by uncertainty from one day to the next, up, down, up, down, a scared acrobat on trapezing time? Surely you enjoyed the firm *earthed* feel of domestic love? Even at the price of a little stiflement?'

It wasn't Linda that replied but a very young, hurt, sullen woman saying with tipsy melodrama, 'Of course she did. She had her good man and true. He wore her like a rose in his buttonhole and she wore him like a golden shield. But *you* can never be like that. You're not the kind to be loved like a rose. Don't kid yourself.'

'Well, what then?' I asked. 'Don't you come on the warpath as well. I thought you'd gone your ways for good.'

She struck me as peculiarly unattractive. I almost felt she'd got what she deserved. And then, mercifully, I remembered that given half a chance she wasn't too bad, she'd never completely lost the capacity to enjoy herself.

And as though my thought had prompted her, she got up and wandered to the bureau, this obstinate young woman, and rummaged and found her own very small collection of photos of a kind that could, just, be put beside the contents of your memorial albums. And she stared at them for a long while and I think, for all her fighting words, she was hoping to convince herself she might almost have qualified as a rose, or at least a brightly coloured lily.

21

There we stand, Robert and I, on the Pont de L'Alma, Paris, August 1956. I'm smiling at the man behind the camera, a genuine relaxed smile full of a funny happiness which is nothing more than the animal energy of youth on holiday and the effect of this lovely city. Robert is less exuberant. His expression is grave but not dour, not on the edge of aggression as it so often was. He is giving his considered approval to this moment and this scene. He is almost happy.

I look long and willowy, hanging onto Robert's arm, a whole new stance and posture developed unawares in the course of a few days. A few days of dressing well, eating well, idling and being admired.

What is all this – a second honeymoon? Well, not by intention. We did nothing to help ourselves that summer but fate handed us a little present, as if to say 'well done' for patching up our patchy marriage and staying together.

Robert was asked at short notice to replace his head of department at an international seminar on modern poetry. So we went to Paris, expenses paid by an American organisation with money to throw around. For once he actually seemed anxious to have me along. 'You'll have to do the talking, Carla, I canna get my tongue round a word of French.' My French was pretty terrible, but I was prepared to stumble or mime my way through most situations, while Robert was reduced to hissing every few seconds, 'What's he saying? What's he saying?' I liked it that way, having my uses, my moment of being in control.

Paris was wonderful. We stayed in a charming small hotel on the Left Bank. During the daytime I was left to my own devices while the literati conferred. Map in hand I walked, I looked, I wrote postcards in cafés, and I went shopping with money given to me by Stella whose generosity in a good cause – that of conjuring up the Carla of the old days – was unstoppable.

I bought, among other things, a little dress of sleeveless flame-coloured linen cut with impeccable chic, high-heeled sandals, sheer stockings, and patent leather pochette with an elegant gilt clasp. I also bought a pair of sunglasses with wide white rims and safely hidden behind them sauntered through a city largely emptied of its inhabitants. In spite of its untypical languor, I still thought it was the most wonderful city that man could devise.

I sent Esther a vulgar postcard of a girl wearing nothing but a G-string and a large plume of ostrich feathers apparently sprouting from her bottom, writing, simply, 'They don't have much *class* nowadays' – Esther's standard critique of modern show-biz. I also bought her a pair of beautiful black suede gloves, guessing hopefully at the size, for she was due to go to a niece's wedding, deigning to return for the occasion to her estranged family. She was distraught at having no proper gloves to wear. 'The rest you can fudge up,' she said. 'But gloves and shoes, no.' I posted them off hoping they would arrive in time.

It was fun buying presents. For Nicky I got a little clockwork boat which played 'Il y avait un petit navire. . .' and for Stella I bought a silk headscarf in pastel colours. For Tom and Liz, Robert's brother and wife who were looking after Nick, I bought a gaily glazed Provençal casserole.

It was fun rediscovering my face. Mirrors became allies again, boosters of morale. Someone vaguely like my student self looked back at me. I took to making up my eyes again, inspired by the French girls round me. Robert said tartly I looked like a demented insect but in fact walked proudly enough beside me watching men's glances swivel. I took immense care where I myself looked.

All the same, one day I bought a picture from a street-artist painting, just as he should be, by the Seine, not an old man in a smock but a young sun-burned man in an open shirt. I coped as best I could with a lot of gallant banter but turned down flat the suggestion that we should celebrate the transaction over an aperitif. I was on oath to myself, and still liable to feel terror at certain recent memories. Still, it was a pity to end on a note of such cold disdain, a rejected Frenchman's wickedly successful way of snatching victory out of defeat. 'You poor limp creature,' he seemed to say. 'Fancy turning *me* down because of some boring preoccupation with virtue.'

Never mind, I had a picture. Of boats and trees reflected in water. It was hardly original but there was a sense of light and dazzle, and the impudent freshness of a young artist dashing away with his colours and his palette knife. It gave me, I am sure, some premonitory thrill about the passion and the playtime of art. It marked the first stirring. I no longer have it and just as well, I think. I'm sure now I would only see that it was derivative and naive.

That evening there was a reception for delegates and their wives or girl-friends, my first presentation to conference members. I had a lovely time. I got the impression that while half the membership were still locked in intense discussion and even more intense battles of a savagely personal nature, the other half, the younger poets, perhaps, were just as glad to forget about poetry altogether for the space of a few glasses of champagne. My corner got rowdy. Someone invented a brilliant variation on chess with the canapés, winner eats all. I don't know where I figured in all this, except that I hadn't laughed so much in years and had eventually to be rescued by Robert. He suggested I slow down a bit. I did. But eventually about ten of us went off to eat together, then on to dance, and finally, stumbling and exhausted, ended up at the tail-end of a cabaret show high up in Montmartre with more champagne. Next morning I thought I was dying, but it turned out to be only indigestion. Robert said 'serve you right' but not unsympathetically.

Yes, Paris was a reprieve. We talked no more of splitting up. And I took the kind of photos that could have been part of an album with the camera father leant me. Here they are –

amateurish shots of Paris; a few of myself taken by Robert, a few of him taken by me. In spite of the holiday mood he has managed to look grim in most of them. Embattled Scottish manhood scowling defiantly in front of the great west door of Notre Dame, at a café table in Montparnasse, in the Jardin du Luxembourg. Apart from the photo with the two of us, there is only one other that gives a glimpse of the man who could, circumstances being entirely favourable and his defences down, actually be happy. I mean *happy*, not engaged in some kind of ranting debauch. I don't even remember what provoked that rare smile of well-being. He was probably talking to the Americans we'd made friends with at the conference, and I must have caught him as he looked up and across to something that clearly pleased his poet's eyes. Or perhaps he was enjoying the sweet taste of praise. They thought a lot of his poetry, did the Americans. The conference had gone well for him. Useful contacts, the possibility, hinted at, of a visit to the States next summer. The door onto the big world which from home stood at a thin-angled crack pushed open a little wider.

So – there you are. There's my collection. And I haven't a single photo of you, not one. Well, there seemed no need. The camera was no part of our relationship. We never stood back from each other or ourselves for long enough to think about *recording*. Of course, if we'd gone on that long trek through Europe, promised for the time after my graduation, I expect we'd have started building up our own dossier of shared life.

In fact I'm just as glad I have nothing. I don't think I could bear to have witness to the basic certainty we lived in, in spite of all attacks of doubt, that destiny had pointed us at each other and said 'There! You've found, each of you, the one face in all the millions that you instantly and fully know.' Love is, after all, nine-tenths recognition.

It would finish me, to look at photos of that certainty, on my own.

22

We got back from Paris towards the end of August. Esther was at her door the minute she heard our footsteps but there was no cheerful welcoming of returned travellers. She looked pale and ten years older.

'Whatever's wrong?' we asked.

She came out flat with it.

'I've had a bereavement.'

I knew before she said it who it was. Ahmed.

Shocked, we brought her into our flat. It smelt warm and stale. Robert immediately went out again saying he'd be back right away, but we needed something to drink after news like that.

Timidly, uncertain of the forms of condolence I asked, 'What happened?'

'He had a heart attack.'

'How did you hear about it?'

'She 'phoned me up.'

'Oh!' I felt an acute spasm of sympathy. 'I hope she behaved decently.' I didn't even know if 'she' was still the ex-chorus girl from Rothesay, but I presumed so.

'Well,' said Esther grudgingly, 'yes, I suppose under the circumstances. She's the hysterical type. But he dropped dead – and I mean *dropped* – as they were getting ready for bed. So there was something to be hysterical about.'

She sat down wearily in the big chair.

Robert came back in with beer and whisky in a paper carrier, and got busy with glasses.

'Did you attend the funeral?' I asked, hoping the black gloves had come in useful.

'*Attend*? I organised it.' There was a stunned silence. 'Well I mean, I was the person to do it. We'd often talked about – how we wanted it to be, whichever should go first. And the funny thing is, although he was younger, we spent more time planning his than mine. Maybe it's the kind of thing you know, in your bones.' She sighed tremulously. 'He wanted a French flag on his coffin if he died abroad, and he wanted to be embalmed and his apache make-up and costume put on.'

We continued speechless. Finally Robert plucked up the courage to say he thought it was only the military who had flags on their coffins, though I'm sure his mind like mine was on the other part of the request.

Esther took a good gulp of whisky.

'Ahmed wanted a flag. I don't see no reason why he shouldn't have one. He had his flag.'

'And – the rest?'

Esther looked at me.

'He got that too. I told that woman she'd lived off him for ten years, the least she could do was fork up for an embalming. I made the arrangements.' She paused. 'And I did the make-up.' She had another gulp. 'I'm not sure whether I did right. I don't think Ahmed realised – ' She put her glass down and her hands came up to her face. Robert went over to her and put his arms round her. She was the only person I ever saw him touch in a friendly, natural way. I stood there watching them, her face buried in his stomach, and I felt a little hurt when I thought of all our tangoes. After all, I'd almost known Ahmed.

Into Robert's stomach she sobbed out the worst blow of all.

'It didn't make any difference, he hasn't left me a bean' – as if the dead man, seeing her faithfully carrying out his wishes, should have had the power to alter his will hastily in her favour. 'Everything's gone to her. I don't know how I'm going to make out. He didn't pay very regular, but it did come in now and again and it helped.'

I wished and I *wished* it was in our power to say, 'Never mind, we'll help you out.' I could think of nothing except to ask my father if he knew of a cleaning or care-taking job. Meanwhile Robert was taking out his wallet. He was putting a fiver into Esther's reluctant hand. I thought frantically of that plus the cost of the drink. I could feel the old churning of the stomach, my reaction to the threat of no money. It was all I could do to stop myself from hoping that Esther would succeed, as she was trying to do, in handing back the note. She did not. I tried to remember what was left of my spending spree in Paris, Stella's bounty. One or two small traveller's cheques, perhaps? I hate what lack of money does to you – the fear, the caution, the nag of mean-ness. On your own it's different. Now I'm a spendthrift when I'm in cash, pull down the blinds and lie low when I'm not. Then I lost sleep over the non-existent stuff. However, I'm glad to say I held my peace over that fiver.

I did ask my father if he knew of anything for Esther, explaining the circumstances. He had no suggestions to make about work but he offered to contact Ahmed's lawyer if I could get the name and see if a bit of pressure on moral grounds could be applied. And eventually, after various delays, Esther did get a small lump sum from Ahmed's estate. I can only suppose that the ex-chorus girl wasn't a bad sort and recognised Esther's right to claim, or that between them my father and the other lawyer leaned on her. Anyway, Esther was amazedly grateful and endowed my unknown father with a halo. 'That blessed man' she called him thereafter.

For the rest of that year Robert and I lived in quite a decent state of tolerance, maybe even something a little stronger. Esther's troubles created a sort of bond, and then she got ill and had to be nursed and we both spent a lot of time with her. When she was better she used to come and sit with me and Nicky. She had taken up crochet, an old hobby from childhood, she was determined to make a blanket for me. I have it still, a patchwork of many colours.

Things were more peaceful. Robert spent more time with Nick, determined he should learn to kick a ball at the earliest possible age. And he was writing again, encouraged by the conference and some good reviews of his last collection of poems. It seemed to be a less furious process than usual.

Occasionally he even sat at home of an evening, reading, sometimes scribbling.

And I? Well, I had been to Paris, and as well as the good eating and drinking and the novelty of money in my *pochette*, I'd had a glimpse of the brighter side of penury. For one evening we were invited to the home of a Jugoslavian poet, a tiny sixth floor flat in Montparnasse where he lived with his French girl-friend. It was even more cramped than ours but its tiny space was – not filled, but in some way hollowed out by colour, colour on all sides, paintings, weavings, tapestry, embroidered cushions. Lovely living stretches of colour. It suddenly threw open a window in my mind. I had to get up and finger or peer at everything.

'I wish I could make things like that', I said to the girl-friend.

She shrugged (it was mainly her work) and said in her halting English, 'But it is not ve*rry* difficult.'

'Who taught you?'

'*Personne.*' She shrugged again. '*Ça s'apprend* – you learn yourself.' And then went off to prepare us excellent coffee, tossing a long lock of shining hair over shoulder.

Quality. Paris was all about quality, whether on the boulevards or in the attics, or in the neat slick patterns of the waiters swooping and swaying with trays and flourishes. Quality and style. Where to begin?

I hung up my painting of boats on the Seine and then realised the rest was up to me, to introduce quality and colour, to create Bohemia out of beery squalor. '*Ça s'apprend* – you learn yourself.' I was doubtful. I started unpromisingly by getting Esther to teach me how to crochet. But I saw no future, no possibilities in crochet. And then one day I got the idea of imitating that neo-impressionist's brush-strokes with stitching and material. Paints were out of the question. You can't pick up remnants of paint but you can – and I did – pick up all sorts of junk that can be sewn onto fabric. I fixed everything fixable onto material; buttons, sequins, wools, threads, single earrings, tassles, beads, laces. And out of this started to grow strange plants and creatures, strange landscapes, strange shapes, things that emerged from a part of my mind I knew

173

nothing about. I worked like someone obsessed, as though I had some vast mythical task to complete. I sewed my pictures (samplers, banners) whenever I got a moment and when finished stuck drawing pins through them and onto the mouldy oatmeal walls. My task – surely nothing less than papering over the whole of drab 'reality' with a net of fantasy?

As a matter of fact they are quite powerful, these little relics. They carry a quality of private ritual. I appraise them now from a critic's and collector's viewpoint, very far indeed from the state of mind that hatched up these oddities. They remind me a little of peasant art, something superstitious, hopeful of weaving spells against the odds, yet like all dwellers on the margin grasping at tangible things, wood or stone or fabric, to express the intangible.

Someone – Germaine Greer, I think – described women's art as 'biodegradable', i.e. it's made of *stuff*. Yes, because like peasants we have only tenuous control over our environment. We're not on sure enough ground to be abstract. There are gods between us and the levers of power. Shabby bewildered gods now. But not always. Last century they grew bigger and bolder with every decade. Now the only great ones are themselves turning full circle and admitting mysteries beyond the grip of mind. However, that has little to do with some curious fabric pictures whose power, nonetheless, has the unmistakeable quality of the powerless; they invoke, they do not impose.

All I was trying to do was keep drabness at bay. I combed the junk shops – such rich collections of life's forgotten droppings – spending minute sums. It was such odd trash I bought that sometimes shopkeepers gave it to me for nothing. Even so, without the connivance of Mary who turned out an unexpected ally, I doubt if I could have gone on, certainly never tackled the big bold pieces which really did transform the flat. One day, visiting my old home, I asked her if she could spare me any pieces of material or if she had any old necklaces or beads she didn't want, and I showed her one of my embroidery-patchworks.

She was quite impressed.

'It's like a picture for a fairy-tale,' she said. 'I didn't know you could do that sort of thing. You were always hopeless with a needle as a child. Well, let's see what we can find.'

In her housewifely assortment, nothing of interest. So she led me off to a closet the size of a small room where the fruits of the household policy 'Never discard' were piled on shelves and hanging from rails. Old curtains, old linen, old dresses, old suits, old shoes. At the far end I saw things that gleamed, evening-dresses, dance-shoes with diamante buckles.

'What's all this?'

It was what are discreetly called 'personal effects', my mother's things never cleared out after her death, merely stored away out of sight. I blinked and felt a most peculiar sensation, almost like lust. There was loot there beyond imagining. Still, I hung back uneasily, halted by superstitious fear such as any novice tomb-robber probably feels. Also, I was a bit alarmed. The kind of 'I want – ' I was feeling, it wasn't civilised. It didn't care a damn.

'You might as well,' said Mary, looking at me sideways. 'Nobody's been near this stuff for years. Your father once asked me what we should do with it and I said send it to the church mission aid sale but he didn't like the idea and we've never spoken of it since. If you can find a use for it, Carla, I don't see why not – it's not doing anyone any good lying here, is it?'

I suppose it was an odd thing for her to do, let me loose among all that finery. We neither of us mentioned Stella, each for our own reasons. There was no love lost between Mary and Stella. For myself, I certainly never foresaw the kind of rage that possessed her when she eventually found out, but I knew she might be none too pleased. As for Mary, perhaps she was glad enough to get rid of stuff which was in some sense a permanent reminder of her second-best status. Perhaps too, she was glad to see me reviving. She was quite fond of me.

Whatever the reason, she let me rummage free-handed among my mother's clothes and watched without comment as I somewhat barbarically helped myself, cutting into old gowns, wrenching off bead-work and lace, pocketing the jewellery – oh, not the valuable stuff, that was in safe keeping

175

in the bank, to be transferred to Stella and myself at father's discretion. (Stella, I think, got some of it quite soon after her marriage. Shrewdly enough, he held back on my share.)

No, what I found were the trinkets, costume jewellery, semi-precious stuff. There was a big box full of necklaces, crystals, moonstones, Venetian glass beads, rough-cut turquoise. Why hadn't we been allowed to play with them as kids? But I would play with them now. I saw them already making patterns, dream flowers, apocalyptic beasts – and I plunged my hands into that box and I took. And then I went to work with scissors and went back to the flat that day with two bulging bags of plunder, the first of a trail of such bags. My feeling was pure and simple jubilation.

I have an idea that I may have shocked you, Marius – such disrespect for the dead, the close and personal dead. My own mother's belongings simply dismembered to make a few wall-hangings? Possibly you think Stella's anger was justified. I can still see her face, pale and livid, stammering with rage and astonishment, that Sunday she found out.

But my mother meant nothing to me. There was nothing to connect me with that portrait of a straight-featured beauty in the drawing-room. If they'd wanted to keep her memory green why did they never speak of her, father and Stella? Why didn't they tell me stories about the early days?

That I have never discovered. It was not until I realised that everyone doesn't bury their dead with quite such total silence that it occurred to me to wonder why they never did. At one time, when I was about fourteen, I did ask a few questions, hit by a wish to fill in the mysterious gap which was all I had in the way of a mother. They were not encouraged. I was told she died of pneumonia caught after a skating party, and from somewhere or something, a tone of voice, a look, or simply an intuition, I got the impression that she shouldn't have been there, that father disapproved. I think I did spin a few fantasies, about lovers and rendezvous, and the possibility that she died in disgrace, but they didn't really take hold. She looked most awfully correct in her portrait, not a hint, not a crack in that deadpan mask to suggest a hidden touch of mischief.

176

Probably she did nothing more disgraceful than die, a pretty serious offence if you believe, as the good bourgeois does, that life – not merely people or their aspirations but the actual naked flame of existence – can be brought under control by a set of rather humdrum rules of procedure. For a class so reputedly cautious in its thinking, this is a claim of megalomaniac proportions, but no one seems to see the discrepancy. And it holds good, more or less, till death comes along, death which brings awe and fear and mystery and blows the lid off the tidy scheme of things. Very anti-social and disruptive, is death.

So – my mother transgressed and was consigned to silence. I really have no remorse about what happened with her clothes. And I don't think Stella had a leg to stand on, in that row.

After my looting, the flat was strewn with snippets of velvet and satin, spilt pearls and sequins. I don't know how many beads Nicky swallowed, thankfully none large enough to obstruct his gut. He too got enamoured of things that glittered and to Robert's alarm insisted on wearing a necklace of beads he and I put together one afternoon. I said I thought he had nothing to worry about. Had he not also successfully demolished the rabbit-hutch and terrorised the rabbits the last time we went to visit Tom and Liz?

My mother's finery turned into my biggest creation to date, a jungle full of mythical beasts peering through spiked and tufted plants. They had brilliants for eyes which caught the firelight just like real animals at night. Nicky thought it was wonderful and so, privately, did I.

And then I launched out into portraiture – a sewn portrait of Esther as I imagined her in her heyday. From the gaunt face of the present I created a bold younger woman, jutting cheekbones and thick-bridged nose making the link. She was fascinated. It was the first thing that seemed to rouse her from her lethargic preoccupation with Ahmed's death. Yet in some way it did honour to the life they'd shared.

It was for this work that I finally applied scissors to a magnificent jet-bead-encrusted dinner-dress, the flashpoint for Stella's later fury. And there she sat in my portrait, made up of patches and great wool stitches and the kind of glitter she might have worn and somehow it had worked. She looked at us both with a kind of wary confidence, a brave woman, a *grande dame* whom life has decided to rough-hew with a fairly persistent series of axe-blows. It was Esther now looking out of the woman she had once been.

Even Robert was impressed. He'd paid very little attention to what I was doing up till now but the Esther portrait intrigued him. He said he wanted a friend of his to come and have a look at it, someone who ran a small private gallery. On the appointed evening I fidgeted around, proud and nervous, waiting for them to come, heating and reheating the coffee. I should have realised it wouldn't be till after pub-shutting time. Silly to have started preparing at eight o'clock.

They arrived eventually, both a little the worse for wear, nothing unusual. What was unusual was that the friend was young and well-dressed with piled-up blonde hair. A woman. The first to visit the flat. I had not been prepared for her. Robert's outside world was, in my mind's eye, all-masculine.

I looked at her with the natural antipathy of dark for fair women. She hardly noticed me. Instead she swooned around my work, the portrait of Esther, the fabulous beasts, various other little pieces hung up or lying on a chair. I should have been gratified by the gush and the superlatives, except that they were all addressed to Robert, as if all this was his cleverness.

Eventually she turned to me.

'I'll take the lot. I'm collecting up for an exhibition of new work. This is quite unusual, you have a weird talent, darling. I charge fifty per cent commission on anything sold. All right?'

'No,' I said startled. 'It is not all right. I haven't decided that I want to sell anything.'

She stared. I don't think in the first mumbled introductions she'd clearly heard my voice. Now it rang out, clearly an educated voice. She looked at me more closely and her expression, for all her sophistication, was comically easy to read, 'What is that voice doing coming out of someone who looks as if she dresses from jumble-sales?' This was, of course, well before the days when dropping out or living macrobiotic-ally have made such out-fits commonplace.

'The fact is,' I said, 'I don't know anything about your gallery. I've never thought of exhibiting. And fifty per cent sounds a very large cut.'

I can only think some spirit of the future was speaking through me. Never in a considered moment would I have spoken like that, but my blood was up, all this pawing over my work as though I were invisible.

'Darling – ' she fixed me with a lazy green eye, 'I can tell you people are pretty keen to exhibit with me. It would be a pity to pass up a good opportunity. Not everyone's willing to back a beginner.'

'Don't be a fool, Carla.' This was Robert. 'Marilyn hasn't time to mess around with people who can't make up their minds.'

'But you never told me – you just said you were bringing a friend to look at the Esther picture. I didn't realise – '

'Well, are you going to show your stuff or aren't you?'

'You can show Esther if you want, but no selling. I've promised it to her as a present. The rest – ' I looked around at my jungle and all the other little banners with strange devices. No, no! They were too precious. Finally I let her take three.

After she had gone Robert said tartly, 'Considering how you're always complaining about being flat broke I'd have thought you would jump at the opportunity of making some cash.'

'With fifty per cent off? That's not making cash, that's being exploited. Your friend's going a bit far.'

'She's got big overheads.'

I felt like saying something rude about other big things, but refrained. It did occur to me to wonder why Robert would have as a 'friend' the kind of woman he purported to loathe. But on this subject my defences were watertight. The last thing I wanted to do was grill him. I did not want to address myself to the details of Robert's out-of-home life. It was all remote and unpalatable and overlaid with the issue of drink, the big issue. The rest didn't matter. I did not like his art-gallery woman and I did not go to the private view of the exhibition which included my work. I don't know whether he did or not. When, after a couple of months, I got a very small

179

cheque and a request to collect unsold work, I suggested that Robert pick it up since he knew the woman.

'Who?' he asked, puzzled. 'Oh – that bitch.'

I collected the portrait of Esther myself. I hope no client of mine has ever been treated as offhandedly.

23

That autumn we saw a lot of brother Tom. Tom, small, wiry and energetic, was rising steadily to prominence in the Communist Party. He came through quite often to Edinburgh to address meetings or give lectures. We went once to a meeting where he was talking (this was part of his private campaign to get Robert active in the Party again) and I was astonished. This little man, speaking with savage passion and the confidence which is born thereof, was he the same Tom who played with my son and teased me about making 'wee patchworks'? Just the same, he came in for a lot of heckling from his audience.

Afterwards I asked Robert, in my naivety, why, if they were all members of the same party, was there so much quarrelling? He tried to explain about the Twentieth Congress of the Communist Party of the Soviet Union, and the cult of the individual, and how Stalin had been denounced as the agent of terrible mass crimes. 'People are very shaken. They don't know what to think. It's tearing the Party apart.' It was the first I had heard of the forced labour camps and the purges.

Tom came back and stayed with us overnight, dossing down on the living-room floor and catching an early train back to Glasgow, a routine that became familiar over the next few weeks. Sometimes he can't have had more than four or five hours' sleep, he and Robert arguing on into the small hours. Although my part was as usual a fairly silent one and I yawned my way to bed long before they did, I enjoyed those visits, Tom such a contrast with Robert, it was difficult to believe they were brothers. When not engaged in political debate he was humorous and easy-going and he brought out a better, less bitter side to his elder sib. You could tell there was a long affectionate wrangling relationship between them, that they were comrades, not in the Party sense, but in matching of wit and sharing of loyalty. Robert's own wry sense of humour, hardly tasted since courtship days, was re-aroused. There was a sense of family bonds never in evidence when we paid our occasional uncomfortable visits to his old home.

I even felt – and was glad to feel – that this sense of family was extended to me. I may have been a silent listener but I was not excluded. I sewed away while the battle for Robert's allegiance, his proper Party allegiance, went on. Tom wanted him to be a real comrade, in the true political sense. He came back and back at him for his lapses, his failures to commit himself to regular party work. 'I'm starting to think yer nothing more than a fellow traveller.'

Robert bristled at that, but still stalled on the question of further commitment. Particularly now, he said, there was a lot he wanted to think over. Besides, he had enough on his plate. He hadn't time to to go to meetings. He could work for the revolution in his own way.

'What way?'

'What I write, what I teach.'

Tom shook his head.

'Yer a good poet, Rab, I know that fine. But it's action we need, man. *Action*.'

Tom was a good speaker, platform or fireside. He had passion. He had learnt from men who had fought in the Spanish Civil War and had hoped it was the prelude to the battle which would be fought on Clydeside. He was more ardent, more fanatical than Robert – I would watch the fanatic take over from friendly easy-going Tom, a man of kindness if ever I knew one. Yet he seemed to find no need for the personalisation of conflict I so resented. Of course, as Robert would have been quick to point out, he hadn't had to marry the enemy.

Only Robert was not getting at me so much these days. And the arguments with Tom, as the autumn progressed, were becoming tougher, more acrimonious. The issue of Stalin's 'errors' was splitting them further and further. Yes, Tom agreed, there had been atrocities, a terrible scale of destruction. He did not choose to try and deny the enormities as some of the Party still did. Still Russia remained inviolate, the one country which had bowed to historical necessity under a great and courageous leader.

'Courageous?' Robert looked at him vexedly. 'You call it courageous, to liquidate millions and turn millions more into broken beasts?'

'Aye. It takes courage, moral courage. To hold to your vision. To accept the price that has to be paid for purging a society of its internal enemies. But even great leaders get swept on too far in the wave of events.'

'Och, cut out the cant, Tom. Just stop talking about "historical necessity" and "internal enemies" and think for a minute. D'you suppose there's much picking and choosing when it comes to dealing in millions? And this price you talk about – who pays? Who pays? Not the leaders, just ordinary people, as ever. And if *that* is the price, well I'm not sure – '

'Not sure of what?' Tom asked sharply. 'This is no time to be swithering, Rab.'

'I'm not swithering. I just need to think about things.'

And Robert's jaw set into silence for the rest of that evening.

So in a sense their antlers were already locked by the time Hungary suddenly became headlines, in every newspaper, on every news bulletin. Things were suddenly happening. There had been an uprising, a demonstration in Budapest which had turned into an armed uprising. Imry Nagy, the new leader, was calling for help to the Western world. Russian troops were approaching. There was an urgency about the even-toned BBC reports as there had been during bad moments in the war when, as a small child, I caught it from adults' faces if not from the actual announcer. Robert listened and read obsessionally. He even was moved to exclaim and explain to me, for I was in the dark. I knew nothing about what had been happening in Poland, about Tito's defiance, about the growing restiveness of individual Warsaw Pact countries under the thumb of Moscow. I don't think I grasped very clearly what was happening, simply watched in amazement as Robert went through some kind of tearing apart of himself. We were listening together when Nagy's last public speech was broadcast: 'At daybreak, Soviet forces started an attack against our capital, obviously with the intention to overthrow the legal Hungarian government. Our troops are fighting. The government is in its place. I notify the people of our country and the entire world of this fact.' Robert was quite white.

'That's it then,' he said. 'The poor buggers. It's all over bar the shooting. More deaths, more slaughter. Does it never end?'

A few days later Tom came through. He had a bad time at a local meeting, to which Robert also went as a member of the audience.

'I didn't see you springing to my defence,' Tom said morosely.

'No, nor likely to over this one. I don't know how you can make yerself say the kind of things you were saying. They would stick in my craw.'

'Wha' do you mean by that?'

'I mean that I'm tired of hearing about counter-revolution and chauvinism and disciplinary measures when what's happening is that a genuine popular uprising over real grievances is being ground out by Russian tanks. All the time you're yacking away about the need to control the forces of revisionism – a "sacred duty" I think you had the gall to call it – all *I* can think of is those poor brave sods without a hope – '

'My God, you've turned yellow. Or maybe it's blue. Bright nationalisitic blue. D'you suppose I enjoy the idea of the Hugarians being shot to pieces? I'm not a war-monger. But quit I will not. There is need to uphold the true Revolution. If it needs Russian tanks, it needs Russian tanks.'

'Well, here's where we part company.'

They stared at each other.

'D'you mean that?'

'Aye.'

Tom's face went blank and numb. I hadn't realised the strength of what existed between them, brotherly things by blood and conviction, solidarity. Tearing apart now. They both looked stricken.

'So you're quitting.'

'I'm working to get refugees out and over to the UK. It's a university set-up. We'll try and place any students that manage to get here. For once I'm glad I'm an academic.'

And that was all he would say. Tom refused to stay the night as he usually did. He'd hoped, he said, to persuade Robert, as a poet and an intellectual, to lend weight to a platform party at a meeting to rally the faltering and split membership. It was more than he could stomach, to curl up with his defeat on our living-room floor. The rift, for the time being, was total.

'So what did you make of all that?' Robert for once turned to me. He looked glum and broken up as the door shut behind his brother.

'I – I don't know.' Cautiously I added, 'I think you've done something that was very hard for you.' Silence. Then – 'I'm glad you're going to help them.'

He put his hand for a moment on my shoulder. 'Thanks.'

24

I suppose it must have been about six weeks after that, certainly not long before New Year, that Janos first came to the flat. He was very quiet that first visit, sitting among the old crowd, John Graham and the rest, Robert's cronies who in their migratory fashion seemed to have found their way back again. The drinking sessions, punctuated by tea and sometimes food, had come round again. I did my bit with slightly better grace and a good deal more efficiency than in the early days. I was pretty good with a chip-pan by now.

From my viewpoint in the kitchen, the door open into the living-room, I stared at the newcomer. He was pale and fair-haired, a slightly sallow paleness, not blue-tinged like Nordic pallor. He looked small and slight beside Robert who seemed to have taken him under his wing.

'Come on, Janos, drink up,' I heard him say paternally, holding the beer bottle over his glass. And the fair-haired young man smiled and held out his glass.

I couldn't stop staring. There he sat, so ordinary, so normal, a young guy among older men, wearing a big wool sweater under a jacket of curious cut and shoes, too, of a curious cut and very worn. A refugee. A man with nothing, nothing to fall back on, no network of familiar faces and places, simply himself. I watched him smile, then break into a laugh, then say something himself. More laughter. His English seemed to be pretty good, good enough to laugh at jokes in broad accents, to reply and cause his own laughter. He didn't know, of course, that he was being watched so attentively, that when he wasn't laughing his face had the look of someone hearing his own voice in a cave, a look of total loneliness, not as self-pity but as a condition of life. Does it strike at once, then, the fact of exile? Yes, even I knew that.

I tried to believe that the young man in my living room was connected with the matter of all those broadcasts and news reports and photos and found it difficult. Found it difficult also to take in the fact that he had nothing and no one to vouch for his existence, only himself. He was a man without a frame, a setting, a condition of vagabonds and tramps, not of decent young men with clean hands and neatly cut hair. And for all his normality, it showed, a certain nakedness and watchfulness, a little space round him where a frame should have been, as he sat among men whose voices rose and fell with the cadences of those whose lives are filled only with the familiar.

That first evening I think we did no more than say 'hullo' when Robert mumbled, 'This is Carla – ma wife', and quickly passed on to more vital matters. But we smiled over the handing out of tea, and he got to his feet to take the big tray from me. A nicely mannered boy.

Robert had told me a bit about him. He was a science student but had also studied English in Budapest. He wanted to continue. Robert was urging the administration to bend the rules governing combinations of subjects. Meanwhile Janos was sitting in on one of Robert's courses. 'A bright lad' said Robert approvingly.

The next time he came round with the others, when it came to tea-making he asked if he could help. I said certainly.

In the kitchen we stared and smiled at each other.

'I'm Carla,' I said, feeling the need to start properly, on my own feet so to speak, not just as a mumbled aside.

'And I'm Janos.' He held out his hand and we shook hands firmly. 'You are younger than I expected.'

'Oh?' I was amused at his frankness. 'I suppose you were going by my husband. He's ten years older.'

'Only ten?'

It was the first time I'd thought of Robert as looking older than his age. Certainly he was putting on the beef.

'Yes. Could you put that bowl of sugar on the tray, please?'

He did so, then looked across at me. He had very clear blue eyes. He seemed to be waiting for something, or asking for something.

I blurted out, 'Is it all very strange?'

'Yes.' He nodded, in thanks. 'Pretty strange.'

'Were you in the fighting?'

'Yes, part of it.'

'We heard about it – over the radio,' I said awkwardly, 'but that tells very little.' There was silence. 'Anyway, I'm –' what did one say that did not sound wrong, pitched for something quite different? 'I'm glad you got safely out of it.'

'Thank you.'

He didn't smile. I suddenly realised what I'd said. That imprecise triteness 'out of it' meant escape from death, as it also meant loss of country, of home. I was congratulating him on surviving, not saying, 'well, just as well to be out of that spot of bother.'

He still seemed to be waiting. I was busy cutting and buttering scones and could have kept my head down all the time, asking him little things about his course, where he was living, and so on. There was that temptation. But I looked up and said, suddenly sure of myself, 'You must still be very shocked. So much, such violence, in such a short time, and all the passions, it seems to have been such a passionate business – '

'Yes,' he said quietly, 'it was. Some day if you will let me, I shall tell you about it. You are one of the few people who has asked any questions. You, and Robert. Other people, the good professors and their wives, they go so carefully, like walking on needles. They don't ask anything. They have been very kind. They invite me and my compatriots for dinner but we must forget we have nearly lost our lives and seen our friends blown up. I understand. I know it is not for pretty conversation. But pretty is not very real at the moment. I think – either I am not real or they are not real. We cannot both be real.' He looked at me gently. 'There is not that problem with you.'

I gave a wry smile.

'Probably because I'm not pretty enough.'

'Oh *no*! I was not saying that!'

188

'I know. I'm only teasing. I'm glad – I really am – if you feel you can be relaxed here. Please feel at home.'

This was the first time I'd ever offered to anyone except Esther a quality that only tenuously existed for myself in the place where I lived. I felt suddenly warmed by the possibility that unnoticed the quality might be creeping up, that there *was* something to offer.

Janos was busy stacking mugs on the tray. He quickly got the hang of things.

'Why did you choose Edinburgh?'

'Because my father was once here, before the war. He is a good scientist. And I thought maybe someone will remember his name.'

'And did they?'

'Yes. It helped. Connections are always useful.'

So, a tiny thread of network had after all led him here.

The kettle boiled. I made up the huge brown pot of tea and left it to draw.

'How about something to eat, Carla?' shouted Robert from the other room.

I shouted back, 'I've buttered some scones. Will that do?'

'Oh aye, I suppose so.' He came to the door and leant in. 'What are you two gassing about? Come on through, Janos. You'll get tea in a minute.'

'Yes, I will come through. In a minute.'

Janos smiled but stood his ground. He had somehow appointed himself my helper. It was all very inoffensively done.

That evening, as always, he carried the big tray for me. As he took it from me he said, 'I feel better. Thank you.'

'I'm glad.'

'Can we talk again?'

'Oh yes.'

He gave a funny, delightful smile, small-boyish. I wanted to give him a big protective hug.

That was in January. As I remember things, it seems that the next few weeks were obsessively taken up with me and Janos talking. It can't have been so, of course. Twice a week at the

189

most, I suppose, when the others came. I dare not ask him to come on his own although everyone's honour would have been as safe as houses. Instead, we would settle down on opposite sides of the kitchen table, leaving the fraternity of the boys (age range anything from thirty to fifty) to gossip and sling mud and sometimes discuss poetry. Even to Robert it was abundantly clear that we were nowhere near the region of dangerous intimacy. He minded Janos forsaking him for me, but it was a grumble, a mild displeasure only.

In any case they had their own sessions of talking, Robert with his questions to ask, political rather than personal. Janos thought a lot of him, so sharp, such a splendid teacher, for all his strange behaviour. Sometimes his lectures would run on by as much as an hour, sometimes he failed to give them altogether. His tutorial groups were either uproariously funny, or terrorised by the quest for a scapegoat, oh, so he was still at that, one of his nastiest tricks. Loyally Janos forebore to comment, simply said, 'I hope it is never my turn.' Between the laughs and the intimidation there were stretches of good stimulating argument. I remembered from my own student days. If you actually had something to say, a real point to make, the floor was yours. Robert was only a tyrant over stupidity and lazy thinking.

Janos talked so nostalgically about his beautiful Budapest that I went to the public library and got out travel books about Hungary to identify for myself all these places of his life. Yes, it looked a beautiful city indeed, full of buildings with curling graceful scrolls and bulbous baroque domes and jaunty spires and balustraded bridges. A place for elegant romance, wine and music and leisure. An operetta world. Even though life had been lived in terms very different ever since he could remember, Janos said it was still a city that had champagne in its heart, a place that celebrated lightness and pleasure, a city for artists. Through the pictures in a travel book of the 'thirties, he pointed out to me the landmarks of his life and without transition sketched in some of the events of the uprising. 'Look,' he would say. 'Here I passed every day on the way to classes. That was where my friend Stefan was shot, with six others. The tanks came round – here, this corner, see?

There is a patisserie there. My mother used to meet me after school on Fridays when I was a little boy, for a treat.' I like to think it helped a bit, my curiosity, that by provoking this zig-zag reminiscence between the recent horrific past and the longer quieter views of childhood Janos may have found some means of believing the unbelievable. For it strikes me that nightmares and all the torments of mind are to do with avoiding the brand of finally accepting, that such and such a thing has actually happened, as if we put up glass, and on the glass gets etched in fine detail what we are begging not to burn into our souls.

Janos had nightmares, but they were not – yet – about the fighting.

'It is about this city,' he said.

'What? Edinburgh?'

'Yes. Forgive me. I should be grateful, nothing but grateful. Only dreams have no manners, have they? I dream – that I am walking and walking, alone, there is no one, down these black streets and there is something very odd about the light. And I see there are two suns in the sky, one in the east and one in the west, and so everything is casting two shadows, and where I walk the two shadows meet, so in spite of two suns I am in the dark, caught in the dark. And I see no way out. For there are so many high buildings here, and long spires, that no light can get in.'

'You don't like Edinburgh much? Not a beautiful city?'

'Oh yes, it is, very beautiful, but also frozen. It is just the kind of beautiful city to figure in a bad dream, the kind where nothing moves. Sometimes, just walking round in the day-time wide awake is a bad dream.'

'Oh, Janos. Are you so unhappy?'

'Sometimes. Only sometimes. Look, you are not to get upset. I am a fool to talk so much. I am – look, any place would be like this. It is not the fault of poor Edinburgh. I am just missing everything. And I worry about my family. My father tried to stop me from joining the protests. He said it would be dangerous, for everybody, himself and my mother and my sister. I wouldn't listen, we quarrelled quite badly and you know I suddenly saw him as an old man, finished, and now it

191

was my turn, I was the Man. It gave me a sort of courage, for a time. Now, all I can think is "Are they all right? Has something terrible happened to them because of me?"'

'Do they know you're alive?'

'I don't know. I can't write. In case that's bad for them.'

He was only nineteen, an evocative age. I remembered how green and thin my adulthood felt when I, for different reasons, also found myself pushed out of childhood. But Janos would be a better survivor than I. He might even have another crack at being young, once he had recovered from his experiences. He was resilient, basically an optimist, even though he dreamed of perpetual dark and his dead friends were too much with him, and he said he felt like a freak.

' – you know. Like something in a circus. A baby with an old man's beard. Some part of me knows, too much about death and defeat. The things of old age, the end of life. The other part is still crying for its mummy and daddy and saying "Help".'

'It'll get better, Janos, slowly. You'll get more interested in life around you, here. You'll make friends – why, you already have made friends. Robert says you're very popular.'

Robert went to endless trouble for him; he found him better digs where he could share with one of his ex-patriots, he introduced him to the pubs of Edinburgh, helped him over text-books, gave him extra coaching in written English. Janos was the first friend we had shared.

He was the first friend I had made in three years, bar Esther, a fact that helped to manage certain other emotions which were giving trouble. It was all very well being mature and motherly, exaggerating our three years' age gap into almost a generation. That held for the daylight hours. At night, in the dark, last thing before sleeping, all restraint was upended, desire and fantasy ran riot. I was besottedly in love with him not only because he was blonde and fine-looking but because he had brought me his sufferings and accepted my comfort, as he brought his jokes and made me laugh. I, the sad sullen creature, had something positive to give. I, the all-purpose skivvy, was worthy of chivalrous treatment. Even still, my terrible superfluousness in Robert's life for any but practical purposes could weigh my spirits like lead. Janos made me feel needed; more important than that, he made me feel I gladdened him. Best of all, we made each other laugh.

That was the saving grace, the steadying thing. Even in the middle of a great imagined love-scene I would remember some nonsensical remark which had set us both off. *That* was real, and it might happen again tomorrow or the next day, and *that* was as much a basic lack in my life as the other thing. The other thing, great unsubstantial fruit of imaginary rapture, competed with the experience of ardent friendship, and for the most part lost.

So 1957 started fair. It was not until towards the end of February that certain small symptoms of physical unrest, a touch of biliousness, a tenderness about the breasts that made me sure the missed period was coming any day – but then it was followed by another – summed up to the fact that once more my body had played me traitor.

25

'Not again!' Robert's horror, when I told him, matched my own. 'Not again!' It rapidly changed to fury. 'How could it happen?' He stood over me, breathless with anger. 'Have you done it on purpose?'

'No', I said stonily, 'I have not. I don't want another child any more than you do. We've been unlucky.'

'You've been careless.'

'I have *not* been careless. I don't want another child, I tell you. But diaphragms aren't a hundred per cent certain – '

'Spare me the details.'

'All right, I'll spare you the details. But one detail you can't be spared and that is the fact that we'll have to move. We can't go on living here. I can't face it, three flights with a baby as well as Nick. And it's cramped enough already. We'll have to find somewhere more suitable for a family.'

'Family – ' Robert said it softly like a swear-word. 'You think you're going to get me that way? Turn me into a family man?'

I set my jaw sullenly.

'I can't turn you into anything. You're turning yourself into some kind of oafish Peter Pan, trying to pretend nothing's changed since you were a student. Look – ' I pleaded suddenly, 'if we're to have any hope of keeping our sanity we *have* to find somewhere bigger than this to live.'

Robert's jaw also set.

'We are not moving. I will not cripple myself with debt and mortgages just so that you can swan around in bungalow-land.'

'I don't want to live in bungalow-land. I just want us to get out of here. There's no *room*, Robert. Can't you see for youself?'

But if he could he wouldn't. Oh we were back on form again – but don't be taken in by that faint suggestion of relish. Robert (as well as Joaquin) may have had his moments of trying to persuade me I totally misunderstood myself, that I wasn't after peace and quiet, I was a fighter in my bones. It would certainly explain our fervent antagonism and our eerie understanding of each other. Maybe he was right. But as far as I knew myself I was, at this point, simply sick with dread and this hideous sense of *déjà vu*. Another child? Never! It had just got to the point where the combination of Nick and myself and Robert was possible without flailing anger on someone's side, all of us given to explosions of one kind or another. And now this precarious harmony was shattered, truly shattered, by the sly meeting up of sperm and egg.

If Tom had still been around, maybe he might have been able to intercede, persuade Robert to contemplate what Robert seemed unable to contemplate without suspecting a long conspiracy laid step by step to ensnare him. But there was no point in approaching Tom. They had not spoken since the day in early November when he had walked out of the flat.

Instead I turned to Esther, in tears, and she did try to intercede for me. All she got for her pains, poor soul, was the kind of bawling out usually reserved for me. She said I was a 'good girl trying to do her best by Nick and the next little one. You can't ignore your responsibilities, Robert luv, not on and on – ' and he told her savagely to keep out and mind her own business and whose responsibility was it anyway, that there was another child on the way? As if a woman were by her very pregnability a guilty creature.

And somehow from then on the forthcoming child was referred to, if at all, as something entirely to do with me, my child, my fault. And if I had only realised it, through the dazed months that followed, I was nourishing two offspring inside my rounding body, the healthy buoyant baby that Louis turned out eventually to be, and another lusty thing, the steady black passion of my hatred beside which all the earlier

195

versions, the anger and the brooding and sense of neglect, proved to be whimsical stuff. It grew as gradually and as quietly as the other, its enormity largely hidden from me. The days were too stretched with anxiety, with silent avoiding, with wondering how I was going to cope. My embroideries gathered dust, no pictures moved in my mind. I was overtaken by a kind of animal fatalism. I simply did not know what was going to happen.

Much, much later Tom said, in one of his rare attempts to defend his brother, that Robert had always been scared and disgusted by pregnancy, that the whole threat and menace of uncontrollable fertility, meaning more hardship, more desperation, was something that sent him into panic paranoia. And, man's right to gratification being unquestioned, the fault was of course to be found in the passive malevolence, the ultimate power to burden, of a woman's body.

I refused to listen to Tom. I was not prepared to try and see the barbarous treatment I'd experienced as some aspect of a symbolic war against my whole sisterhood. Even in crisis, perhaps particularly in crisis, one's claim to unique harm must be upheld.

That was much later. At the time it was Janos who took on the impossible task of trying to soften my attitude. I hadn't intended to tell him about being pregnant, not to begin with, anyway. But he soon saw through my forced attempts to jolly on as usual. And when he did eventually succeed in making me laugh truly it ended up with crying. Instinctively I made for the part of the kitchen where I couldn't be seen from the living room. He asked distractedly what was the matter, and I told him. I just blurted it all out, about the unwanted child and Robert's fury and his refusal to move. And meanwhile the bardic voices rose and fell in the other room, itemising the many and complex stages of Scotland's cultural annihilation.

Janos had noticed, he said, that Robert was treating me unkindly. It distressed him very much. He had been so good to him, so extraordinarily kind.

I was past caring whether I split their friendship. I told him the story of my marriage. Bit by bit, over the pots of coffee or tea when he was helping me tidy up in the kitchen, I told him everything – everything, that is, except Joaquin. And he listened, night after night, and I could feel his distracted helpless wish to do something miraculous and make things better. It helped, a little, and so did the fact that he never made me feel that my little personal disaster of a wrong marriage was petty compared to what he had experienced. And so did the fact that he didn't want to cut and run when I cried, which I frequently did. The corner beside the cooker by the shelves with the pots and pans was the best place to retire to, to keep out of sight.

Poor Janos! I can see his face, pained, sympathising, bewildered, caught between the two of us. There was Robert, coming to the kitchen door, 'Come on, no need to do the chores, man. Yer pints behind the rest of us' – gradually as the weeks passed becoming gruffer, more resentful, hurt, I suppose. More outrageous. 'You can leave that cow to her own devices. If she's so tired she should get to her bed, not have you skivvying for her.'

'I will come, I will come. Just in a minute.'

Thus Janos, trying to pick his way along this tightrope that would one day snap. But his guts were on my side. He couldn't bear to see me carrying things. He fetched the coal, he filled the kettle and made the tea. The big tray he had always carried. He tried to pour his physical energy into my life to make up for Robert's sulking avoidance. Nick still needed to be lifted at about ten o'clock. It was Janos who lifted him.

And yet still he remained loyal to Robert.

'He is such a gifted man, you know. His poetry, some of it is marvellous, strong and passionate. And he has a kind of fiery vision. Like a prophet. He says one day, when we have learnt the art of living, when we stop wasting all our time and energy in existing, then life will be always poetry, always inspired always magnificent – '

'Perhaps,' I said viciously, 'you have to learn the art of existing first.'

And to myself I cursed Robert for his passion and his visions, leaving me to get on with the brute facts of existence. I too had had my visions. I had wanted to be Mary sitting at the feet, passing the time in vital discourse, mind and spirit

197

uplifted. Nobody consulted me about becoming weary, nagging, thankless Martha.

Janos quickly changed the subject. But another evening he came back to it. He had come across Robert a day or two before sitting quite alone in a pub near the university. He had gone over to speak to him and Robert had turned slowly and said, 'Go away, Janos, I'm not fit company for man or beast.' And Janos, who had never before been treated to one of Robert's black moods, said he had never seen anyone look so desperate.

He asked, 'Are you all right?' and was told to go to hell. Next day Robert said he was sorry.

'I think,' he said in a puzzled way, 'that he is quite frightened of something, something painful, and also very frightened in case the pain is seen. He is like a fugitive, hiding and running away, hiding and running away. You know, I feel very sorry for him. He is an enemy to himself.'

It was brave of him to say that, and to meet my eyes as he said it.

I was sitting sprawled on a kitchen chair, my feet out in front of me. There was a ladder in my stocking and my shoes which had once been wine-red were a scuffed mahogany and needed heeling. My feet were not helpful, so I tucked them out of sight beneath the bulge that was to be Louis. Something warred and locked in my chest.

I looked at Janos. Even if it smashed our friendship, our lovely curious friendship still with its pre-loverly adolescent quality in spite of everything, I could not admit the thought of Robert in distress. What about me, my distress? And so my voice came out childish and high-pitched as I said, 'Well, if you're so sorry for him, go and comfort him. I shan't. I *can't*.' And I turned away from him.

He just stood there. I think I expected him to rush to the task of winning me round. I had forgotten that this was not just any young man of nineteen. He was older by far than me. He had had a rough taste of death and what it does to the little order of the living. Perhaps he did have the kind of insight that usually comes from living long. All he said was, 'Carla, Carla, is there no way you can be a little bit forgiving? It will only damage

198

you, this bitterness. It will eat up your life, your only life. Carla, you are too–' he paused, suddenly at a loss, 'I–look it is important. You are a lovely person. With the power to be joyful.'

'How *can* you say that?'

'Because I have seen it. When we laugh together. When you show me a picture in a book. When you listen. When your mind is not angry or frightened. Don't kill that.'

I think I literally wrung my hands.

'I don't know how. I don't know how to think about forgiving, not after the way he's reacted to the baby coming.'

'Then leave him.'

'What – like this?'

I looked down at my stomach.

Janos put his hands up to his temples and squeezed them. He breathed hard.

'If I had money, if only I had some money I would take you away. I would give it to you. I would make it possible for you to leave. I would help you altogether.' He turned away. 'But since I have none, those are only words. I had better go through now, before Robert starts getting angry.'

26

At the end of August Louis was born, a late summer baby, an easy delivery, eight pounds of fair healthy humankind, an amazing gift of natural joy and pride at the end of that stormy gestation. All the wonder of neatly folded ears, miniscule fingernails, fine line drawing of lips and eyelids on this new, glistening new face, blank yet cleanly printed here and there with the person-to-be, a curve of curiosity round the nostrils, peaked furrowlets where eyebrows would be – all this was mine for the first time. I had been too drugged and battered over Nick's birth.

Louis had the questionable gift of winning hearts before he could properly open his eyes. Stella was enchanted. Esther said he looked like a fairy baby. The nurses had christened him 'the little prince', because of glinting golden down growing in a kind of shadowy tonsure on his fine round skull.

Some hearts he did not win. Robert was rather drunk when he came to see me and the baby for the first time. He stood swaying a little, looking in some disgust at this pink creature already with some of the angel-child quality which was to haunt his boyhood and enrage his brother.

'That is no son of mine,' he declared emphatically.

The nurse who was standing by the cradle which she had just wheeled into my room, for it was near feeding time, laughed a little uncomfortably.

'You think we've got the name tags mixed? Don't worry, Mr. Carmichael. Many a parent gets a shock from a recessive gene.'

'Ah,' he said sarcastically, 'we're educated, are we?'

The nurse, whose nostrils were alert and who was now looking disapproving, said brusquely, 'Do you suppose nurses are morons?' and left us to it.

Robert sat on my bed. He smelt of fags and drink and wet weather. His raincoat was damp but he didn't bother to do more than unloosen it. He didn't touch me except to pick up a strand of my hair, dark as his own. 'And how has this shining blond infant managed to emerge from your swarthy loins?' he asked.

I laughed in the stilted uncertain way one does when in doubt whether something is a joke or not.

'In the usual way.' To myself I thought: 'Oh, you can sneer. But you told me this child was mine, nothing to do with you, and so it is – all mine.'

'But who's the father, Carla?'

He leant towards me, lurched, rather, but steadied himself upright again.

I laughed again, even more uncertainly. If this was a joke he was taking it too far by half.

'He's a surprise, isn't he? A throw-back to my mother's side, I suppose. A lot of her family were blonde. Unless you've got some fair genes somewhere in your family?'

He looked at me owlishly.

'Not one. Not a single blonde gene. And I'm having no truck with a blonde son – ' he looked scathingly across at the cradle – 'that peeled shrimp – '

My easily swung emotions rose angrily.

'Hey – just a minute. You can call me what you like, but leave the child alone – '

'Leave the child alone!' He mimicked my voice squeakily. 'Oh my God! The great and wonderful powers of mother-love. But I'll call him what I like. Yes. It's a free world, so they say. I'll call him what I like. I'll call him a bastard.'

He frowned, fumbling a cigarette out of a packet produced from the damp raincoat.

'Look, you're not supposed to smoke in here, not when the baby's – '

'Oh shut up.' He lit up after two or three scrapes with the

match, and flung it on the floor where fortunately it went out. 'Now, the thing is, we've got a problem.' God, how I loathe the pseudo-solemn phase of drunkenness. 'Here is the problem, Carla. Even bastards have fathers. We have to find a father for your bastard. You know, just to keep the record straight.' He swayed again and I wondered whether to ring the bell and get him kicked out, but held back, thinking how awful it would be to have one's husband escorted away drunk and disorderly from visiting hour.

He sat and smoked in silence for a few minutes, his breath coming out noisily, his heavy engine breathing. I lay quite still keeping an eye on the baby who was still sleeping.

'I have an idea,' said Robert at last, his voice gravelly. He seemed to be getting drunker. 'I think that baby's half Hungarian.'

'Robert – ' I felt myself getting hot. Milk trickled like sweat from my breasts. 'Stop this horrible game. The baby's yours. You know it. It was conceived before – before Janos had even come to the flat. And there's never been anything – anything. How could there be? He's your friend. He thinks the world of you.'

'Well, he has a very funny way of showing it.' He was sounding pontifical, self-righteous now, pulpit-drunk. 'He all but carried your slops for you.'

'And was that so terrible? Such a breach of friendship?'

'Friendship? What's friendship? There's no such thing. Every man for himself. Help yerself to the next chap's wife. Why not? Aw – shit, the lot of you! I shit on you!' His voice had risen.

'Robert – please, don't shout – '

The baby made a sudden little wail. I scrambled out of bed and went to pick him up and immediately I felt calm and peaceful and quite unscared. I looked at Robert over the small bundle in my arms.

'Perhaps it's nothing more sinister than common decency, the way Janos behaved. Perhaps he simply didn't like seeing a pregnant woman carrying buckets of coal and hanging around to feed you and your so-called friends late in the evening. If that makes him the father of this child, then he is. At least he kept me from going altogether crazy. But don't you dare take it out on him!'

Robert subsided, shrugging and muttering. Perhaps an angry woman with a child in her arms struck some chord of matriarchal power, something before which macho drunks traditionally lose their nerve. He said no more on the subject of Louis' parentage.

'You'd better go now. It's time for me to feed the baby.'

He dowsed the cigarette he wasn't supposed to be smoking in the orange drink on my bedside table. It made a faint sizzle and left a stench in the air.

'Give my love to Nick.'

Even that felt like something far too personal to pass between us. Nick was with Esther, the breach between her and Robert having been partially healed for the purpose.

Robert left without a word.

I slept badly that night, dozing uneasily between feeds. Of course he would forget what he'd said. It had been a piece of drunken malice. It would be lost by the time he'd recovered from his hangover. Still I felt thoroughly jangled and un-nerved by the keenness of his nose for the unsaid things of my life. Not, I may say, that even my straying fantasies had made any kind of allegorical connection between Janos and my surprising blonde baby. No, if there were any fantasy involved it was that I had produced him alone, quite alone. His colouring only served to emphasise that Robert was insignificant in his creation. To that extent, we were in agreement, Robert and I. This was no son of his. I think it was the only way I could redeem the past months. And after all, I had pulled triumph out of humiliation. I had produced this magical princeling, delivering him properly with the midwife saying, 'Good *girl*, you're doing fine, you're doing just lovely' – not, as with poor Nick, a matter of having a stone dislodged with much pain and a lot of tearing. Secure in the world of women and babies, I could afford to feel scornful, victorious.

Janos came to visit me bringing freesias and fern and chocolate cake. I don't know what he lived on for the rest of the week, for the cake was large and delicious and came from

Fuller's. I insisted we have some straight away and gouged out slices with my fruit knife serving it on paper hankies. In my pretty nightie, a present from Stella, leaning back on pillows, free for a day or more to cry and laugh and enjoy my child, I felt transformed – back into girlhood and irresponsibility rather than onward into maturity. After the cake-eating was over we sat holding hands, while Janos made me laugh with stories of his land-lady and her friends.

As visiting hour was drawing to an end I asked him, 'Would you like to see the baby?'

We went along together to the nursery where I persuaded the nurse to bring Louis to the door – which as a mighty favour she agreed to do. Janos stared down at my little pink son with the gold fluff on his head, and the baby obligingly opened his unseeing blue eyes and gave that full disconcerting stare of blank omniscience. Janos said, 'He's lovely – ' and then laughed. 'But what a surprise! As if an olive tree had suddenly produced a peach.' And like Robert a few days before he picked up a strand of my near-black hair, but unlike Robert he kissed it. The nurse was staring at us curiously.

'Feeding time in fifteen minutes, Mrs. Carmichael' she reminded me as she turned away with Louis.

We walked back along the corridor from the nursery, our arms round each other, lovers of a sort with all the vital bits unspoken and understood, the prohibitions and impossibilities swallowed obediently like medicine, passions banked down, but there in the small touch, the tender concern, the feeling that a smile was a gift, a winged shaft coming from the sun. It was a very odd sort of lovers' lane, with dressing-gowned women shuffling around in various stages of post-natal tenderness and a cleaner mopping over the floor with an O-cedar mop. The pungent smell of polish followed us back to the little private ward which my father in one of his erratic gestures of kindness had negotiated for me.

Janos stood uneasily. I picked up his coat and said I thought it was probably time to go.

'When do you come home?'

'In about ten days' time, I think.' I paused. 'I shall go to my sister's when I leave here for a few days. You know, I don't think you had better come round to the flat for a bit. It's going to be – quite difficult, I think, settling in with the baby. Robert – he's taken a sort of dislike to him.'

I glanced at him anxiously, fearing that even in this guarded way I was getting far too near revealing Robert's outrageous idea. He nodded sadly.

'He's not very friendly now. I don't know what I've done.'

'Helped me too much. That's all. You've done nothing wrong.'

'Carla, I – '

'What?'

'If things get too bad for you – I hope they will not – but if they do, will you *promise* me you get in touch? I will do anything to help. Surely I can help some way?'

We kissed and parted as friends, passionate friends. There was no point in letting restraint crack now.

27

On my last night in hospital I dreamed that I had run away, I and my small new baby. We crossed a town at night, and I went into a café to ask for baby food, odd since I was in reality breast-feeding. And I was worried all the time about his catching cold. He seemed to be too scantily clothed. His blanket kept slipping off him. In the cafe it was warm. They would prepare baby milk for him.

It was one of those dreams which give up slowly. I woke still deep in its reality, wondering indeed where I had run to. Then the ward formed itself round me. Early light squared off the window behind the shutters. Stella was to pick me up in her car later on, around ten o'clock. We would go back to her house for a few days until I was properly on my feet again. As I lay there it seemed crystal clear. Do not go back. Run with your baby. Run away. Where?

Once or twice at Stella's I thought, 'What would she say, what would happen if I just said out loud, right here and now: "Stella, I've run away. I'm not going back. Things are too bad"?' Presented her with a *fait accompli*. But I doubted my powers to make the fact stick. I could see her face, lifted sudden and startled as it had that time before, and the cold anxiety wiping out the friendly concern. She was very friendly just now, enchanted with Louis, fussing over me. Chicken that I was, I couldn't stand the thought of all that vanishing. Stella's voice would go cold and say things like, 'You always exaggerate, Carla, you always have. When you were a kid you'd bring the tiniest scratches to be *bandaged*, or say you'd fallen twenty feet when it was only two.' Yes, but paradoxically I also went around once with a broken bone in my foot having fallen out of a tree I wasn't supposed to climb. In the interests of concealment I could be stoically, ridiculously brave, that is to say, foolhardy. 'Why ever didn't you say?' Mary had asked in dismay when X-rays had eventually revealed all. It was the broken branch I'd been more concerned about, father staring at it angry and mystified. I was a real coward about facing displeasure. Yet it never kept me from doing things that provoked it.

I said nothing to Stella, not directly. She was upset when I announced I was leaving three days earlier than we'd agreed on.

'Why? Wouldn't you be better to get really rested before going back?'

'I daren't put it off any longer. In case I lose my nerve.'

That was her opening. She side-stepped it neatly. 'Well, all the more reason to be thoroughly fit. You stay on here till the end of the week.'

'No. I can't. Really I can't. Esther's probably at her wits' end with Nick.'

I had heard nothing from Robert. Stella said, at long last, 'Are you really so dreading going back?'

'Well – ' I began slowly, my stomach churning at the thought of telling my tale of humiliation in all its sordid detail and possibly, probably, having it pushed aside, spurned, something tacky and objectionable but not grounds for action, of the kind that has repercussions. 'It's been very difficult. Very, very difficult. Because he's so mad about having another child.'

'Yes, but surely now he's seen him, I mean, Louis is the most lovely baby. No one could be anything but proud, surely?'

You will notice that Robert had become 'him'.

'It's not like that. He – he says it's not his child, and he doesn't want anything to do with him because he's blonde.'

'But that's absolutely – he must be – ' Stella stopped short. Her eyes suddenly flicked towards me and away again. I could almost hear the buzz of the thought she was trying to suppress, like a sneeze in church.

'No,' I said drily, emphatically. 'I have not. And he isn't. He *is* Robert's son.'

Stella blushed.

'I didn't really – ' She tried to resume her loyal outrage. 'He must be out of his mind to say a thing like that. But then, insults are his speciality, aren't they?'

'Yes, they are. I suppose – I can only hope he'll cool down. He was drunk when he said all that.'

I don't know to whom I was offering crumbs of comfort, myself or Stella. They stuck violently in her throat.

'*Drunk*? When he came to see the baby?'

'Yes.'

She looked appalled, weak with it. She put down her needlework and wiped her hands.

'Oh God, Carla, you really are in a mess, aren't you?'

I was so taken aback at the effect of this revelation, a commonplace of my life, that I failed to make the most of it. That was the moment. That was the moment to have pressed home the impossibility of going back.

My sister sat looking into painful space. She seemed to be struggling with her thoughts. Finally she said carefully, 'I'll keep in touch. We'll see each other regularly. You can bring the kids here. I'll come over and get you so that you don't have the fret of the journey. I do want to – help, Carla?'

There was that upnote of pleading. It seemed to say, 'Will that do? Will that count as help? Without me having to go the whole hog?'

It was absurd, but shaky and scared as I was I saw that she was more so. I felt I had to protect her. To keep her intact as my older sister with her certainties and her confidence. I knew she didn't know much; that her confidence was brittle and based on shutting out. But such is the hold of traditional rights. That's what families are all about, primogeniture and the stacking of generations and the almost mystical power of older over younger. Why did it seem so important to safeguard *that*? When the other matter, my own life, was urgently signalling danger?

That said life seems to have been nothing but a daft dialectic between fatal rushings in and equally fatal hanging back. I missed my moment, again. The next day I went back. Stella left me at the foot of the stairs. She offered to help me up with the baby's things, but Esther, whom I'd 'phoned, came down and we managed between us.

The flat. Best not think about it too clearly. It stank, not only of its usual smoke and dregs but of rousing biological decay. This had been accomplished quite easily in the twelve days of my absence by the simple means of never throwing out any rubbish, and since it had coincided with a spell of late season warmth – 'Indian summer' we all said idyllically at Stella's, lazing out on her lawn – the bacteriological activity had been tremendous. Robert was never an orderly man at any time, but this mess was a special effort, a filthy gesture like saying 'up yours' to any idea that a woman who had just had a baby required any kind of special consideration.

I was fortunately as strong as a horse. With Esther's help we got the place more or less cleaned up over the next few days. I hardly saw Robert. He came in to sleep and eat breakfast and that was more or less that. Stella was as good as her word. She came round quite often to take us out, either over to her house or for a drive into the country. I would be waiting for her at the foot of stairs, or she would toot and wait. I knew she hated coming inside the flat and spared her that. It was very strange, this split-level living, falling back for the space of an afternoon into the leisured moneyed ways of Stella's life and then climbing the stairs back again to Hades.

Robert was not bringing his friends round any more. I saw almost no one. I longed to know how Janos was getting on. I missed him appallingly, but didn't dare ask for news. And then, one day, I got a letter from him. I suppose it was a love letter, for it started 'My sweet Carla –' but it was full of proper queries about the baby and my health, and some news about himself including the fact that he'd dropped out of Robert's course – 'it seemed better'. It ended with decorum. 'I am your true friend for always, Janos.' And then, under that, dashed off obviously at a different time, one single passionate sentence. 'If I could be in your arms that is my heaven.' Oh God! Coming in the middle of this desert, grey desert of approaching winter, slate-banked days of late autumn, how can I not clasp this precious piece of paper literally to my heart? I wore it tucked into my brassiere for the rest of the day, then transferred it to the torn lining of my handbag folded small, a process of weaning which was to end up in a litter bin.

Only it never got that far. Why should Nicky suddenly have reverted to an old habit, an old game we used to play more than a year ago when I first brought all the exciting beads back to the flat? I would empty my handbag and hide beads in the pockets and under the torn lining and he would dig down into it, excitement of a Christmas stocking, to find treasure. And now, one morning after a particularly broken night with the baby, Robert and I both white-faced and exhausted, here is Nicky emptying the contents of my handbag on the kitchen floor and digging with his strong little hands. And suddenly he starts to cry and says: 'No beads!' and flings a little folded wad of paper across the floor in disgust and it lands at Robert's feet. Perhaps there is something too deliberate about that folding, something not casual, for he hesitates, about to kick it into the grate. He bends down and picks it up. I notice even as I stir the porridge with a hand suddenly stiffened, that he is getting clumsy, thick fingers funbling with the scrap of paper. He is starting to blow up all over. I try to say something offhand like 'Oh, put that rubbish in the coal hod', but my lips too have gone stiff and my mouth sticky with a sudden drying up of saliva. It is too late to curse myself for most astounding folly, but I do just the same. And then all inner things stop. For Robert has unfolded the paper and has read it and he raises his head slowly and says, very deliberately, 'You cunt! You bloody lying cunt!' And his jaw suddenly masses down and I see the inevitable speeding towards me.

I saw it speeding towards me with such certainty and such terror that everything slowed down, down, down. . . . I had time to think, 'Get the gas out, push that pan as far away as possible. Move away from Nick.' I got as far as the other side of the room before Robert grabbed my shoulder and then, smash. He hit me in the face, *his* face looking as if every nerve were a string and someone had suddenly pulled them all squint. And then, from some tangled gut of fury, words –

'You cunt! You think you can do it twice and get away with it? You stinking bitch! I'll mess you up good and proper,' and his hand lammed into my face again.

Yes, he beat me up good and proper – though not, as these things go, viciously. No kicked-in ribs, no blunt instruments, just a solid thudding round my head and face which felt as if I was being dashed against something vast and solid like a house or a cliff.

Then Nick started screaming. At least, I've always believed they were his screams. I have a vision of him running like a demented little clockwork toy from one side of the kitchen to the other, then finally hurling himself at my legs in his old baby rugger-tackle clutch.

'Mind the kid – ' I managed to get out.

Robert did mind his kid. He stepped back gasping, and I don't know any more about his actions, for, reeling and sick, I made for the bedroom and the carry-cot with the baby, grabbed poor sobbing Nick by the arm and staggered across the landing to Esther's.

It was early for visiting. I wondered in a ghastly panic whether she'd even bother getting out of bed, so as well as ringing the bell I clattered and clattered at the letter-flap and shouted, 'Esther! Esther! Let me in. It's me – Carla.'

I almost fell inside when she eventually opened the door, flattened against it in a panic that at any moment my own door would burst open and flight be cut off. She was in her slippers and dressing-gown, hair tangled and mouth sunk in (by this time those heroic dental survivors had been replaced by the inevitable glass-by-the-side-of-the-bed), a frown of sleepy irritation which vanished when she saw my face.

'Oh my God – oh my poor girl – ' there was a sort of hushed horror in her voice and a hint of seeing an old familiar enemy. She brought us in, lifting Nick and cradling him like a baby – some weight for an elderly woman – while the shock seemed to loosen some long-stored dread for us all.

'I tried, Carla, I promise you I did – oh God, what got into him? Oh my poor girl! And the baby, only weeks old. Why in God's name were they made so vicious? I *told* him, before he

211

bawled me out – it wouldn't work, not all squashed in together. Oh, he's a devil with that temper! I've been afraid for you, luv – '

By this time she had steered us into the kitchen. 'There, there – ' she kept saying, stroking Nick's hair, patting my shoulder, then back to Nick and his asthmatic sobbing. Finally she eased him onto a chair and went, inevitably, to put on the kettle. At some point she got in her teeth.

As I sipped my tea, having to use two hands to lift the shaking mug to my lips, I knew what I had to do. It sounded clear through the throbbing dizziness and shock. Pain and collapse came later, much later.

'I have to 'phone home.' I must get home, back to father. Only he would do. Only he was strong enough. Stella? No. Robert's fury could get past her any day. I saw him coming after me, raging across Edinburgh, the job uncompleted. I needed to be inside a fortress.

'I have to 'phone home.'

'Can you manage?'

Esther helped me get up, steadied me, and held my arm as I made my way to the 'phone. It was Mary who answered.

'Mary – ' It was easier to say what I had to say to her than to father. There was a shocked pause.

'Stay where you are. I'll come and get you in the car.'

'No, no.' For some reason I wouldn't have that. 'I'll get a taxi.'

There must be a gap. I must cross the city myself, make my wounded flight, years too late, on my own.

Esther 'phoned for a taxi. I had no money but counted on father or Mary to pay. I wouldn't accept Esther's money knowing how little she had and not knowing when or how I would get it back to her.

'This is the end,' I said.

'Yes.'

She sounded utterly defeated, as though recognising the futility of hoping the worst won't happen. She'd done so much to try and help us, Robert as well as myself, but she didn't venture a word on his behalf.

'After this you can't go back.'

212

I shut my swelling eyes for a moment. Somebody had at last said it. Decisions didn't come into it.

We kept peering down into the street for the taxi.

'I'll be in touch' I said again and again. 'We mustn't lose touch.' I was still clutching the handles of the carry-cot with Louis sleeping like a rosebud after being fretful half the night. But Esther, now dressed, insisted on carrying him down when the taxi arrived. She was frightened, as I was not, by the state I was in.

We crept quietly out of her front door. My legs were spongy with terror as we made our way slowly, oh so slowly, across the landing and down the first flight of stairs. At any minute I expected to hear the sound of my own front door bursting open. But there was silence, uncanny silence, and the door remained shut. Perhaps he'd gone out to work – good God, think of facing a room full of chattering students with your fists still tingling from messing up a woman's face. Or perhaps he was still inside. A horrible idea. Beast in its lair, minotaur in the maze, menace at the heart of silence. I staggered out onto the street and a cold blast of air proclaimed the outside world.

The taxi-driver stared and stared.

'Oh come on,' said Esther boisterously, 'don't pretend you've never seen a bashing before. Just take them to Lauderdale Gardens – what number is it, ducks? Twenty, number twenty. And no questions – understand?' Sudden ferocity which caused the neck of the driver to pinken.

It was not yet half-past eight when we reached my old home, a dull raw November morning drenching everything with that peculiar sullen light in which every line less emphatic than a vertical and every shape less tailored than a right angle disappears, colour a lost concept.

I told the taxi driver to wait while I asked inside for some money. My battered face seemed to quell any argument. I held Nick by one hand and the carrycot in the other, as strange a parade as ever walked up my father's well-kept garden path. And of all things I suddenly had a picture of myself walking up this selfsame path rather drunk and very dishevelled after a student fancy-dress ball. I had gone as Harlequin. It was a chance to show off my legs in domino tights. I remember my friend Susie cursing over the painting of those tights which took the whole afternoon and left me dominoed for another week. I'd kept my mask on and hidden my hair under a cap and no one had recognised me until the fun hotted up and I was forcibly unmasked and decapped. And then in the early daylight I staggered aimiably up the garden path while the gaggle of friends who had walked me home disappeared down the road. And the cold stone house had the same air then as it had now – of remaining in a kind of glacial trance, a trance of unassailable dignity aloof from the heat of either fun or pain.

I remember, in my jolly inebriated state, rather enjoying the swimmy feeling of wondering which was real, me, fagged out but still high and excited from the party, or that tight solid house with its path of flagstones and its two oval beds of roses. The same reality couldn't hold us both.

And once again, I felt it, struggling along with my two sons and my head beating and throbbing. The house stood aloof, expressionless, disowning this extraordinary apparition as it had disowned tipsy Harlequin. Oh but you *must*, you must not reduce me to some mental aberration! This is it, I am real, let me in!

Nick was shivering and whimpering in the cold. He held my hand so tightly I had to put Louis down in order to ring the bell.

'It's all right, Nick,' I said. 'Someone's coming. You'll be warm in a minute.'

Mary opened the door. We walked in without saying a word. She took the carry-cot from me and put it on the hall seat. Then she put her arms round me very gently. I thought I should have burst into a flood of tears but they were frozen stiff. I was, after all, a daughter of that house.

28

We stood back from each other.

'I'm getting rooms ready for you and the children,' she said at last. 'I think you should go and see your father.'

She sounded nervous, uncertain. I was aware that she was waiting for some kind of pronouncement from him, perhaps a definition, a clarification.

'Don't worry about the baby. I'll keep an eye on him.'

Louis had opened sleepy blue eyes and was starting to make faint sucking noises against his fist.

'I'll have to feed him soon.'

'Well, just go and have a chat with your father first. He's in the dining-room.'

So they still had a full-spread breakfast every day, did they? The silver was out and shining. The room was warm. Father was busy buttering toast when I went in, a Jove-like absorption in grave matters, such as getting the slicing into three equal fingers exactly right. He took one look at my face and his knife dropped.

'Oh my God,' he said in a funny high-pitched voice, just as he had when I told him I was pregnant by Robert.

'Oh father – ' I ran towards him, but he stopped me from putting my arms round him by holding out his hand and grabbing mine. We held onto each other, gripping hard. I could feel his fingers working in mine, whether affection or nervousness I don't know. They were bony, spare, hard.

'Sit down, my dear.' Nick was hanging onto my skirt. 'Mary's getting things ready for you. Not your old room, I'm afraid, because that's rather too near to my own quarters. And frankly, I was never very tolerant of the sound of infant wailing and have made no progress over the years. We decided the rooms in the basement.'

I sat down, pulling Nick onto my lap. He dug his fingers into me and stayed motionless, clinging like a little monkey. I appeared to be sitting at Mary's place. In front of me were her unfinished yoghourt and half-drunk glass of fresh orange juice. She struggled perseveringly against her weight.

'Have – have you eaten?'

I said no, but I wasn't hungry.

'Some coffee, then. What about coffee?'

Yes, I would like that. No, don't get a clean cup, Mary's will do.

At last he said huskily, 'Your face looks – very painful. They say raw steak, don't they? I never know why. I wonder if we have such a thing? Do you think you should – er – bathe it? Warm salted water, perhaps?'

I shook my head very slightly.

'I just want to stay here and get warm.'

'Yes, yes, of course.'

He looked uneasy. I waited, mutely asking to be asked something, anything. I would stand in the dock if necessary. I didn't care if he thought I was the guilty one, I just wanted him to *ask* something. I didn't care if any man, even my own father, thought I was at fault because I knew, absolutely in my bones, that my basic flaw was simply to be a woman who had not got the hang of things, who did not know how to melt into invisibility or slither into new shapes to try and find favour. That was why I had got beaten up, because I was what I was, not because of poor Janos's little letter. It would have come. It was always there, the possibility.

'Carla, what – '

At that moment the telephone rang. Father got up to answer it. It was Stella, to talk to me. They had already told her.

'Are you all right? Are you all right?' She sounded dreadfully agitated.

'Well, I'm pretty shaken up – '

216

'Yes, but thank God you sound like yourself. I was afraid – look, we'll talk later. I'm just ringing up to find out what you need. I don't suppose there was much chance to – '

'We ran, Stella. We've got nothing. There's just me and Nicky and the baby in the carry-cot. I haven't even a spare nappy for him.'

'Right.' Her voice had steadied up. 'I know where to start, then. I'll come round, after I've been shopping. Now don't *worry*. I'll see to everything.'

We sat around for the rest of the morning, Nick and I, as though we were the survivors of a shipwreck. My milk had not all suddenly dried up with shock, so I fed Louis as usual. Nor did it seem to taste of gall or other bitter things. His new sturdy little life ticked placidly on, apparently unaffected by the upheavals of the morning. Mary thought I ought to lie down but it was easier coping with Nick on my feet. There was no question of separating him from his hold on my skirt, my pullover, my knee, or whatever other bit of my person he could grab. Around noon he fell at last into a deep sleep.

'My dear,' said Mary timidly, 'I do think we should do something about your face.'

She looked exhausted, having worked all morning to get the rooms in the basement clean and ready. We were too much, we were already too much, one beat-up mother, one half hysterical child and one very new baby. I felt the inner house, the web of routines and private order, listing like an over-cargoed vessel. I was genuinely concerned for her.

At that point Stella appeared, parcels under each arm, carrier bags in each hand. When she saw my face she went pale. I was too much for her too. She took refuge in anger once Mary had left the room.

'That idiotic woman – why didn't she tell me you'd been *hurt*? All she said was "there's been an incident". Incident! And why hasn't she *done* something about it?'

'Oh, you're not to get on to Mary. She's been running all morning. We were just going to see to it – my face. Anyway Nick's only just gone to sleep. He's so upset, I couldn't do anything.'

'Well, I'm going to 'phone for Fergus straight away.' Her

lips were trembling. I think she wanted to cry. 'You've got a cut over your eyebrow which might very well need stitching. And he might know of something to help take down the swellings – '

To tell the truth, I simply had not dared to look at myself. I didn't know what I had, exactly, in the way of cuts and bruises. My mind had been all on the children, such mind as I had left.

'He's coming round right away.' Stella reappeared looking slightly better. 'Now for the Lord's sake, Carla, come downstairs and get to bed. Mary's getting a hot bottle ready.'

She helped me down the stairs to the basement. There was a gas fire burning in the room that was to be my bedroom. Radiators were clicking and honking into action. It was strange coming down into this part of the house. It had never been properly used by us as a family. At one time maids had slept down here. At another, briefly, it had been let out, almost a self-contained flat with its own door in from the garden. Most of the pipes in the house appeared to originate from here. It was my first impression, pipes, and coconut matting.

Stella helped me get undressed. She'd brought over a nightie among all the other things for the children.

'Don't go,' I said urgently, once I was tucked into bed. 'Don't leave me alone.'

'No, no, all right. Just try and be calm. You're all right now, you know, you're quite safe.'

Tears were at last rolling down my face.

'What a mess, Stella, what a horrible mess!'

I wept into the fresh scented hankie she lent me. She looked almost as devastated as I felt. She took me in her arms to comfort me but I felt her fear and even a sort of repugnance.

'Why didn't you tell me,' she almost whispered, 'that this is what you were afraid of?'

I pulled myself away and looked at her.

'I – well, there are – you don't always – there are some things you don't spell out to yourself.' I tried to leave it at that but couldn't stop myself. 'In any case, I don't suppose you'd have believed me.'

Stella stared back at me without speaking. Her lips parted and closed again. She seemed to readjust her face over the unsaid thing, whatever it might have been. Then she got up and started opening her parcels.

'Where shall I put the things I've brought for the children?'

'Oh, in here, anywhere you can find. We'll all be sharing this room for the next while.'

The door bell rang somewhere above us.

'That'll be Fergus.'

She went hastily out of the room. I heard their voices a few minutes later, a duet of high-key dismay and low-key reassurance, as they came down the stairs.

'Well, I'll leave you to it,' Stella said on the other side of the door.

I hadn't seen Fergus Johnson, our family doctor, since the time he had declared me pregnant. After my marriage I'd re-registered with a practice in the area where we lived. He was an iron-grey man who would not get old, he would simply weather and become a little gaunt, perhaps eventually a little bent. As far as I could see, he was unchanged by the passage of four years.

'Well, well, Carla lass.' He warmed his hands in front of the gas fire, knobby practical hands more like a tradesman's than a doctor's. Then he took hold of mine in both of his warmed ones. 'You've run into something pretty hard by the looks of things.' There is nothing like a voice, a gentle practised voice, to calm and settle the whirling litter and dust of a shocked mind. 'Let's have a proper look, then.'

After probing gently round my aching, ringing skull he did rather painful things to the cut above my eye, cleaning it up. After a few minutes thought he said he thought bridging it with little bridges of sticking plaster would do the trick instead of stitching. Stitches would mean going into casualty – oh no, I agreed instantly to plaster bridges. I did not want to take my face, which I had at last seen, and it looked like a cross between some kind of Hallowe'en turnip and a map with a lot of high ground marked in purple, anywhere outside the house. I have a faint scar but it's a small price to pay for avoiding that extra humiliation. (You used to caress it tenderly, wandering your

219

fingers over my features, 'drawing' my face, you used to say. A childhood accident, I said about the scar, running into a doorpost in my excitement at finding a nest with small blue eggs in the garden. Forgive me. It was not an absolute lie, just a transposition. I did run into a doorpost, but it did not produce that scar. And I kept the lies, the inventions, down to a minimum.)

After dealing with the cut, Fergus gave me a very thorough examination, pulse, lungs, blood pressure, the lot. He even took off a sample of blood.

'What's all this for? I've just had it done at my post-natal.'

'Might as well get a total picture while we're about it. It's a hunch of mine, but it seems to me that women quite often get – er – knocked about when they're in lowish health. I don't know – perhaps something going back to our animal past. Animals, a lot of them, are roused to aggression by signs of weakness or sickness . . . on the other hand, it's more likely that tempers are shorter when you're not feeling a hundred per cent. Arguments flare up, that sort of thing.'

'How much do you see of – this?' I pointed towards my face. 'Not a lot, I shouldn't think, not in a practice like yours.'

Fergus sighed.

'More than you'd imagine, my dear. Anyway, I haven't always worked in this kind of area.'

'And how do they, the women – how do they usually react?'

He sighed again.

'Most women don't have much choice, do they? They may go away and stay with their mother or their aunt for a little while, but sooner or later most of them just head for home again.'

I felt physically sick at the thought.

'Well, not me. Never. Never. Father can put me out in the street, but I won't go back.'

Fergus looked troubled.

'You know your father will never do such a thing.' He got out his prescription pad. 'Here, these are for some sedatives which you'll need if you're going to carry on feeding the wee fellow. I'll call in again tomorrow, though as far as I can make out there's nothing worse than bruising. You're certain you haven't had any trouble with your vision?'

'Yes, quite certain.'

'No obscured patches, disturbance of outline? We can't have you going around concussed.'

'No, nothing. I'm seeing quite normally.'

The only trouble is believing, but that's a different branch of disturbance.

'Well then, I'll be off. Take as much rest as you can for the next few days. And – oh my dear, I am so very distressed to see you in this pickle. I remember when you got pregnant with the first kiddy, hoping it would work out for you. I suppose it didn't?'

'No, it didn't. It most certainly did not. I've lived the life of a non-person, somewhere between a drudge and a robot, for four years. What's happened since is biology and hatred, a wicked combination. My guess is that most women who get messed up are non-persons. I don't think men are brave enough to beat up someone they haven't already reduced to crumbs. Because they're all bully-boys, whether they use kid gloves, velvet gloves, bare knuckles or whatever – bully-boys, the lot of them.'

'Now don't say that, Carla. I know you're upset, you've had a terrible experience, but you have the rest of your life to live. You're still a very young woman. Don't declare war on us all because of it. We may be a patchy lot, but some of us have hearts. Really.'

'Yes, I know. Big superior hearts.'

'Come, that's unfair.'

He sounded sharp for the first time and started packing away his things.

'I'm sorry,' I said humbly, realising this was no time for biting the hand that was trying to comfort me. He was, after all, the only one who had so far said, plainly and out loud, how upset he was that I had a face that looked like a cross between a Hallowe'en turnip and a map of high ground.

Later in the day I got up. There was no point in trying to rest. Nick screamed if Mary tried to keep him away from me for

221

any length of time. And anyway I was frightened of being left alone. I wanted other people round me, to distract me from the compulsive shocked replay of the morning's events, oscillating between believe and disbelieve, accept, it has happened, no NO. Not true, not to *me*.

At about six o'clock I heard father coming back from the office. His voice, irritated, answered by Mary's explaining. I found out that Nick had upset and broken a vase of flowers. The water had made a stain on the wooden sill where it had been standing.

'Well, he mustn't be allowed to scramble on the seat, that's all.'

Mary's face, which I caught sight of as I came up from below, was all mute with misunderstanding. But it was not in her nature to protest. We were already too much for them.

Fortunately Nick was played out by seven o'clock. He slept and we dined. Yes, I sat and ate dinner plying my heavy knife and fork in father's wine-and-beige dining room full of solid, fine things but curiously without grace. I felt as if we were all sitting in some kind of bubble, some time-limbo, an hour-glass with the sand stuck in its neck. There was the bafflement of all those unchanging things, the fat silver candlesticks on the sideboard, the wine silk shade round the central light and the little matching wine hats on top of the wall brackets. Father of course was sitting at the head of the table in the carving chair. Behind him hung a portrait of his mother, his Italian mother who had passed on to me my dark hair and skin but mercifully spared me her ugly jaw and her enormous bust. There was something monstrous about this repetition. Did my dreadful bruised face count for nothing? Surely one of the cravings satisfied by classical melodrama is just this passionate desire to see the natural order swept aside by the impact of events – owls hooting in daylight, graves yawning, rivers running backwards. Oh, I'm not pitching my life-crisis on quite this cosmic scale. A picture hanging squint, a broken glass or two, father faltering as he poured wine – that would have done, I think, just any sign of the splash marks of my shock. Well, Nick broke a vase. I'm not surprised he broke a vase, in fact I was quite glad. And yet I'm aware I asked the impossible, that everything *was* to be unchanged and rocklike in order to pronounce me safe.

We ate for the most part in silence. It hurt me to eat and I had very little appetite but I sipped at the claret which father – oh my dear, dear remote father with one of his curious touches of love – had opened for my 'homecoming'. After dinner we met in his study, he and I, whether by previous arrangement or intuition I don't know. But now I come to think of it, he must have intended it for Mary brought in coffee for two and two glasses for the brandy he kept in his corner cupboard.

'No thanks,' I said to his offer of Remy Martin. 'I have an idea alcohol isn't good for head injuries, and I've already had wine.'

'A pity, a pity. Perhaps you're right. Though they say it's a good pick-me-up. Well, another time, my dear.'

'Yes. Another time, I'll be delighted.'

'Will you pour coffee for us?'

'I – I don't think I can. I'm sorry.' I laughed nervously. 'I've got the shakes.'

Judging by the way the cup rattled in its saucer as he handed it to me, father also had the shakes. So, after all, here was a slight dent in the cosmic order. He sat down with his own coffee and stirred and stirred. He seemed about to speak, again and again, a big indrawn breath let out in a sort of sigh but no words. At last he managed to make a start.

'I take it – ' he cleared his throat, and it seemed to give him courage. 'I take it, you want to stay here? For some time at least?'

'If you think you and Mary can put up with us.'

'Oh yes, we'll manage.'

I was sitting forward in my chair, aged about ten but without ten's rollicking confidence that tomorrow is another day and we can all start happily over again.

'It's a big house,' said father, 'too big for the two of us. It's more habit than common sense that keeps us here. There should be room enough for all of us. We'll just have to work things out as we go along. Eh?'

223

He gave me a half-smile, trying to convince me this was all a matter of being level-headed and practical.

'But father – ' I sat even further forward. My head was aching horribly.

'What is it, my dear?' He looked at me with some tenderness, then drank more brandy. 'What's on your mind?'

'You do realise, don't you? I can't go back. Ever.'

He gave his petulant sigh.

'You are one for putting things bluntly, Carla.'

'Well, with a face like this, is it a moment for finesse?'

I was trembling. I knew I was rushing him, that he liked a foregone conclusion to emerge in its own time, but I could not sit there in uncertainty.

'I can see,' he said very soberly, 'that you have been very badly treated – '

'Oh this – yes, it's bad, but it's nothing to what's been going on.'

'Do you mean this is not the first physical assault?'

'No, I don't mean that. I mean that my life for the past four years has been something that I don't think I shall ever get over. My face will heal, I suppose, Fergus says there's nothing serious – '

'Yes, that's what he told me.'

'But my life, myself, that's another matter – '

'Carla.'

It was my father who now leaned forward.

'It is now *my* turn to speak bluntly.' He was trembling. 'I do not wish to know about your life. I do not wish to know. I have always detested the man you chose to marry. . . .' (Oh that was unkind – unkind, father. And was it actually true? Did I choose? When I tried out the word 'yes' for size, when you asked me if I loved him? Was that a choice? Jesus Christ, we make choices, then, with numbed shocked fragments of our consciousness. We lurch, we flounder, and that turns out to be a choice with a long, long train of consequences. Is such carelessness because we are spiritually idle and materially spoilt? Or have all sorts and kinds, rich, poor, feckless, or philosophically grave, made the selfsame kind of lurches?) 'I do not want to be privy to matters that I suspect would only make me incoherently angry, and do you no sort of good at all. What you have to do now is get on with life again, as best you can. Of course this won't mend overnight, an experience like this – ' Father's level, rational, not unsympathetic voice went on in this vein for a bit longer. My attention had turned in, to the raw whimpering bit that was feeling worse and worse the more he reasoned things out so methodically. '. . . you and the children are welcome to live in your old home for as long as you like.'

'Thank you. Thank you for that, father.'

'But remember, *your* part of the bargain is to get strong and well and put all this unhappy time behind you.'

I got up. Under these circumstances there didn't seem to be anything more to say.

'I think I'll go and see to the baby now, if you don't mind.'

'Very well, my dear. I hope you all have a good night.' He extended his hand as I passed his chair and we exchanged another of those bony handholds. 'By the way, I should keep inside the house till your face has cleared up a bit. No need to give people anything to gossip about, is there?'

Much later, he came down to see if we were all right in our basement quarters. Nick was curled up in my bed where he was obviously going to sleep for the next while. Louis was awake lying in his carry-cot. His hands were waving with entranced aimlessness, his vast blue eyes following the movement a fraction late like a butterfly catcher flitting after his elusive prize. I was sitting on the edge of a low couch occasionally adding my finger to little Louis' life puzzles. I may even have been smiling a little, corners of consciousness carrying on as normal.

Father stood in the middle of the room looking at us, after knocking quietly. I had the feeling that he too was a stranger to this part of the house.

'Have you got everthing you need? Mary fix you up all right? Are you going to be warm enough? It's starting to sleet outside.'

'It's very cosy, Dad. We're all right – fine.'

He sighed.

225

'I can't help thinking – things seem to have come full circle, don't they? I feel rather conscience-stricken. I shouldn't have said what I did upstairs, about you choosing to marry – ' (so he'd seen I was hurt). 'If I hadn't pushed you into such a corner, if we'd taken a little time – but then time doesn't wait in such circumstances. Still, I could have done better by you, not let you get panicked into this disastrous marriage. . . . And now, the irony of it, two children. My dear, why did you have another if things were so bad?'

I shook my head.

'He wasn't planned for.'

It was not easy talking about my accident-prone fertility with father, even in this strangely unguarded mood.

He peered over the carry-cot and let the waving hands clutch his finger.

'Well, anyway, he's a lovely baby, this little Louis.'

He watched him quietly for a few seconds, then straightened up and made a funny face, half lifting his arms and then letting them fall. It could have passed simply for a shrug, but I got up from the sofa and the arms came up again and round me. We hugged each other hard and close and he put his bristly cheek very gently against my bruised face. It must have been the first time I had ever held and been held so close by him since I was a fully-grown adult, for I'd never before realised how small and small-boned he was. I could wrap my arms round his little torso.

I longed to let the tears roll onto his neat shoulder but I am in some ways my father's daughter. In any case, tears would have been too simple. That long embrace was about all the impossibilities of sharing love once the wind has twisted two people so differently. Love each other we might, and did, but now there was fear, and to manage fear there must be silence. In which case all love can say is 'good-bye, good-bye, good-bye'.

'I hope you get some rest, my dear.'

Father disengaged himself gently. He passed his hand very tenderly over my hair and it rested a moment on my neck. Then, pulling himself together, he gave my earlobe a tiny tweek the way he used to do when I was a child. I smiled briefly. Then he was gone.

226

I got myself slowly ready for bed, warming the nightie Stella had lent me in front of the gas fire. It was difficult finding a bearable angle for my head on the pillows. And having at last found one relatively comfortable I undid all the good work by crying cautiously into the dark, cautiously because of Nick beside me, because it hurt, because I had come back a bruised stranger to my old home.

29

Exit Robert, from my waking life. I have never seen him since the day he beat me up. It has meant a long involvement of go-betweens, principally Tom, without whom the situation would have been impossible, but Esther did her share too in the early years. It was my first experience of something I can only call animal determination, for I felt it pig-deep, something squealing but overpoweringly stubborn, this vow that nothing and nobody was going to put me in any kind of contact with Robert Carmichael.

It took me by surprise, I may say. There I was, about two weeks after I had run back home, waiting for Stella to come and pick me up. She had offered to accompany me while I went back to the flat to collect my own and the children's belongings. I had 'phoned Esther and asked her to make sure Robert was out of the way. And I was sitting waiting in the hall, sun-glasses on – my bruises were by this time pale primrose and green and I had actually ventured out once into the street – with every intention of going on this dreaded errand.

At two o'clock on the dot Stella came briskly into the hall, silk scarf over newly dressed hair.

'Ready, then?'

She held out her hand to me, her face encouraging and sympathetic. I thought she looked wonderfully serene and pretty, and I liked the expensive sweet smell coming from her hair. But I couldn't get up. My stomach was behaving in a way that demanded all my attention. I could not get up.

'No.'

'Well,' she said patiently, sitting down beside me on the hall seat which was like a miniature church pew. 'Could you hurry a bit? I've got to be home by four and that doesn't leave us very much time.'

I tried again. If I let go my grasp of the pineapple knob at the end of the seat arm I didn't know what would happen. Finally I shook my head.

'I can't do it. I can't go back to that place.'

'I see.' There was a pause. Stella's face lost its sympathetic expression. 'I know that look. I know it very well.' She got up and walked towards father's study, as if to summon the supreme presence, then remembered he wouldn't be there.

Something in me simply could not budge.

'I'm sorry. I'll 'phone Esther and ask her to pack up for me – it's only Nick's toys and my fabric hangings and workbox I want anyway – '

'Don't think it might be – good for you to go back?'

'*Good* for me? What on earth do you mean?'

'You know, to get your nerve back, like getting behind the wheel after you've had a car crash – '

'You're not suggesting I might go back and live with Robert, are you?'

'Don't scream, for God's sake. No – *no*. I realise – but just the same, you can't run away from what you're doing. You're leaving your husband. And that's a serious matter.'

She blinked her pretty grey eyes at me. Suddenly it wasn't Robert I was leaving but a kind of infallible, the accolade of womanhood, a 'husband' – never mind if they came good or indifferent, cracked or crazed. Stella loathed Robert, but somehow there was Robert and there was this other thing – trophy, justification, lifeline to identity – a husband. And leaving him was – perhaps? – as awful an act as the bashing-up?

'You seem to forget that living with him was also a serious matter. Seriously damaging. Forget about it. I'm sorry I asked you to help. Don't worry. I don't need your help. Now or at any time. But *do not* think you or anyone else is going to get me back inside the flat.'

'Carla, don't turn on me. Don't – I'm not against you. I want to help – I'm not a monster. Stop *looking* at me like that. I do know, I understand, you've been through hell – '

I cut in coldly, 'You don't know. You don't understand. You've watched me go through hell and pretended not to see. It was more comfortable for you that way.'

Stella stood quiet for a moment, pulling the fingers of her gloves into shape. Then she said, with considerable dignity, 'It's apparently unforgivable in your eyes that my life has so far gone more smoothly than yours, that I've been more or less contented while you have not. I'm not going to apologise for being contented and I'm certainly not going to apologise for being lucky, if it is a matter of luck. If I've been unfeeling I'm sorry, really sorry. But here's one other thing to think about, and then I'll go and get your stuff. You can't expect anyone else, even your own sister, to take on your life for you. Not any more. You wanted me to make it all better the way I used to do when you were little. But good heavens, it was your mess – it *is* your mess, bad luck and all. And if I was uncaring, or appeared to be, it was mainly because I was scared. Rigid. Someone like you *is* scaring.'

'What do you mean, someone like me?'

'Someone with no instinct for self-preservation, who doesn't know what's good and what's bad for them. Someone, if you ask me, who makes for trouble.'

And with that she left me.

I stayed huddled on the hall seat with my dark glasses on, mulling over the less pitiable aspects of being a victim. *Why* was I so helpless? Why didn't I know what was good and what was bad for me? I didn't come up with an answer, not then, and not really ever since. I was raging with Stella, but also recognised tremblingly some element of truth. I did not really believe in a will of my own, any potency to shape my own experience. Whether this was an endemic flaw or the result of too-heavy odds, or a failure to grow up, I didn't know. Was it lodged somewhere in the darkness of pre-memory when my mother died, the great hand of black loss wiping out a three-year-old's world? Oh, but that was a cop-out, that kind of thinking. I think – and I didn't reach this point sitting on that hall seat – that few people commit or invite frightful crimes against themselves but an awful lot of us collude with what harm is done to us, through others. And I suppose that's the real reason I never gave you any hint of all this, Marius, not so much for the final humiliation of being beaten up but the worse one, self-inflicted, of hanging on until it happened.

I was still sitting in the hall when Stella came back. She looked different, dishevelled was the word that came to mind, but I don't think it had anything to do with messed up hair or untidyness about her clothes. It was just that the air of serene integration was no longer there, and her eyes were unusually wide open.

'Can you help me bring the stuff in from the car?'

She sounded sharp and in a hurry.

'Yes, of course.'

It was rather pathetic. Defined in material terms, Nick's, Louis' and my lives amounted to a few cartons, a battered suitcase, a wicker shopping basket fraying at the handles and a large stuffed elephant. But then even housefuls of antiques and objets d'art look as arbitrary and unimpressive as junk-yards, packaged up for removal. Silently we took them out of the car and down into the basement. I felt conscience-stricken.

'I'm sorry. You must be exhausted hauling all this stuff down those stairs.'

'Your eccentric neighbour gave me a hand.'

'My – oh, you mean Esther. How did she know you were there?'

'Heard the noise, I suppose.'

'Noise? What noise?'

'Your husband shouting and yelling.' Why should Stella sound as if she were accusing *me*? After all, wasn't I trying to be rid of the man?

I was shocked, though.

'Robert – he wasn't meant to be there. I told Esther to warn him. And anyway, he should have been teaching – '

'Well, she said she'd done her best, but it wasn't much good because by all appearances – I mean, he was very – ' She put down one of the cartons with a sigh. 'He'd obviously been drinking for some time, some *considerable* time.'

Again, a mixed expression of shock, of acknowledgement, and then a stiffening away into pure distaste.

'I'm sorry,' I said humbly, but thankful to my core that I had refused to go. Perhaps the self-preservation instinct was at last getting to work.

'Oh, you couldn't know – but I must say, it was not pleasant to let myself into what I thought was an empty flat and find myself arguing with an exceedingly drunk and angry man.' She shivered. 'I really was going to give up but then – what's her name – the frazzle-haired old woman – '

'Esther.'

I tried hard to say it in a way that would stop these dreadfully dismissive descriptions.

'Well, she came rushing over and talked to – Robert, and managed somehow to get through to him. Anyway, he shut up and seemed to lose interest and we just grabbed what we could. I must say she was very helpful, your neighbour, even if she does look a fright. She went down to the corner shop for cartons and found things I'd certainly never have found. She kept saying, "Carla'll want her bead-box, she must have that" – and "Nick'll need his meccano" and she found a whole lot of it at the back of some cupboard. Oh, by the way, she sends her love. She seems very fond of you.'

'Esther's about the only friend I have.'

'Really?' Stella's voice went cool and her eyebrows lifted.

'Yes, she's a wonderful person,' I said defiantly. 'Terrifically interesting. She used to be a cabaret artist – '

But Stella was busy with other things. She was distractedly unpacking a box of assorted children's clothes, not very clean, some torn. 'We'd better go shopping as soon as you're properly better. Most of these must be just about outgrown, anyway.'

'No, you've done your bit,' I said stiffly, with that quivering and senseless pride which must make a stand before giving in to inevitable – and essential – favours.

'Oh look here.' Stella took my face between her hands, in the old way. 'This is one thing I *can* help with. And you – just accept you're going to be financed by the rest of us for a while until something's worked out. After all, isn't that what families are for?'

A gush of tears filled my eyes. Back in the family, safe, protected. Wasn't that what I'd always wanted?

30

For a few hours, sometimes even as much as a day, home was truly home, the place where I'd been a child, a familiar part of me. But that day I arrived with my terrible face, that first day seemed to set the basic pattern for the next five years. We didn't seem to be able to shake off that curious muted frenzy in which we had milled round trying to swallow at one impossible gulp the fact of crisis while keeping the expression smooth. We seemed merely to repeat the unease, the curious sense of waiting without purpose, the apprehension, the sense of living past each other rather than with. The old home went. Such places can only live freshly in memory. There is nothing more completely dead than the actual place.

Most days Nick did something which caused a row, a row between him and me, his temper tantrums back again in force. Mary point blank refused to confront him. Whatever happened while I was out – at work, eventually – was stored up till I came home. Father gave tetchy scoldings but knew too well that he must not risk losing his temper or heaven knows what might burst forth. They were loyalty personified, he and Mary, there was no question of moving us on, but nothing stretched or adapted to fit us in. We were, myself and my two children, simply parked on them by circumstance; they had rescued us and we stayed in a curious state of recent rescue all the time we were there, except that a sort of battle-weariness set in.

After the first shake-up of my reappearance father never referred to my marriage, to Robert, or to the state I was in when I reappeared. Silence was the *cordon sanitaire* to be drawn round these events. He had obviously briefed Mary as well. If ever I tried to tell her anything about those last months when I had been pregnant with Louis she would shut me up briskly by saying: 'Well, that's all in the past now.' I can't help feeling that left to herself curiosity, let alone any kinder emotion, would have prevailed.

Thus I was cared for and made comfortable and given as much material help as anyone could ever expect, but I was to have the horrors in private, please, except that I don't really think they had much idea of the state of my mind until one mischievous windy night in January, some two months after my return.

It had been a bad day, Nick rampaging and beside himself with inarticulate anger. I had gone to bed exhausted and was just dozing off with the roar of the wind in my ears but still conscious, I could swear, when something moved behind the curtains, moved and stirred and was still again. In the dark my skin twitched and bristled with an old terror, terror of childhood, terror of the bison creature, hairy, shaggy and red-eyed, that lay in wait for me in dark places. It was standing there now, behind the curtains, waiting, taking its time, something huge and gaunt, the primeval beast of darkness.

I lay still as a mouse, waiting too, without power to move or speak.

It was coming over to the bed padding softly across the room, sniffing, sniffing me out, for all that I prayed the bedclothes would protect me. It was coming nearer, nearer, yes – ah, don't! I've done nothing, nothing so very bad! And then he was on me. I could feel his weight. It pushed me deeper into the bed, I had difficulty breathing. I was suffocating, pinned down, buried alive. There was repulsive moistness, breathing, agitation, faster, faster . . . *No!*

I woke up with such a ghastly sense of horror that I was out of bed and running upstairs before I had time to realise it was father's bedroom I was making for so madly. The door burst open. In the dim light of a single bedside lamp two amazed figures rose up like astonished ghosts in a double act – a sight so convulsively funny that a giggle broke like a fart in the middle of my panic.

'Carla – whatever is the matter?'

I flung myself on top of father and the book he had been reading, weeping violently.

'Robert – '

'*What?*'

'He was there behind the window curtain and then he came over – I can't keep him away, father. He's gone, but he'll be back, he knows how to get at me – '

Father was shaking me slightly.

'You've had a nightmare, that's all. Come on, child, sit up.'

He looked tense and pale and vexed. He still had his reading glasses on.

'Oh father, I can't go back – '

'But of course not, no one's asking you to.'

'I can't go back to *that room*, in case he's still hiding behind the curtains – '

'Now pull yourself together. This is *absurd*. You have had a bad dream and now it's over. Mary, my dear, do you mind? I think a cup of something hot would be a good idea.'

Mary bundled herself out of bed, sighing. She too had had a long exhausting day.

'I'm not going back down there alone.'

I made to get under father's eiderdown, still beside myself with terror, not one person but a sprawl of quivering pieces.

'Sit up, Carla,' ordered my father sternly, in his turn preparing to get out of bed. He fished around for his slippers, little bare elegant blue-veined feet with high arches and mobile toes, moving around till they found what they wanted (I had never seen my father's toes before.) Then he put on his camel cord-edged dressing-gown. Then he took me by the shivering arm and firmly walked me across the landing down into the hall with its churchy atmosphere and on down into the basement.

'There,' he said, switching on the overhead light which glared 150 watts of common sense on the scene. Nick stirred in his sleep. Thinking it over later, I realised he'd probably rolled half on top of me and started off the dream.

'No one could hide behind that curtain anyway,' said father, going over and twitching it aside. At that moment a branch flew past the window. He started back. Then, recovering himself, said, 'It's a dirty night, just the kind of night that brings bad dreams. Things blowing against the window – '

'And the angry spirits walking the storm – '

'Robert is not an angry spirit,' said father firmly and patiently. 'He is not dead, he is very much alive. Ah, thank you, my dear – ' Mary had come in with a cup of Ovaltine and a sleeping pill. Father took them from her and put them on my beside table. 'Now get yourself tucked in and drink this.'

I protested about the pill. I might not hear Louis. Mary said emphatically it was more important that I get a good night's sleep, the baby would come to no harm. I think she was really saying she wanted no more flying intrusions into her and father's privacy.

The next day I received a sort of ultimatum. Sanity and secretarial training, or madness and 'treatment'. It was not put quite so bluntly but that was the gist of it. Father was rattled by the nightmare incident and the fact that I had weeping fits. Perhaps I needed sedation or – er, the help of someone professional, I seemed to be rather confused. On the other hand, it might just be that I did not have enough to keep my mind occupied. Mary was prepared to look after Louis but Nick would have to go to nursery school. 'Anyway, think it over, my dear. Sooner or later you'll have to start earning your living.'

I did not want the help of someone professional. I only wanted father to know what it was like to have four years of fear and unwantedness in my system and for him to show some human non-Jovian compassion. On balance I decided I would rather be a secretary than a psychiatric patient, and so I suppose I correctly diagnosed myself as not-mad.

Nevertheless the door was now wide open to those nightmares. They came, they came like some sort of occult harvest from the marriage years, and Robert had no need to be dead to be an angry spirit. I suppose one might say with some oversimplification that by night and on my own I was, if not mad, then edging in that direction, and by day and in company

237

I was sane. It was, of course, the final triumph of my upbringing over the forces of disintegration.

So, for the next five years nothing really happened, except in my private underworld, dreams and drawings, drawings and dreams. Mostly I sketched the children but looking back into old portfolios I realise that already there were signs of later themes, particularly some smudgy pastels which were groping their way towards that picture which you so disliked, which I later called 'The Bad Dream City'. (You thought I should stick to abstracts, those clean bright things I did in accordance with the fashion of the moment. You were always hoping, I think, to cure me of my habits of 'morbid' thought.)

It's quite mysterious, the way in which time ceases to move, a kind of non-movement which makes any kind of happening an impossibility. Of course there were events. Nick went to school. I learned to drive. And I took that secretarial training, sitting earnest and anxious among all the sprawling teenyboppers, a veteran of twenty-four. I got a job in my father's firm, working for one of his junior partners who stiffly invited me out to dinner a few times and even stiffly proposed marriage, at which, I'm sorry to say, I giggled. He will never understand that that giggle was more hysterical than callous, but he took it very badly. I started applying for jobs elsewhere, but father simply found me another partner to work for, having expressed a certain reserved chargin that I had turned down a solid and sensible fellow. However, he said that the pension scheme in his office was superior to most others I'd find. Father did an awful lot of knowing best and I knuckled under. I was already, apparently, to start saving up for being an old woman.

There were events, incidents, but nothing happened. I've heard people who were in the fighting or the blitz of World War II say something similar – 'Nothing's ever really happened since' and that can swallow up marriage, birth of children, the lot. No landmark in the spirit's journey. Perhaps no journey, the spirit fled to recuperate by the banks of the Styx.

I know you thought my ideas about depression were crazy,

but I stick by them. It is necessary, sometimes, to visit the stream of death, at least go near enough to hear the sound of its waters as it flows quietly through life, at the heart of things, the thing that draws you when life itself has become opaque and low-quality. There's nothing sick about it. It is more sick to deny our amphibious nature, to pretend that we can stay on dry land in daylight for ever. But it's a dangerous excursion. One may give in to the temptation to plunge headlong for the other bank, or simply to stay hidden there, in the semi-dark. The difficulty is to struggle back, not stay too long as I did, thinking the only place for me was among the black poplars and the willows.

As a living embodied person, I never saw Robert again. I refused point-blank and no one insisted. And he has never, then or since, showed any indication of wanting to see me either. Tom and Esther took on the management of contact between Nick and his father. Louis didn't figure in that at all, of course. I have no doubt in my mind that I owe my survival to those two, my brother-in-law and my ex-neighbour, their loyalty and friendship one of the few life-giving things during those five slow years before the New Dawn of Alma Crescent.

I never saw Janos again either. I couldn't face him after what had happened. I did hear from somewhere that he left Edinburgh once he had graduated. But he is present in 'The Bad Dream City'. It is partly his vision which lies behind the picture, his huge suns casting the long shadows and his sense of a frozen place as well, perhaps, as echoes of the Budapest fighting in a city reduced here and there to rubble. The glimpses of infernos behind tenement windows, the lost souls leaning against the dark mouths of closes, they are all mine, and mine the cracking Georgian structure with the earthquake tilt in the right-hand corner.

That picture, incidently, got me my first London exhibition. It was spotted by a man who did not share your qualms about expressionist art, and it gained me a rather successful exhibition in this gallery that I now run. I thought for a while that I was all set to have a career as a painter, but it was not to be. Or perhaps I simply became faint-hearted. It seemed immeasureably easier to be good at assessing the work of others, less harrowing and sleep-disturbing, though still with enough risk to make it piquant.

I do still paint a little, mild stuff on the whole, to keep my eye in more than anything else. Perhaps, though, there is one important picture still to be painted, especially after last night. I have never yet painted Alma Crescent. I think I have an idea how it might be, a great sprinkle of clear bright colours with here and there shapes, the twist of the staircase, the foliage on the cornice, the strange old anchor Louis found, the beautiful Goddess of Mercy you found and bought for me. Some of these things, in a maze, a confetti-shower of colour. Something like that. And for all that lovely empty dream of last night, I shall call it 'La Vie en Rose with Marius'.

You shall have it, if I ever paint it, to counterbalance this long angry story I've just been telling you. For you made me extraordinarily happy, you and the house between you. It is only the blind incomprehensible grip of that marriage vow made in bad faith, and the creature in me who runs amok and bears the face of my husband that defeated us. But then, bearing whatever face, that is me, a woman who can't ever again live in the shadow of a man, not even yours, my once beloved.